DIRTY FLIRTY ENEMY

PIPER RAYNE

Cover Design: Okay Creations

First Editor: Joy Editing

Second Editor: My Brother's Editor

Proofreader: Shawna Gavas, Behind The Writer

Dirty Flirty Enemy

He's the arrogant Manhattan realtor with billboards advertising his six-pack more than his expertise in negotiations.

I'm the competing broker who stupidly moved across the hall from his office.

From day one, I've been his sworn enemy. Okay, so I might have accidentally stolen one of his clients. Well, is it stealing if the client comes to me?

Even our vicious banter and loathing gazes can't hide the chemistry between us. Who can blame me? He has enough charisma to make every hot-blooded woman in the city melt with a single word.

Just when I think a mutual respect could be born between us, the biggest developer in the city offers us an opportunity that pits us against each other.

Time to forget Carmelo Mancini's dreamy eyes and tight abs.

Game on.

DIRTY
FLIRTY
ENEMY

CHAPTER ONE

Bella

I step out of the taxi only to be front and center with Carmelo Mancini's ridiculous new billboard ad.

First time? I'll be gentle.

Along the bottom, it says, *I LOVE first time buyers!*

Real subtle. He's always using his sex appeal to try to gain clients. Probably offers sexual favors if they sign on the dotted line. If I were a spiteful woman, I might find my way up to that billboard late at night and spray-paint something juvenile over that cocky smirk of his.

But I'm not.

At least today I'm not.

I can't let him get any farther under my skin though, because I'm bound to run into him, what with my new office being across the hall from his. Is the location ideal? Not at all, but I needed a new office and this building had an unexpected immediate opening, which meant the landlord was desperate to fill the space. Cheaper rent weighed against a few run-ins with Carmelo Mancini made it an easy choice.

I roll my eyes at the ad and make my way into the building. A man in a suit opens the door for me, and I smile politely. "Thank you."

"You're welcome." He nods.

We file into the elevator, and my hands clench around the handle of my briefcase. I lean forward to press the six button, but he beats me to it. He heads to one corner of the small shared space and I head to the other. As the doors are sliding shut, a cute brunette stops them with her hand and enters with a bright cheery smile. I try not to show my relief at not being alone with this strange man in the elevator.

"So sorry." She glances at the floor buttons, doesn't hit one, and takes up residence between the guy and me.

I feel her eyes on me, so I turn and smile. I already have one enemy in this building, no need for another.

"Hi, I'm Annie." She puts out her hand.

I shake it. "Bella."

"I know."

"You do?" My head tilts to the side.

"Sorry." She waves her hand in the air. "I work at the Mancini Agency."

"You work for Carmelo?" I ask.

Her eyes widen. "God, no. He's Mancini Real Estate. The Mancini Agency is an ad company owned by his brother, Enzo... er, Lorenzo Mancini."

"There's two of them in this building?" I ask.

She laughs, an infectious one at that. "Just be thankful the third brother, Dominic, isn't here. He's kind of a buzzkill." She leans forward. "I heard you were taking up the vacant office on our floor. I've seen your ads, so I recognized you."

I grab a business card from the outside sleeve of my briefcase, and I hand the card over to her. "Well, if you're ever in the market to sell FSBO is a great option..."

She smiles sweetly, a look I'm all too familiar with. The one where someone is about to nicely decline my services.

The real estate market in New York isn't for the weak. When I left a traditional brokerage to start a For Sale By Owner company that only charges a fee for putting a property on the MLS, I hadn't realized how hard starting over would be. Sometimes I second-guess that decision—until I remind myself of the reasons why I stepped away.

"In the interest of full disclosure, I should probably mention that I'm in a relationship with Enzo—Lorenzo Mancini." She cringes as if she's sorry for sleeping with the enemy.

The guy in the corner chuckles lightly and Annie whips her head around, but the guy pretends to be engrossed in his phone.

"That's convenient." I keep my voice light, so she knows I'm not being snarky.

Annie waves me off. "Yeah, well, long story there, but as you can imagine, our real estate business has to go to Carm —Carmelo, what with the Italian family thing."

The guy chuckles again and Annie peeks over her shoulder.

Thankfully, the elevator dings, signaling that we've reached our floor and the doors part for us to exit.

I step out of the elevator then turn to face her. "Nice meeting you, Annie."

And it was. She seems nice, and I could use someone who's not hostile toward me in this office building.

The guy hovers around the outside of the elevator,

staring at the small sign on the wall as though he doesn't know where he's going.

"Nice to meet you. We'll definitely have to plan some kind of after-hour drinks together." Annie waves to me and turns on her heels.

She's so carefree and at ease. I feel like a ball of thread wound so tight no one can unravel me.

The man stays by the sign as I walk to my office. The hairs on the back of my neck stand up because it seems odd. He knew he had to be at floor six and there aren't that many offices in this building. Four, total, on this floor.

I'm about to open the door to my office when I feel a grip on my elbow. "Excuse me."

I swing around, deliberately smacking him hard in the leg with my briefcase.

He stumbles back and bends at the waist to hold his knee, and I quickly step into my office, letting loose a relieved breath when I spot Max at her desk. She looks at me over the rim of her glasses, probably wondering why my back is plastered to the door.

"Is the Mancini guy out there?" she asks, sliding her chair out from her desk. She tosses her glasses onto her paper-ridden desk and rounds her desk.

"No. I think I might've overreacted."

A knock sounds on the door behind me a second later.

"I'll see about that." She places her hand on my hip and slides me away from the door before opening it a crack. "Hello?"

"Hi. Is Bella available?"

"And who may I say is asking?" She eyes me then looks back at him.

"Kevin Henderbrook." The man's voice is deep.

My face heats from the embarrassment of hitting him with my briefcase.

"Is she expecting you?" Max asks.

"No. But I had an appointment with Carmelo Mancini until I heard what she offers."

My stomach flips. How does this man want to do business with me when I very well could have broken his kneecap?

Max opens the door and ushers him in. "By all means, come in. Sorry, but we're two women and new to this building. You can never be too careful."

Mr. Henderbrook glances at me. "It's quite all right. I have five daughters. I should've known not to approach you like that." He bows his head in apology.

He's sophisticated and attractive for a man who's probably in his fifties. I didn't get a good look at him until right now, which my self-defense coach would reprimand me for.

"Please, I'm sorry. It was instinct. Come on in. Would you like something to drink?" I wind through our small office. Small meaning it's me, Max, and two other part-time real estate reps who handle outside appointments and pictures if need be, so they're rarely ever here.

"No, I'm good. I just wanted to hear more of what your company can offer."

We enter my office and I shut the door. He sits across from me, and I give him my best pitch with the hope he's actually interested. When I moved in across the hall from the Mancini Real Estate agency, I never intended to poach a client from them, but when opportunity knocks, you can't say no.

You can apparently hit them with your briefcase though.

An hour later, Mr. Henderbrook signs the contract and

slides the papers toward me. "Now comes the hard part. Letting Carm know I went a different route."

I cringe, although I'm not really upset about it other than I feel empathy for my new client. Carm hasn't exactly been quiet about speaking against companies like mine, saying we can't properly represent our clients and a bunch of other bullshit. He wouldn't walk away from a nine-million-dollar penthouse deal that fell into his lap and neither should I.

"Good luck."

He waves me off. "None of your concern."

We both rise from our seats. "I do apologize again for hitting you."

Again, his hand waves to shoo off any concern. "I would've told my daughters to do the same thing. I was hesitant to approach you because Carm's always been my guy, but the for-sale-by-owner thing has always intrigued me, and hearing you talk with that woman in the elevator... well, it felt like the universe trying to point me in the right direction or something."

I open my office door. Max's hands are flying feverishly across the keyboard.

"Do you know Annie?" I ask Kevin, leading him out.

He chuckles like he did in the elevator. "I've heard about her. Carm is a pretty animated guy, and well, you can't get to know him over the years without hearing about his family. So I don't know her, but I know *of* her if that makes sense?"

I giggle because I understand. It's true that a client and a realtor end up sharing a lot over the process of buying or selling. "Interesting. I've yet to actually meet Carmelo, so I wouldn't know."

Mr. Henderbrook stops at the door. "You haven't met

him?" He glances at the door across from mine. The plaque next to it says Mancini Real Estate.

"We just moved in and our paths haven't crossed. I only know *of* him."

His eyebrows rise. "Be careful, Miss Scott. He's so charming, it's hard to know if he's the prince or the villain." He winks and sticks out his hand while I'm still processing the meaning of his sentence. "It's been a pleasure. Looking forward to seeing how this turns out."

I shake his hand as the door across the hall opens. There stands Carmelo Mancini in the flesh. I loathe that he looks better in real life than he does on those damn billboards.

I watch him wrap his mind around the scene in front of him. His eyes narrow on me before a smile appears. A bright, toothy smile. If someone told me it twinkled like in those princess movies kids watch, I wouldn't refute it. It's then I understand Mr. Henderson's warning.

Carmelo Mancini is like poison wrapped in the most delectable chocolate. By the time you realize your mistake, it's too late.

CHAPTER TWO

Carm

After Kevin messaged me to say he was running late, I kept busy by looking up comps, but I see now that the enemy has successfully poached my client and I wasted my time.

"Kevin, great to see you again." I cross the hallway, hand extended, boisterous voice and permasmile plastered on my face as always.

He hesitantly looks at the she-devil then back at me, extending his hand. I pride myself on reading people and I don't need Braille on Kevin's palm to know that I've lost his account. He's asked me time and time again about the for-sale-by-owner companies popping up in this city like damn Starbucks. He's a smart businessman and with success comes confidence. I admire the fact that he thinks he can sell his own condo, but I know I can sell it faster and for more money than he can. Not to mention handle the vetting of prospective buyers. The fact is, no one sees my value until they don't have me. He'll learn his lesson the hard way.

"Can we talk?" Kevin says.

The worst part about my job is the fake bullshit that comes with it. I can't just say go to fucking hell and good luck with Gingersnap over there. She's not going to stage the property, nor does she have Manhattan's best photographer on speed dial to make it look as though it's worth the inflated price he's demanding. Instead, I smile, open my office door, and allow him in, giving Miss Scott my back as though I couldn't care less that she stole my client.

Jot this down—don't ever let the competition see you upset. Horrible rookie mistake.

I don't bother taking Kevin to my office. Instead, I pull him into the conference room while my right-hand man, Justin, watches from afar, probably wondering what the hell is going on. There are clients you wine and dine and there are old faithfuls. Kevin was in the latter category until five minutes ago. Hell, maybe I messed up and should've wined and dined him.

I shake my head. Nah, I'm never wrong.

"So you're trying your hand at going FSBO, huh?" I ask, sitting at the head of the table.

Kevin slides into the chair to my left, his hands clasped in his lap. He's not going to act ashamed because he's not. To him, I provide a service to fulfill his needs. In his mind, he doesn't need me. But I'll see the ashamed Kevin when he comes crawling back in three months because no one has bought the condo he thinks is such a hot commodity it can sell itself.

"I have to, Carm. You know I've been wanting to."

"Anything I can say to change your mind?" I ask.

"I've already signed the contract."

I nod and put out my hand. "I wish you luck."

He smiles and extends his hand. I use my friendly, confident handshake. The one that says, "Hey we're still friends, no worries."

We're not, for the record.

"Thanks for understanding, Carm."

"You gotta do what you think is best for you." *Think* being the operative word in that sentence. "I'm here should you need me—and actually, hold up a second."

You're about to witness why I'm better than any other agent in New York City.

I leave Kevin at the conference room door and approach Justin. "Pass me the market analysis on Kevin's place."

He picks it up off the corner of his desk. "Is he ready to sign? I have the paperwork ready to go."

I rip up the contract I had written up. "Nah, he's going FSBO."

Justin's face distorts into a what-the-fuck expression. I smile, wink, then walk back to the conference room.

"Here." I hand the papers to him.

Kevin thumbs through them and looks at me in disbe-lief. This will ensure that when his "sell my own place" experiment is over, he'll still come back to me. I'm not arro-gant enough to think someone else couldn't steal him from me with a lower commission rate. "Thanks, Carm. Sorry you went to all that work for nothing."

He's second-guessing his decision right now, so I'm going to fuck with his head. I slap him on the shoulder. "No big deal. Who knows, maybe it'll sell by tomorrow."

It won't.

We both chuckle.

"And if not, you know where to find me," I add.

"You're the best." He holds up the papers.

I walk him to the door. I just lost a potential hundred-grand commission. Time's ticking and I have to go make up that money until he returns.

"Good luck." I open our office door and walk him to the elevator. I even press the down button for him. "Let me know how it goes. Maybe one day I'll hop on board the FSBO train and actually have a social life." I laugh. Not my real laugh. The one reserved for clients.

He steps into the elevator, presses the ground floor button, and waves as the doors close.

Instead of going to my office, I head right into my brother's Enzo's advertising firm's office. I need to cool the fuck down before I go apeshit on the redheaded she-devil across from my office. I barrel into the Mancini Agency, the door slamming behind me alerting their five employees of my arrival.

Annie glances up from where she's talking to the receptionist, a smirk on her face. "You look flustered."

I narrow my eyes because I can't help but think she knows something about why I am, but why would she? Still, that look on her face...

"I need to get she-devil evicted. Will you be my accomplice and say she's running an escorting business out of her office?"

Annie glances at their receptionist and says her goodbye before sliding her arm through mine and escorting me to my brother's office. "I met her, and I think she's lovely. Very friendly."

"Yeah, she's friendly. She stole my client who was on the way up to see me."

"I saw them both on the elevator and she wasn't even talking to him," Annie says.

She opens the door without knocking and Enzo holds up his finger, phone to his ear. Annie takes the chair across from the desk, and I sit on the couch by the window, which has a shitty view of an alley. Sometimes I think Enzo fell so fast from his Manhattan skyline view because of what? The woman sitting next to me. How scary is that thought? He left a partnership offer to start his own company and all because of love.

Enzo's acting much like I did moments ago with Kevin Henderson. Kissing ass with the hopes of hooking a client.

I return to Annie's comment. "Whose side are you on? Do I need to remind you that I'm basically family?"

She laughs, the one only Annie can get away with without pissing me off more. Sometimes I see why my brother fell so hard. Not that I like her like that, but I can appreciate why my older brother does.

I shake my head. "I think I'm going to plant a desk in the lobby, so my clients don't have the option of running into her."

She laughs again, eyeing Enzo. He winks and smiles, his hand on the receiver as though he's preparing to finish the call.

Annie stares at my brother as though he's a god, all dreamy eyes and desire oozing out of her. "He's trying to get this client to jump ship from Jacobson and Earl."

"You're no better than the she-devil. No wonder you like her."

Her eyes shoot my way with that look of judgment I swear she learned from my ma. "It's not the same. I don't think she's trying to steal any of your clients. Like I said, she didn't even talk to him in the elevator."

Enzo hangs up, stands from his desk, and sits next to me

on the couch. I'm sure he's pissed he's sitting next to me and not Annie.

"So?" Annie's hopeful voice conveys that she cares more about this client than the fact that I'm going to be out of business if the she-devil continues to reside across the hall from me.

"He's willing to hear our pitch." Enzo smiles and winks.

A low moan falls out of Annie like she wishes I would disappear so they could celebrate in private. Not today. They'll have to taper down their ridiculously high libidos. "You're the best."

He winks again.

I hold up my hands. "Enough. Let's talk about me now."

Enzo blows out a breath and my head volleys between their non-verbal conversation. I'm not sure if it's about me or about how they're going to fuck as soon as I leave. The whole fraternization thing is going to bite them in the ass when two of their employees think it's okay to lock the office door and screw like bunnies.

"Hello?" I say, waving my hand between them.

They both snap out of their lovesick haze. God help me if this ever happens to me.

"Sorry, what's up?" Enzo relaxes in the corner of his couch, loosening his tie.

"She-devil just stole one of my clients while he was on his way up to sign listing papers with me."

"And?" Enzo asks.

I hate that love has mellowed him out. He no longer runs on high like Dom and me. It's annoying as fuck.

"And it's my business. So I was talking to Annie... we need to sneak in there and destroy the place so they evict her, or maybe we complain to the landlord that strange men are coming and going at all times." I'm still thinking of how to orchestrate this when Enzo and Annie burst out laughing.

"We're not fifteen, Carm," Enzo says once his laugh is stifled enough that he can speak.

I point at Annie and stand from the couch. "You ruined him."

"Me?" Her eyes dart to Enzo as though she's telling him to deal with his brother.

"Yes. He would've been on board with this before you. But you and your body and your constant sex has put him in some orgasm-filled hypnosis."

Annie's eyes widen, and she bites her lower lip to stop herself from reacting. "I'm... sorry?"

I roll my eyes. "You should be."

"Handle it like an adult, brother." Enzo doesn't even look at me. He pats the couch next to him, eyeing Annie.

She shakes her head. He pats again.

"I'm out of here. I'll leave you two to play your cat-and-mouse sex games. Thanks for nothing."

Laughter rings out of them both until the door shuts behind me. Their employees watch me leave.

"Put your earbuds in, folks. Enzo's about to crown Annie employee of the month again."

They laugh because they can't be so naïve they don't know what's going on in that office during work hours.

As I leave the Mancini Agency and step into the hall-way, she steps out too.

The she-devil.

The hallway is long, but she must feel my seething eyes on her because she stays in place instead of heading to the elevators. For a moment, I wonder if this is what it felt like, back in the Wild West, to be in a standoff with your hand on the gun.

Then her heels click on the floor as she makes her way toward me and the elevator. I step forward and match her pace, not willing to be outdone by her, even on this.

"I think we need to get a few things straight."

She giggles. "Carmelo Mancini, I presume?" She smiles and extends her hand when we both reach the elevator. "Huh. I thought..." She inspects me, her eyes moving down and up, then leaning around my body to gain another view. "So you used a body double for the billboards, huh?"

She just amped this fight up another notch.

CHAPTER THREE

Bella

I've never been able to play the banter game. I'm the girl who thinks of a comeback five minutes later and curses myself for not being quicker on the draw.

So although I'm not a mean-spirited person, I kind of want to high-five myself for that jab at Carmelo. The man is even better-looking in person than the blown-up version plastered around the city for millions of people's viewing pleasure.

"Yeah, right." He puffs out his hard chest a bit, trying his best to put on that smile he probably practices in the mirror every day.

"Oh sorry." I shrug as if I couldn't care less that I hit a sore spot.

The elevator opens and I step in, praying he doesn't follow.

Of course, he does follow. He's a fighter. That's his

reputation. I might not know Carmelo Mancini, but I know *of* him. The rumors—the good and the ugly. He's well known in this city, in this industry.

"Tell me, Ms. Scott, why did you choose this building for your office?" He crosses his arms, his blue eyes searing right into my green ones.

"Miss," I clarify.

"Really?" He arches a brow.

I hold up my left hand. "Not married."

"Yeah, I figured you were probably divorced."

My mouth is so wide open, a hippo could slide in unnoticed. But I know the way men like Carmelo Mancini work, and I don't want him to know he got a reaction out of me, so I snap my mouth shut. He didn't assume I was divorced; he assumed I'd be some nightmare of a wife no one could stand.

"You should do better research, I guess." I give him a saccharine smile.

His gaze bores into me as though he thinks that will intimidate me. "You were a *real* broker once upon a time. Why go FSBO?"

He knew of me? I'm surprised. Back in the day, I was a very small fish in a massive ocean of killer sharks.

"Tired of the game? Money upfront?" I shrug. "There're a lot of benefits to switching gears."

"You wanna talk money? Maybe we should compare paychecks at some point."

This man seriously wants me to stab him in the eye with my pen. Let's see how sexy his billboards are after eye surgery.

The elevator dings and I breathe in relief that the elevator didn't get stuck. That'd be my luck.

"Well, it's been enlightening meeting you." I step out into the building's lobby.

He follows me. "I think we should set some ground rules."

I laugh, opening the front door and stepping out into the beautiful late spring day. It's gorgeous out, and I plan on grabbing a sandwich and spending an hour in Central Park. It's the one day a week I refuse to work through my lunch.

"Call my office and schedule an appointment." I walk down the sidewalk.

"Pretty sure your calendar is wide open. Let's figure this out now." He walks alongside me, flicking his wrist to check the time.

Hopefully he has some dire meeting to get to.

I stop at the street corner although I briefly debate if getting hit by a cab is better than talking to Carmelo Mancini.

I tilt my head and blow out a breath. "Listen, I'm sorry about Mr. Henderbrook. It was never my intention to steal him. He overheard a conversation in the elevator and approached *me*. I know it must look bad, but I'm not the type to steal clients."

His sour mood dissipates slightly for a moment. "Still. Let's agree that neither of us will hand out cards in the elevator."

I shake my head at him. The white pedestrian sign flashes saying that I can cross. Don't need to tell me twice.

I step off the curb, but he follows me. Again.

"I won't give out my business cards, okay?" I say.

He glances at his watch once more. "Maybe we need some other guidelines, like no advertisements downstairs or in the hallway."

I stop on the other side of the street, outside my favorite sandwich place, but he's not going to know that. "Fine."

He nods a few times, stuffing his hands into his pockets and studying me. It looks as though he wants to say more.

Women walking by glance at him from the corner of their vision. I don't blame them, he's alluring. Too bad he knows it.

"Let's discuss it in one of our office's after lunch?"

"Sorry, I have plans."

"Client?" he asks.

"Yeah," I lie because a man like Carmelo will only accept defeat if it's something he can relate to. If I said I'm going to grab my tuna on wheat, head to a park bench, and enjoy one hour of serenity to help keep my sanity, he'd try to weasel his way in, and I'd probably allow him.

"Okay. Well then, we're on the same page? I don't see any other way we can coexist in the same building without those rules."

I nod. "Sure. Okay."

He waits for a full minute, staring at me. I'm not sure what else I can say to convince him. "I should go too."

"Bye." I wave and swivel on the ball of my shoe.

I wait for him to be lost in the crowd before I slide into line, pissed off that he took ten minutes from my solitude.

THE MINUTE I situate myself on the park bench and open my sandwich, my phone vibrates.

I look at my mom's name and sigh, pressing the voice-mail button.

A minute later, it's vibrating again. If I talk to her

briefly, maybe I can salvage a little time to myself. I slide my thumb across the screen and hold the phone to my ear.

"Hey, Mom," I say.

"Bella. How are things?"

"Good. I'm just having lunch."

"I have great news," she says, and her mood is surprisingly chipper—which means she's met someone.

"Who is he?" I ask.

She giggles as if she's thirteen and a boy just said he likes her. My mom is a true romantic, but she keeps kissing frogs. If she didn't manage a successful bakery she loves, I think she'd die of a lonely heart. She desperately tries to find someone. Unfortunately, she needs someone else to pick the person. Her type of man isn't the grow-old-with-me type.

"I'm blushing right now. You always know when there's a man in my life."

Call it twenty-seven years of observation.

I bite into my tuna because let's be honest, my mom isn't going to complain if I'm chewing in her ear. "Who is he?"

"You'll get to meet him because he's bringing me to New York! I'll be there either Wednesday or Thursday, then he's taking me to his house in the Hamptons." She squeals.

I roll my eyes. "He does *own* the house, right? This isn't like the time that guy broke in and the owners found you both naked on a bearskin rug in front of the fireplace?"

"He didn't break in. He had a key."

"He stole the key from their hiding place."

"Well, they should've changed the hiding spot after they fired him."

I sigh. She's legit sticking up for a man she later found in her bed with some street-corner florist. "Anyway, let me know when you're flying in and we'll plan dinner or something."

"Perfect."

"What's his name?" I take another bite of my sandwich.

"Greg Throttle."

I choke on tuna fish. A small girl in her Catholic school uniform gives me a look of disgust as she walks by, holding her mom's hand. *Just wait, little girl. The world isn't filled with rainbows and sunshine.*

"Mom," I say. "Where did you meet him, and do you know who Greg Throttle is?"

She sighs into the phone as though she's remembering, and I wait for her version of their perfectly orchestrated meet-cute. Every one of my mom's boyfriends has come with some cutesy story about how they met. "He kept coming into the bakery every morning for a coffee and my frittata. He'd tuck himself into the corner by the window and read the paper for a half hour before heading out. I was in the middle of this book I couldn't put down, sneaking pages between customers. He saw me reading and asked about the book. I told him it was for my book club and he asked if he could join."

I roll my eyes for the fifth time in this conversation. If she was here to see it, she'd tell me they're going to get stuck facing the back of my head at some point. But honestly, how does she not see the warning signs? "And you do know Greg Throttle is a huge developer in New York? Why is he in Florida, asking about book clubs?"

It totally doesn't hold weight. Someone is acting like him and my mom is buying it.

"He said he's here to look at a few properties on the ocean. You know how so much was wiped out by the hurricane. Our smaller hotels and motels are struggling."

I suppose that could be true, but the book club? A mogul like Greg Throttle does not have time for a book club.

"Well, I'll be happy to see you," I say. I can get a read on the guy when I meet him.

"Me too." Her tone holds that airy quality it does when she's in love. Which only means she'll fall that much harder when his true colors are shown. I have no idea how she can continue to pick herself up time and time again. "I'll figure out the details and let you know."

"Sounds good." I hear her mixer start. "Mom?"

The mixer shuts off. "Yeah, sweetie?"

"Just, you know... be careful."

She laughs. "One day, Bella."

"What?"

"One day a man is going to come into your life. Then you'll believe."

I take another bite of my tuna sandwich. She thinks because I'm skeptical about men, I don't believe in love or even want a relationship. That's not true, but I have a lot on my plate right now. Including a business to build, which she should understand. A love life is last on the list—although I could use a man in my bedroom, that's for sure.

"And he'll want to join a book club with a middle-aged woman who's not an heiress?" I ask.

"Nice, Bella." The mixer starts again.

"I'm sorry."

My dad died young. I can't fault my mom for wanting to find whatever they had with someone else. It's not that I doubt someone like Greg Throttle could fall for my mom, she just doesn't have the best track record.

"I have to make a wedding cake for this weekend, so I'll touch base with you next week."

"Okay, bye."

She hangs up with no goodbye, and I mentally kick myself for being so cynical with her. But come on, there have been so many men throughout my life that she thought might be the second love of her life.

Now my lunch is ruined because the guilt of being bitchy to my mom hangs over me like a storm cloud, blocking me from enjoying the sun. I finish my tuna sandwich, toss the wrapper into the trash, and head back to my office, crossing my fingers that I don't have another run-in with Carmelo Mancini.

CHAPTER FOUR

Carm

Every Thursday, my two older brothers and I lunch at the Trading Post. As I walk through the lunch crowd to our usual table that Dom always secures, I shake hands and slap the backs of some other regulars.

"About fucking time," Dom groans. Seriously, could the man be happy for once?

"Then let's do dinner instead of lunch. I am a real estate broker."

My older brother places his fork down and wipes his mouth, his tie swung over his shoulder in case he spills. He's my brother and all, but he looks like a dick.

"He finally made it." Enzo eyes Dom across the table and winks, downing a big gulp of water.

"Um... not to be mean, you don't have shit to do except get your girlfriend off."

"I just snagged a big client today," Enzo says. "Annie and I are going to celebrate tonight."

"Cool. Maybe she'll give you a hand job under the table."

Dom high-fives me. He's about as sick as I am by how much those two go at it. When will the dry spell happen so I can make fun of him?

"Jealousy looks like shit on you," Enzo says.

Our usual server, Kate, interrupts us, and Enzo should be thanking his balls. "Usual, Carm?"

Her hair is down and curled instead of being in a pony-tail, and her full face of makeup looks ready to slip off her face. Must be hot in the kitchen, or she's been busy this lunch hour.

"That'd be great. Thanks."

She smiles, and I turn back to my brothers, who are looking at me with expectant eyes.

"What?" I ask.

"She likes you," Enzo says, cutting up his goat cheese pizza.

"And?"

"Are you going to ask her out?" Dom asks.

"No."

"Why not?" Enzo pries.

"Maybe because I'm not you and I like variety."

He shakes his head, biting into his pizza. Dom puts a fork into his pasta, surprisingly laxer than he usually is at lunch.

"What about you? How's the whole fuck buddy thing going?" I ask Dom. Other than my news about scoring a meeting with a powerful developer next week, I don't want their attention on me because I'll only rant about the she-devil. Even I'm sick of listening to myself complain about her.

He smiles. "Perfect."

Enzo and I exchange a look. We've seen it before. Dom gets bored easily.

"Still?" I probe.

He piles another forkful of pasta into his mouth and nods.

"I'm impressed." Enzo smiles.

"You're about to end up in his boat." I flip my thumb in Enzo's direction.

Dom mocks offense. "You have no idea how great my life is."

I roll my eyes, and thankfully Kate comes over with a Stella but has no time to give me her flirtatious looks. I know she likes me, but anyone can tell she's one of those girls you go on a date with and then she's waiting by the phone. We'd have to find a new place to lunch every Thursday, and I don't want to listen to my brothers' bitching.

"Other than the twenty-four seven sex you're having, which we all know will eventually die a sudden death, why do you actually enjoy being in a relationship?" Dom asks.

I quirk my brow at Dom. "You fell for your fuck buddy?"

He shakes his head and gives me an expression that says, "shut the fuck up, you have no idea what you're talking about."

Enzo puts down his piece of pizza and wipes his mouth. "It's hard to explain. I mean, the sex is crazy good. The more she figures out what makes me tick and I figure out what drives her crazy, the pleasure just increases. But it's not just that. It's her. The way her body slides into my side on the couch, her cute pink toes running along the top of my feet under the blanket, the way she's never afraid to speak her mind—"

"Okay, we get it." I yawn from boredom.

Enzo buries his head back in his pizza. I could razz him about pink toes and snuggle time, but he doesn't care. I get no reaction out of him anymore, so what fun is that?

"Did you hear Mauro and his fiancée are coming to New York?" Dom asks.

"We were on the same group text," I say.

"He said dinner on Friday, I think?" Enzo rehashes.

Now I'm worried about my brothers' memories. We were *all* on the same thread.

"Who's making the reservations?" Dom asks.

We each put down our silverware and put our fists on our open palms.

"One. Two. Three."

Dom shoots paper.

I shoot scissors.

Enzo shoots paper.

I click my tongue on the roof of my mouth, thankful I'm out. Even though we all know Enzo will lose. He always does.

They stare at one another.

"Annie's not here to save you," Dom eggs him.

"One. Two. Three," Enzo says.

Dom shoots rock.

Enzo shoots scissors. He shakes his head, and we laugh.

Told you. The guy can't win to save his life.

He eyes us. "Fine, but no complaints on what I book."

"I don't care where we go. Maybe Annie should take Maddie and go somewhere girly," I say.

Enzo crinkles his forehead.

"Oh, I forgot you can't go an hour without her." I take a sip from my Stella.

"No, it's just we barely know Maddie. Wouldn't it be nice to get to know her? If you dipshits had girlfriends, it'd make this a lot easier."

Here we go. I expected this type of lecturing if Dom was the one to fall first, but Enzo? Well, I guess I thought he'd be the last to fall in love.

I groan. "A couples' dinner?"

Kate places my salad in front of me. "Here you go, Carm."

"Thanks, Kate."

She nods and heads off to one of her other tables.

"It's not like I'm asking you to bring someone, but don't try to kick the girls out and have a guys' night."

Dom turns toward me, and we exchange a look of boredom.

I clap once because any more relationship talk and I'm going to throw up all over my chef salad. "I have a meeting next week with a huge developer."

"That's cool," Enzo says.

His lack of excitement annoys me. "I'm talking huge. Greg Throttle, guys. I mean, he reached out to me. How crazy is that? I swore Justin was fucking with me when he came into my office."

"Great news," Dom says.

"Especially since evil she-devil is stealing my clients on the elevator."

Dom's phone chimes and he pulls it out of his pocket. I see now my life is of no importance to either of them.

"Shit, I better go." Dom takes out his wallet and throws some bills on the table, standing in the process. He pats my shoulder. "Way to go, little brother."

Enzo says goodbye and Dom's gone.

"I celebrate your shit!" I call after him and stab my lettuce with a fork.

"Don't pout, we're just busy. It's great, and if you hook him, we'll celebrate with Mauro." Enzo seems genuine. "Oh, by the way, Annie's talking about wanting to rent a house in the Hamptons this summer. Can you find me something?"

'Tis the season in New York, but they're a few months late.

"Memorial Day is in three weeks."

He chews his pizza.

"You're willing to give up all your weekends?"

"I'm not giving them up. I'll be there with Annie." He sips his water. "Can you please stop acting like some childish douche about me and monogamy?"

I ignore him and stay on the topic of properties. "I'll look when I get back to the office, but it's gonna cost you, and since you left your job for Annie—"

"I didn't leave my job for her." The bite in his tone says he's a minute away from grabbing me by my shirt. "I'm my own boss. You of all people should understand how great that is."

I nod. He seems touchy, so I figure it's better to leave that topic where it is. "Like I said, I'll look when I get back. I need to know how much you want to spend and where you want to be. Does it have to be beachfront? Are you opposed to sharing with others? That's what most people do, since it's so expensive."

His face twists into a grimace. "We're not staying with anyone else."

"Well yeah, how else would you two spend the weekend naked?"

"Jealousy doesn't suit you," he says again, his cocky smirk on display.

I pull out my phone. "Find something original. Jealous? Never. I'm happy."

"Are you?" he asks.

"You're hanging around too much estrogen. We're not going to sit here and talk about our feelings." I search my phone for the few contacts I have in the Hamptons.

I'm a little jealous that he'll be doing the Hamptons. It's something I've always wanted to experience but building a real estate company doesn't afford you the weekends off. That'd be career suicide. The few times I've gone out for a party there, I envied my friends who drove out to the beach every Friday.

Enzo leans back in his chair. "Humor me, will you? Why are you so against a relationship? I had my own reasons, but what are yours?"

I blow out a breath and stare at him. Do we really want to do this now? "I'm twenty-nine. There's no rush."

"But one day?"

"Who are you—Ma? Just because you jumped off the bachelor plane and nosedived right onto the soon-to-be-married landing pad, don't expect me to."

He laughs, digs his wallet out of the pocket of his suit jacket, and tosses down cash. "I'll talk to Annie and get the answers to your questions. Let me know about the place as soon as possible."

I refrain from rolling my eyes at this new brother Annie has constructed with her magic pussy that gets him to do anything she commands. "You know we're in the same building? We can share a cab."

"Annie's down the road having lunch with Mae. We're cutting out early to head to Central Park for a walk."

"You two are growing a new company, remember?"

He's already standing and sliding his chair back in. "Sometimes you have to stop and enjoy what life is offering you."

"Seriously, does she have a spell over you? What the hell?" I ask, pushing away my salad. My brother is someone I barely recognize these days.

He laughs and leaves the restaurant.

Kate grabs his plate and his cup. "Do you mind closing your tab? I'm leaving early today. Or I could have one of the other servers handle it when you're ready."

I take Enzo and Dom's cash and hand her my card.

"We could share a cab?" she asks, my credit card between her two fingers, right by her breasts.

I lean back in my seat. Her invitation is obviously more than just to share a cab given that she has no idea where I'm headed next. It'd be so easy to go somewhere with her. But even I have a conscience. I'm game when the woman involved knows the score, but Kate? She'd want a boyfriend, and that's not a name I intend to go by.

"Sorry, I have to get back to work."

Her lips dip, and she walks to the hallway.

Guess I'll add her to the list of women I've pissed off today. And just think, it's only lunch.

CHAPTER FIVE

Bella

I'm in my office when Max peeks her head in. Her messy bob with blue ombre looks gorgeous on her. I envy her for the self-esteem to do it. Makes me want to give myself a makeover.

"There's a girl named Annie Stewart here for you," she says.

"Dark hair? Cute smile?"

She nods.

"Send her in."

Max opens my door all the way and Annie waves from the other side of Max's desk. "Sorry for interrupting, this won't take long." She smiles at Max.

Annie is girl-next-door gorgeous. She has a face that makes you feel as though you can trust her with your darkest secrets. I've yet to meet the other Mancini in this office building, but I can see why he nailed her down when he got the chance.

Max is about to shut the door, but Annie stops her. "You might be interested in this too."

Max exchanges a look with me and leans her shoulder on the doorframe. Annie positions herself between us.

"So the building is kind of small as far as office buildings go. I come from working in a huge high-rise where you might never see the same person twice. Anyway, I thought it would be fun to organize a get-together?" She hands me a flyer for duckpin bowling then passes one to Max. "They're these little pins and small balls. I rented it out for the night. There'll be appetizers. It's a way for all of us to get to know one another."

"Why?" Max asks like the true New York City native she is.

It's one thing I love about her, but I'm from a small town in Florida, so I get what Annie's trying to do. It'd be nice to get to know the people we ride up and down the elevator with every day, rather than suffer through awkward silence.

Annie stares at Max as though she's the snarky high school girl who wears black every day. "Just for friendship and to make it more pleasant around here."

Max hands back the flyer. "I'm out."

Annie's smile turns down as she casts her gaze on me.

"Sorry, she's not into meeting new people." I shrug.

"Will you come?"

I read the date. Tomorrow. I don't even have the excuse of visiting clients at night or showing property anymore. That was always my go-to. Annie doesn't know me though. I could lie about a significant other or even a dentist appointment. But seeing how deflated she seemed when

Max shut her down, I find myself not wanting to let her down further.

"Sure, I'll go."

"Really?" Her eyes light up.

"Am I the only one accepting this invitation?" I ask.

"No! Most of the people from the accounting firm on the fourth floor are coming, and same with the architectural firm on the second." I wonder who else might be coming and I guess she reads my face because she says, "Carm isn't coming. He has a meeting or something. The guy has no social life."

I find the tension that was building inside me dissipate. "Great. I'll see you then."

"It's going to be so much fun." She turns on her heels and heads to my door but whips around one more time. "And you get to meet Enzo. No worries, he's nothing like Carm."

I smile. "I look forward to it."

Annie and her giddy excitement walk out of my office, past Max, and out the door.

Max twirls around in her chair. "Why would you go to that thing?"

I shrug. "Because we should be friendly."

She stares at me with an expression of boredom, tipping her glasses down to the tip of her nose. "This isn't some sitcom where we all get together and join a bowling league." She bends her arm and swings it back and forth.

"It's a meet-and-greet and who knows? Maybe I'll pick up a few clients."

She takes that into consideration by tilting her head in an I-guess-you-have-a-point gesture. "True. Maybe I'll go with you."

"Really?" I ask, resembling Annie moments ago.

"Calm down there, Strawberry Shortcake. I said maybe." She swivels back around, pushing up her dark glasses.

I sit at my desk, second-guessing my decision and realizing there's a reason Annie works at an ad agency. She can probably sell anyone on anything.

THE NEXT DAY, my phone vibrates on my desk and my friend Evie's name flashes on the screen.

"Hey," I say, swiveling my chair to stare out my window at the dismal view of a brick wall.

"What's up, cupcake?"

"You're chipper."

"I got laid last night," she says.

I nod. "Good to know."

"You should try it sometime. It's fun." She's mumbling over food.

"Is that the point of your call? To harass me about my non-existent sex life?"

Evie is a freelance graphic designer who works out of her house. She's probably in her pajamas on the couch, eating leftover Thai food right now.

"I want out of Manhattan for the summer."

"Okay, and that has what to do with me?" I cross my legs and trace a pattern through the mortar with my eyes.

"If I have to spell it out, I'm afraid this whole FSBO thing isn't for you." She munches in my ear again. Now I hear a mouse click, which means she's working as she talks to me. Which also means I'll be hanging up frustrated after repeating myself ten times.

"You're late. All the good properties are taken." I swivel

my chair to do a search because I know she won't take my word for it. "Not to mention, are you talking about sharing or going solo? Solo will cost you."

"I was hoping to round up you and maybe Max. Who else could we ask?"

I laugh. "We know no one. I just started a company and you work from home."

"Ask Max. I'm sure she's got friends. Half the fun is getting to know your roommates, then we can all become lifelong friends."

"Hmm, I think I've heard of this before. Oh yeah, *Summer Rental* on Bravo."

She laughs. "I might've binge-watched last season, but come on. It looks like so much fun. Parties. Hook-ups. Like when we were in college! You do remember what it was like to get laid, don't you?"

I roll my eyes. "Even if I could find a place, every weekend is a lot of time for me to take off and—"

"Live a little, will you? A pool, the sun, the beach, the guys. What is there not to like?"

I stare at the ceiling. She's not going to let this go. Evie has tenacity similar to a bulldog. "I have a mortgage to pay. Customers to service."

"Keep listing your excuses." Her annoyance rings through the line. "One day, you're going to have to put yourself out there."

I blow out a breath. "I'll look into it for you. I have some connections."

"I'd really love to experience it with my best friend, I'm just saying," she says through another mouthful of food.

I want to scream at the top of my lungs that her best friend has to survive first. That leaving my steady income job wasn't exactly my first choice, but I did what I had to and now she needs to let me get comfortable in my new role. But that's not Evie. The girl was born wild. I love that about her. Hell, I would never have pulled my head out of my book if it wasn't for her.

"I'll think about it."

She blows out a breath. "Okay. You know I'm being as gentle as I can."

I giggle. "I do."

"We could find ourselves some sugar daddies," she jokes, because neither of us wants this conversation to go downhill.

I play her game. "They'd take us on shopping sprees and fly us on their personal jets."

"They'd have to be best friends so we could have mansions next to one another. I'll be the best aunt to your kids—buy them a pony just because I can."

I smile, a genuine one, while reminiscing about how when we were in college, we insisted we'd live within a stone's throw of each other because not being in one another's life every day was too painful to think about. "You'd probably be screwing the pool guy."

She laughs so hard. "Shit!" The phone drops. A minute later, she picks it back up. "Sorry, I spit out my soda."

"I'll let you go."

"Call me later."

We hang up and I click on a few rental properties, but I don't like the idea of Evie staying with people she doesn't know. But even if I considered it, we still couldn't afford what we'd want.

Not that I'm even considering it.

"Max?" I call, and she swivels her chair around. "Do you want to do the Hamptons this summer? Evie wants to rent a place. Or do you know anyone who needs another roommate?" At least if Max knows someone, it'd be safer for Evie.

Her wrinkled forehead tells me I don't have to wait for what comes out of her mouth. "My friends aren't really into the Hamptons scene."

I nod because I kind of figured as much. I met Max in my early twenties when she worked at the front desk of the real estate broker's office. We formed a friendship and when I left to start my own business, she agreed to follow.

"And you can't go why?"

I blow out a breath and look around the office.

She raises her eyebrows. "Jess and Brent can handle things on the weekends."

I bury my head in the computer, looking at the beach and the ocean, the peacefulness pouring out of the pictures as though they're begging me to change my mind. These people are good at selling the Hamptons' summer experience.

"And you could use a little time away." Max is leaning on the doorframe now. "You should go with Evie. Best friend bonding time."

I glance at the clock, wanting out of the pressure of another person telling me what I need. I've had enough of that over the past year to last a lifetime.

"Shit. The meet-and-greet thing. Are you coming?" I ask, grabbing my jacket and purse.

"Nah, you're better with the clients than me anyway." She sits at her desk.

"Come on. You could use a little fun too."

"Believe me, I got laid five times last week. I get out plenty. It's your vag I'm worried about." Her eyes divert to my lower half.

"Five different men?" I ask, shocked but not judging.

She laughs and covers her mouth. "Could you imagine? I wish, but I do have to say the guy last week was like five different men. I swear he fucked different every day of the week."

"Do I even want to know?"

She laughs, glancing over her shoulder at Brent, who's on the phone. "Let's just say it was a lot like the work week. Monday was slow and lazy, but by the time Friday came around, it was party time."

Jealousy slaps me hard. What is it like to lock all your insecurities away and trust your partner? Maybe Evie has a point.

"Okay, well, hopefully we can at least get the word out about us." I take a healthy stack of our business cards from her desk and shove them inside my purse.

"Just have fun. We're doing pretty well." She winks and shoos me out the door.

I open our door and step into the hallway just as Carmelo Mancini walks out of his offices. He's not wearing a suit today. Instead he's in jeans and a V-neck T-shirt that clings to his strong shoulders and biceps. He's putting his arms into a light jacket without realizing I'm watching.

He looks up after pushing his other arm into the sleeve, then he graces me with a smile that almost makes me grab the doorknob behind me like a life vest before I crumble to the floor. He's breathtakingly gorgeous and shouldn't be able to surprise people like this.

We both step forward, but he holds out his hand. "After you."

My heart gallops while I walk in front of him down the quiet hallway, but not for the usual reason it does when a man is following me.

CHAPTER SIX

Carm

Since my client had to move our appointment to a different evening, I was going to head to my brother's office and tag along with him and Annie to the stupid meet-and-greet they set up. Or I should say Annie. No way Enzo had a hand in this. He likes to socialize with others the same way a cat does—on his terms.

But plans change.

The plan now is to find out if Bella Scott is attending the little shindig tonight. I'm happy to follow her while she's wearing those plaid pants and black high heels. Her matching jacket is just short enough that I can watch her ass move as she struts toward the elevator.

Yeah, yeah, I know I'm being a complete douche, but seriously, no heterosexual male could keep his eyes off the luscious view in front of me.

She stops, swivels, and my eyes don't have enough time

to clip up. By the time I do meet her gaze, she's staring at me with her head tilted and impatience in her beautiful green eyes. Her ivory blouse dips between her breasts. If she wasn't my enemy, I'd suggest skipping the duckpin bowling and heading back to my place.

"Mind keeping your eyes up here?" She uses two fingers to point at her eyes.

I swallow, hoping the desire coursing through my body isn't obvious and abates quickly. "Sorry, I'm human."

She presses her lips together and shakes her head. The elevator arrives and she steps in, clutching her purse at her side.

"You heading to the meet-and-greet?" I ask.

"Yeah," she answers, her eyes focused on the numbers above the door.

I'd chance a closer look at her, but she can't know she has a leg up on me. She's beautiful and she knows it, and I'm sure she wouldn't fail to use it against me.

"Sorry to hear you can't make it." It's clear from her tone that she's the opposite of sorry. She actually sounds pleased.

I tilt my head. She was already informed I wouldn't be there. *Interesting.* How did she...

Annie.

I *wasn't* going to go—until one client changed our meeting and the other was stolen. This building is small by New York City standards, but my business breeds on connections with people. Hopefully I'll walk away from tonight with a few leads. "Actually, my plans changed. I'm going now. We can share a cab."

The elevator doors open, and she sprints out.

"I have to make a pit stop first," she says over her shoulder, never making direct eye contact with me.

She opens the front door of the building before I have a chance to hold it open for her. I'm not a complete douche. An Italian mama raised me.

"I don't mind. We're early. I was going to do a few practice runs."

Because I *have* to beat Enzo tonight. Another reason I changed my mind. I never give up a chance to beat my bigger brother.

"I don't think so." She stops on the curb, holding her hand out for a taxi.

"Come on. Might as well get to know one another." I don't know why I'm pushing so hard. Keep your friends close and your enemies closer?

Her eyes zero in on something over my shoulder, and I follow her line of sight to my billboard ad.

"Want me to strip down so you can compare?" I ask.

Her mouth parts slightly. A taxi stops in front of her, but she's still processing my words. Maybe she wants me to strip. Hell, I wouldn't mind a whole enemies-fuck-fest, getting all the pent-up anger toward one another out in a sweaty mess of ripped clothes and love bites. But I'm not sure she's the type of woman who goes for that.

I open the taxi door for her, and she slides in but doesn't move over.

"Come on, what's the big deal?"

She leans forward, shuts the door, and the taxi pulls away from the corner before I have a chance to hop in.

"What's up, little brother?" Enzo asks as he comes out of the building with Annie. Her phone is against her ear, and he's carrying her briefcase.

I shake my head. My, how times have changed. "I'm likable, right?"

Annie glances up from her phone, shifts her vision to Enzo, then back to her phone.

"Yeah, of course," Enzo answers.

"Annie?" I ask.

She puts up her finger and her body slides behind Enzo. She's dodging me.

"Annie?"

She glances up and blows out a breath. "You can be kind of a douche to women. Not me, but I'm with your brother so..." Her shoulders rise like it doesn't really matter.

"By all means, don't hold back." I chuckle, my hands finding the pockets of my jeans.

She glances at Enzo and he nods as though this is a conversation they've previously had. "You're a loyal brother and son. And you'd do anything for your friends. All admirable traits. You work hard, and your clients always come first."

I wave for her to get to the point. Again, her eyes shift. I'm making her uncomfortable, which only spurs my need to hear her opinion.

"You tend to attract a certain type of woman. And to those women, you're likable. But to other women, you're maybe a tad... forward?" she says as though it's a hypothesis she's about to test, but in her mind, it's already truth.

Enzo slaps my shoulder. "It's okay. I was probably the same."

Enzo and I aren't the same. He buried himself in his work until he had no option but to notice Annie because she was front and center. I pick up women. Women I don't intend to have a relationship with. When I think about it, I'm not sure I've ever had a woman as a friend. Anyone I considered a friend quickly fell into bed with me.

"It's fine. Everyone has a type, Carm."

"Yours are the gym and bar girls." Enzo smiles, but something in his tone indicates there's more to it.

"There's nothing wrong with that. Like when you met my friend Mae. You came off as cocky and arrogant and she didn't like it. Those things aren't important to her. She wants a sense of humor and someone who will bring her chicken soup when she's sick." Annie buries her head in her phone again.

"I'm funny."

"No doubt." Enzo slaps my shoulder again as if he's trying to lessen the blow his girlfriend is delivering.

"You are, but that's not the first quality you show people." Her eyebrows fly halfway up her forehead. "If the girl isn't down to fool around, you're not really interested."

Enzo raises his hand to flag down a cab.

"I make jokes all the time."

She tucks her phone into her purse, looks at me square in the eye, and shrugs.

Fucking shrugs. Does she not understand she's insulting me right now?

"It's okay, Carm. You're getting all high-strung for nothing. You're not interested in getting to know the woman. You have a right to that." She pats my arm and slides into the taxi.

"Are you joining us?" Enzo asks, holding open the door.

"Fuck yeah." I slide into the cab next to Annie, who shrinks back when my thigh touches hers.

My brother squeezes in, eyeing his girlfriend beside me. Her back is almost plastered to the door frame.

"Yeah, this isn't going to work." Her hand's on the cab door to open it when the guy pulls away from the curb.

So we take off with me riding bitch.

Enzo leans forward, telling the cab driver the address.

I wiggle my shoulders for some room. "Where were we? Oh yeah, the fact that you think I'm not a people person. How do you think I've become so successful in this business?"

Annie blows out a breath and looks at Enzo.

"Let's just leave it be for now," Enzo says, staring out the window. He knows I'm not going to, and he doesn't want to see his girlfriend upset because the fucking sun revolves around her these days.

"No."

"Jesus, Carm!" Annie snaps, alarming everyone in the car.

Even the cabbie is staring at us through the rearview mirror.

Enzo's head swivels so fast, I'm surprised he can stop it from circling around in a three-sixty.

"What?" I ask like a wounded puppy.

"You're only interested in fucking these women, so why would you think you're leaving a good lasting impression on them? It's not rocket science. You screw them and leave them, probably before you find out their last name or anything about them other than what drink they were consuming when you ordered them a second." Annie huffs and crosses her arms. "You want my unguarded opinion?"

"Annie," Enzo says, which means there's definitely been some discussion about me.

"No." I put my hand up in Enzo's face. "Let the lady speak."

My eyes lock with hers, and just like the Annie I'm growing to love like a sister, she doesn't back down. "You can be a disgusting pig who sees no value in a woman beyond what's between their legs."

"Jesus Christ," Enzo says under his breath.

"Disgusting pig? At least call me a cow, because I am grade-A beef, Annie."

Her eyes lose their fire and she shakes her head. "Impossible." She stares out the window.

I laugh. "Man, you're a ballbuster." I swing my arm around her and find it's a helluva lot more comfortable. "You could definitely be a Mancini. Don't let Enzo shut you up."

She continues to shake her head.

"Get your arm off her," Enzo says in his low, brooding tone.

Lucky for him we arrive at our destination. Once he opens up the door, my lungs can finally fully expand.

"Pay for the cab," he says.

I dig for cash in my pocket and pay the cab because I kind of invited myself along for the ride.

Once we're all on the street, I stare at Annie. "For you, I'm going to try to make friends with my new neighbor across the hall. How hard can it be to befriend the she-devil?"

Annie looks at Enzo, uncertainty in her eyes. We're about to walk in when her hand lands on my forearm, stopping me. I turn, and in her eyes isn't uncertainty or disgust or any of the emotions I've seen there this entire conversation. It's sympathy. I wait to hear what she seems desperate to convey, but she stays silent.

"What?" I ask, the door falling from my grasp.

"I just... I don't want to see you miss out—"

"Enough." Enzo puts his hands on her cheeks and walks her to the wall of the building, where he places his lips on hers.

"You're in public," I say, but Enzo doesn't stop. "Annie was talking to me."

"There you are." Justin heaves for a breath, stopping next to me. "Is your phone off?"

My eyes search out Enzo and Annie, who are still sucking face as though they're fourteen and trying to get in a make-out session before their parents pick them up. And I'm the one who's preoccupied with getting one thing from the opposite sex?

I pull out my phone, and sure as shit, I silenced it.

Justin opens the door, waiting for me to walk in first. Whatever Annie was getting at, I'll figure out later.

I enter and turn to Justin. "What's up?"

"We have an offer on Haverhill."

I clap him on the back. "Finally, some good fucking news."

Twenty minutes later, I'm tucked in a corner, getting the details of the offer from the other realtor. I've forgotten all the bullshit Annie said until she-devil walks in wearing an outfit worthy of a salute from my dick.

Maybe Annie has a point.

CHAPTER SEVEN

Bella

I walk into the building the bowling alley is located in, and of course, the first thing I see is Carmelo Mancini tucked into a corner of the lobby. To my surprise, he's not with a woman. Then again, if he's like every other real estate broker I know, his job will always be his mistress. So technically, he's probably focused on the most important person in his life right now and trying to drum up new business.

I ignore Carmelo and walk up the stairs, thankful I have on jeans. The perv would probably look up my skirt without apology. I hate that I almost get a thrill from the idea of him doing so. His gaze in the hallway today was transparent. He was checking me out, and I can't say I didn't imagine us stuck in an elevator—until reality crashed down on me.

"Whoa, hold up." Carmelo barrels up the stairs before I

reach the third floor. "Not cool, leaving me on the sidewalk." He smiles. A charming one that my mother would fall in love with.

"I told you I had a pit stop."

His gaze travels down my body again. "I see. I'm not sure which outfit I pre..." His words trail off as though he's stopping himself from continuing the conversation. "Want to play some duckpin?"

I ignore him and continue up the stairs. At the top, he opens the door like a gentleman, and I try not to look behind me to see what he's staring at as I walk through the door.

The space is nothing like I expected. It's older, and it looks as if these lanes have been here forever. This isn't some trendy new place hipsters flock to. But the space does look as though it's been decorated for office parties. All the team-building stuff companies preach have made places like this thrive. But maybe I'm just extra annoyed because I've been going to networking events since I got my real estate license. I've had enough club soda with lime for a lifetime.

I recognize a few faces from the building. Everyone we pass smiles nicely at Carmelo and shakes his hand or slaps his shoulder as if he's been voted prom king. You'd think he was the damn mayor of New York, for God's sake. Which makes me feel as though my time here is wasted. He owns the market of our small office building.

"There you are." Annie approaches me, eyeing Carmelo before swinging her arm through mine and pulling me over to the bar and what looks like an older version of Carm. "This is Enzo," she says, pride in her voice as she runs her hand down his arm.

He turns from ordering a drink and flashes a smile as bright as his brother's. His warm brown eyes don't have the same desire that's laced through his brother's blues.

"Enzo, this is Bella," Annie says.

His gaze stays trained on mine as he extends his hand. "Nice to finally meet you."

I shake his hand. "You as well."

"Can I grab you a drink?" he asks.

The bartender places a beer and a glass of wine on the bar top, and Enzo hands Annie the wine. She smiles sweetly at him with a thanks.

"I'll have what Annie's having," I say.

Enzo talks to the bartender, pulling more cash from a money clip in his pocket.

"Here, let me." I open my purse.

"Nonsense." Annie waves me off and shoots Enzo a look.

He smiles and looks at me. "She's the boss."

The bartender pours my wine, and Enzo passes it to me.

"Come on. I'll introduce you to everyone." Annie links her arm with mine again and walks us toward a group of people.

"I see I'm only good enough for some drinks, huh?" Enzo says to our backs.

Annie swivels around but keeps walking. "I'll thank you later." She winks.

"Spare everyone your flirting," Carmelo says to Annie when he reaches us. He eyes my drink and his smile tips down a bit but recovers quickly. "I see someone beat me to it."

"Your brother," Annie says.

"Next one is on me." He solidifies that with a wink that makes my insides go gooey.

I shake off the feeling and allow Annie to take me into the middle of a circle of people. She politely interrupts to introduce me to employees of the accounting firm in our building. I nod, chitchat, and hand out a few cards. One guy asks me if it's my assistant who has the different color hair and dark glasses. I get the feeling he wants to pry for more information, like if she's single, but he doesn't ask.

Annie gets pulled away by the owner of the accounting firm, and shortly after, everyone finds lanes to bowl. Enzo and Carmelo are razzing one another in the far lane. Both of them have pushed up their sleeves and are practicing.

A guy I haven't met walks up to me. "I've been asked to grab you. You'll be bowling with Carmelo Mancini."

"And you are?" I've seen the guy around, though he's usually frantic and has his phone glued to his ear.

"I'm Justin. Carm's assistant." The blond-haired kid— and I say kid because he can't be more than twenty-one yet —holds out his hand.

I take his hand and shake. "Nice to meet you."

"I was hoping Max would come tonight," he says as he nods for me to go first.

My gut twists over the fact that I have to bowl with Carmelo, but my guess is Annie planned this. She's obviously going to bowl with Enzo, and since she's my new insta best friend and ally, I'm not going to argue.

"Yeah, she's not much of a people person," I say to explain Max's absence.

He chuckles. "I kind of got that when I ran into her the other day."

Something in his body language tells me she made an impression on him, but Max is a complicated creature. I'm not going to get this guy's hopes up. With no piercings or tattoos, he's definitely not her type. Not to mention he's younger than the guys she usually hangs with.

"She doesn't bite, but she has been known to growl," I say.

He chuckles again, his hand running through his long blond strands. "Oh... well..."

I wonder how a guy like him can work for a cool and calculated guy like Carmelo Mancini.

We reach the lane Carmelo and Enzo are bowling in.

"And there you go." All the pins fall, and Carmelo turns around, using two of his fingers like guns, shooting them at Enzo. "I so have you."

Enzo stands, shaking his head. "Sit down, little brother. Let me show you how it's done." He grabs a ball.

"Here you go, Miss Scott," Justin says as if he's delivering me to royalty.

"Thank you," I say politely, wondering where the hell Annie is. I don't want to be stuck with these two brothers who might just wrestle their way down the lane.

With a sigh, I sit on the black leather bench, cross my legs, and sip my wine. The people in the other lanes are filling out their score sheets with their player names.

Carmelo sits next to me. "You done with that yet?"

"No, and regardless, I'm not going to have a second."

"Water? Soda? A big pretzel with cheese? Whatever you want."

I study him for a second. He looks genuine about wanting to get me whatever I want, but why? He treated me like the enemy the first time we met. What's his game plan? I know he has one, because a man like Carmelo isn't nice for no reason.

"I'm good. Thank you."

"Okay." Enzo claps and dramatically points at the lane. "I think that ties us up."

His smug look has me laughing.

Annie walks up from behind us. "You two are ridiculous. Let's do girls versus boys before you two end up in a fistfight."

"Deal," Carmelo says.

Enzo crosses his arms. "No way. Couples."

Annie glances at me. "I'm not sure."

Carmelo eyes me. Obviously, the decision rests with me. I'm not going to be the reason Enzo can't bowl on the same team as his girlfriend. Then again, the thought of teaming up with Carmelo sounds about as much fun as getting a pap smear.

"No, it's fine. I'll be teammates with Carmelo," I say, plastering on my friendly "I'm all good" smile. The one I use when I lose a client but don't want to show how frustrated I am.

"Carm," he says. "Only my ma calls me Carmelo."

He's so close, I can smell his cologne. See the stubble on his face that makes it look like he's always sporting a five o'clock shadow. I realize for the first time that his blue eyes are actually rimmed with hazel.

"Okay," I croak before downing the rest of my wine.

He stands. "Want to shoot rock, paper, scissors to decide who goes first?"

Annie's already prepped with her fist on her palm. This must be a thing with them.

"Oh, I don't care who goes first," I say, standing from the bench.

"Yeah, you do," Carmelo... er, Carm says.

"Let the ladies do it," Enzo says from his spot near the machine that spits out the balls.

"The only reason you want the ladies to do it is because you know you'll lose. Annie's your best shot."

I look at Annie, who shrugs and rolls her eyes, silently saying that this is them—crazy competitive brothers.

"Fine, you go then, Bella." Carm nudges me with his arm.

"On the count of three," Annie says.

"One," Carm says.

"Two," Annie says.

"Three," Enzo says.

I shoot rock.

Annie shoots scissors.

"Whoa!" Carm hollers in my ear then swings his arm around my shoulders. "Good job."

He guides me over to the lane and I realize heels probably weren't the best choice, but I had thought I'd gracefully bow out of the bowling part once it started. Annie takes a seat on the bench and kicks off her heels, pulling a package of socks from her bag. She puts a pair on her feet.

"Here," Annie says, handing me a pair. "I ran out at lunch and it's a three-pack."

"They don't have bowling shoes?" I ask.

"Nope, and you can walk as far down the lane as you want. It's pretty low key here."

I nod. *Good to know.*

"Maybe we should start you guys closer to the pins, like a ladies' tee in golf," Carm says.

Annie and I whip our heads around.

"We're just as capable as you," Annie sneers and stands.

Carm holds up his hands as Enzo laughs and slaps him on the back.

"You take offense to everything." Carm rolls his eyes.

"Because—" Annie starts, but Enzo comes up behind her and distracts her with his mouth at her ear.

He whispers something, and she melts back into his strong chest. His hands fall to her hips and squeeze.

"You two are in public," Carm says.

I laugh because I was thinking the same thing. Our eyes catch for a moment, and it takes more of my willpower than it should to look away.

Enzo swivels Annie around and captures her lips in a move that's so damn sexy, I'm jealous. Not that I want Enzo, but a man like that has moves I can't fathom.

"Showoff," Carm mumbles, shaking his head. Directing his attention to me, he motions toward the lane. "Ladies first."

"I've never done this before." I stand, and he follows me to the row of small balls.

He picks up one and hands it to me. "This is my first time too. Put it in your palm and act like you know what you're doing. That's the best advice I have for you."

I smile.

He smiles.

Where is the cocky, arrogant flirt? This isn't the man I'm familiar with.

"Okay." He steps back, giving me some space.

I walk up to the lane pretending as if I have some clue how to do this. I swing my arm back then forward, and the ball flies halfway down the lane before landing on the wooden straightaway, barreling toward pins. Three go down on the right side.

"It's a start," I say.

Carm scribbles on the scoresheet. "Now get a spare." He smiles, his eyebrows raising.

"Come on, Bella!" Annie claps behind me. Obviously, her lip lock is done. "Ouch! What? I don't really care who wins," she says to who I suspect must be Enzo.

"If you're going to be a Mancini, you need to try to win at all costs," Enzo says.

"I'm not a Mancini," she says.

"Yet, babe. Yet."

I pick up another ball, that rush of jealousy over what Annie and Enzo share hitting me once again. I wonder how long they've been dating and how they got together?

What am I talking about? I don't have time for a relationship. My new business needs to be my priority for the foreseeable future.

I throw the ball down the lane and only get three more pins down.

Oh well. It's just a game.

I turn around, and Annie's already stepping up with her hand up. "Way to go."

"Spare would have been better," Carm says under his breath.

I narrow my eyes. Just when I thought we were on our way to a civilized coexistence.

Annie rolls her eyes. "It's just a friendly game, Carm."

He taps the pencil on the paper. "Said no one ever."

I sit behind him and grab my wine before remembering I've finished it. I'm going to need another glass after all to get through the next couple hours.

As Annie goes to bowl, Carm swings around, his hand landing on my knee. A million jolts of electricity zip up my leg to my center. "Sorry. I'm just really competitive."

I nod. "It's fine."

Our eyes lock, and he almost looks as if he's trying to figure me out. Exhilaration swims in my stomach. Would I even be able to turn down Carmelo Mancini if he focused his charm my way? I hate that I don't know the answer to that.

"Strike! Yay, baby," Enzo booms.

Carm blinks, and the moment is over. I knew he was trouble, but I'm not sure I knew how much trouble.

CHAPTER EIGHT

Carm

What is it about Bella Scott that grabs hold of me every time she's around? I hate her as much as I want to fuck her. I need to get it together.

Since Annie pretty much told me I'm a douche, I'm trying to be civil and not flirt, but when my hand landed on Bella's knee, a current of warmth shot up my arm. I remember what Annie said about how I come off, but even so, I'll admit that I wanted to grab Bella's hand and take her away from here, press her against the wall outside the bathroom, slide my hand down to her ribs, and grab her ass as I thrust forward so she could feel how hard I was. The dark pink color on her lips would look incredible around my dick.

Nice daydream, but I need to deal with reality.

I pick up my ball, unnerved by how much headspace Bella has been taking up over the past few days. I throw the ball and try to get a strike. Not just because I need to beat my brother, but because she's watching.

Enzo laughs when my ball goes into the gutter. "I have to bring you around more often."

I turn around only to see Bella's eyebrows raised. "Now get a spare," she says, throwing my words back at me.

I laugh and pick up another ball, throwing it up and catching it in my palm. There's no way I'll allow myself to be distracted and lose to Enzo. Thankfully, Annie only got four pins down.

When I let it go, this time it rolls down the center of the lane, and I throw my hands in the air right before the ball makes contact. It crashes into the small pins, and every one goes down except one on the far right. What the hell?

Enzo's laugh is all I hear when I turn to face them.

Bella's eyebrows are still raised. "Spare would've been nicer." She sips the wine she got from the bar a few minutes ago with a blank expression.

The fact she can keep her smile at bay tells me she's a woman who holds her own.

I shake my head, and Enzo takes my spot in the lane as I fall in next to Bella on the bench. Her perfume reminds me of walking through Central Park when spring is in full bloom after the rainfall has helped every flower sprout throughout the vast acreage.

Wait? What the hell was that? Since when do I compare the way a woman smells to... well, anything?

Is this how it starts?

I should ask Enzo.

I adjust in my seat and pick up my beer.

Enzo gets a strike before I can initiate any conversation with Bella, and she's out of her seat before Enzo has a chance to leave the lane.

The entire game goes back and forth. I underestimated Annie and Bella, because they hold their own, all of us getting a feel for the game after the third frame. But now we're tied, and it's come down to the last frame.

Bella spared, and now she's on her last ball. I stand as it heads straight between the front pin and the one behind it. She did it.

"Shit," Enzo says next to me.

"Relax," Annie tells him.

Every pin falls and Bella turns around, both her arms up, and jumps with an exuberant smile. Before I can think better of it, I run over to her, pick her up, and circle her around. There's no way Enzo and Annie can beat us now. Yeah, I may be underestimating Annie, but what Bella just did is hard to replicate.

Her arms wrap around my neck, and she laughs in my ear. Goose bumps travel down my spine. She feels soft and secure against me, her silky cheek pressed against my neck. Of course the congratulatory hug turns me on, and that vision of us I had earlier reappears like an unwanted nightmare.

This woman will never allow me to sleep with her, and even if she did, I'm not cool with the idea of running into my one-night-only affair across the hall every day.

I lower her, and she tucks her hair behind her ears. There's a slight blush on her cheeks now. Did that hug affect her like it did me?

"Way to go, Bella!" Annie high-fives her.

Enzo mumbles something, but I can see it on his face. He's pissed. We don't even have anything riding on this game. But he knows the best part is the bragging rights I'll earn by beating him.

Bella and I do end up winning, but only by five pins.

"Let's go out!" Annie says once she and Bella have their shoes back on. She finishes her glass of wine.

I'm surprised. Other than one night when my dad over-served her Frangelico after dinner, I've never seen Annie drunk. Even that night, it made her more like a tired cat than a party animal. Then again, once Annie entered the picture, Enzo and I stopped going out to clubs like we used to do.

"Yeah, I think I'm going home. Long day," Bella says.

Annie sticks out her bottom lip in a two-year-old pout. "Come on."

"Babe, it's Tuesday night, there's nothing good open," Enzo says.

I keep my mouth shut because I know there are good clubs open. He knows there are good clubs open so he's obviously looking for an excuse not to go. Glancing at my watch, I see that it's only nine.

She falls into Enzo, giving him the eyes. I've seen them before. Specifically, any time he's putting up a fight against her. They work, and it scares the shit out of me because I'm a pleaser by nature. A helluva lot more than Enzo ever was. Which means that if I ever let myself fall for someone like my brother has, she could make me do things I don't really want to do.

"You're going to complain tomorrow when the alarm goes off," he says, but the fight in his voice is gone.

See what I mean? It's crazy.

"Yay!" Annie claps and sets her sights on Bella.

"No. No." Bella puts up her hands. "I am not a night owl, and I have an early meeting tomorrow."

I cross my arms and wait. Annie is a convincer. She just persuaded Ma and Pa to go on vacation to the Caribbean this summer. We all chipped in for their anniversary. Enzo, Dom, and I thought we would rock, paper, scissors on who got to take the trip after Ma refused. But instead of saying no, they accepted the trip after Annie had a chat with them. Imagine two old Italian people on a white beach, fully clothed and criticizing the food, without a kitchen of their own.

"Carm?" Annie says, drawing my attention back to the conversation.

"What Bella said. I'm not into being a third wheel."

"Perfect. I'll cover the bill." Annie steps away.

Enzo places his hand on Annie's arm to stop her. "I've got it."

"So where should we go?" Annie smiles at me.

I glance at Bella. "You agreed?" My tone is accusatory, and the scowl Bella gives in return says she's not happy about it.

Bella looks behind her. "Is there some knockout behind me who distracted you from our conversation?"

I grin. "Jealous?"

"You wish."

Annie's head swivels back and forth between us as though we're entertainment. With the amount of wine she's drunk, she's bound to get nauseated.

"Maybe I do." I raise an eyebrow, challenging her.

Bella rolls her eyes.

A stream of people come by to say goodbye and thank Annie for organizing the night. Justin lingers. My assumption is that he wants to talk to me but doesn't want to do it in front of the enemy.

I step away from everyone else. "What's up?"

"I wanted to let you know that Mr. Throttle's assistant messaged me this evening and wants to meet you for brunch at The Cobbler at ten thirty tomorrow." He cringes because Throttle is moving up our meeting.

I shrug. "Okay."

"Do you want me to text you in the morning?" He has his phone out, ready to set a reminder.

It's taken me two years to train Justin into the assistant I need him to be, and I can sense his itch to move on. Having him has allowed me to have a social life for the past year. Not the social life of a normal twenty-eight-year-old, but I get out a lot more than I did before he was around. Pretty soon I'll have no choice but to promote him.

"I'm not eighty and senile. I can remember."

He eyes my pocket. "Well, I put it on the calendar."

I purposely don't pull out my phone to set an alarm, just to prove a point. Though I do make a mental note to do so as soon as he's not in sight.

"Thanks, Justin." I pat his shoulder.

Enzo's made his way back to the group, and he and Annie are in a conversation which I'm pretty sure is Enzo asking her to reconsider the whole going out thing. She's still giving him those eyes though, which means we're going clubbing on a Tuesday night.

"I overheard you were going out after, so I wanted to make sure you knew in case you wanted to change your plans."

"Thanks, buddy, but I already have a mother."

Justin nods and runs his hand through his blond hair. "Okay, well, have fun." His eyes shift from Bella to me —twice.

"Do you have a thing for her?" I ask, smirking.

"No!" I swear his voice changes octaves like when I was twelve.

"It's okay if you do." Don't even ask me why I'm

pushing this. I should let it go. Before he has a chance to answer, I shake my head to wave him off. "Thanks, Justin. Have a great night."

"Night, Carm."

My brother waves at Justin as I re-join our foursome.

"You know the clubs." Annie saddles up to me. "Where should we go? I want to dance."

"Dance?" Enzo rolls his eyes behind her, but when she looks at him, he smiles.

Seriously, he's so fucking whipped, I'm losing respect for the guy I looked up to most of my life.

"Annie, I really think I might just go home," Bella says.

"No." She swings her arm through Bella's. "Let's just go for a bit and have some fun."

She escorts Bella out of the bowling alley, and Enzo and I begrudgingly follow, Enzo grumbling the whole time.

"If you're so upset, just say no," I tell him.

Annie and Bella step out onto the streets of Manhattan, laughing.

"I like to make her happy, and she rarely gets the chance to go out and have fun. We spend the majority of our weekends in bed. Not the way you think. We're with our laptops, talking over campaigns and working. If she wants to go dance, I'm gonna dance."

I shake my head, not understanding at all.

He looks at his phone where I see he has the Uber app up. Must've called a car when I was talking with Justin. A dark sedan pulls up to the curb, and he opens the door for the ladies. They slide in and Enzo waits, because he's going to take the front. Of course he is. This time around, Bella's riding bitch.

He chuckles when I slam the door in his face after I get in the back seat.

"Where to, Carm?" Annie asks.

I lean forward and give the driver the name of the club and the address so he can make the change to his system. Seems Enzo put his and Annie's place in when he ordered the car since we hadn't decided where we were headed.

Bella glances at me when my thigh presses against hers. I have no choice. It's a tight squeeze back here. Annie's putting us in a bad situation. There's tension between us, wound so tightly it might break from the smallest action.

I'm man enough to admit I don't possess a lot of willpower when it comes to things I want. I rarely deprive myself, no matter the consequences. But this time, I can't give in to temptation. Tonight, my hands need to remain in my pockets and not on her hips.

Our gazes lock as the cab stops in front of the club. Even I would bet against me tonight.

CHAPTER NINE

Bella

How do I always get myself into these situations? Dr. Newberry told me to assert myself. Not to let people convince me to do something I don't want to or to feel bad because I say no to something. Yet here I am, stepping out of a cab with a man I think of as my enemy, his brother, and his girlfriend.

It'll be nice to have friends at the office. That's my excuse.

Carm, being Carm, glances at the line wrapping around the building and beelines it to the bouncer. Of course he knows him. He probably picks up a different woman every night of the week here.

I watch him talk to the bouncer, his back to me, and can't help but notice that Carm's jeans mold to his ass perfectly.

My belly dips as if I just tipped over a hill on a roller-coaster. What will happen behind those closed doors? Will this club become the location of a memory I'll regret forever? Because when Carm's strong arms and solid chest were pressed against me after I scored a strike, for a moment, I wondered what if he wasn't a high-end broker and I wasn't the FSBO girl? What if we just happened to meet at a coffee shop? Would I have allowed him to take me home and give me a night I'm sure I'd never forget?

"Let's go." Carm waits near the bouncer.

Annie and Enzo head in with me trailing behind.

"You're on a first-name basis, I presume?" I snipe as I pass him.

"A thank you would be nice."

"Thanks," I say over my shoulder, and we step into the dark club with pounding dance music.

Annie and Enzo head straight to the bar. I'm about to follow when Carm grabs my elbow and pulls me to the side. A big body runs into me from behind, and I lose my footing on my heels, falling into Carm's chest. His hands grip my upper arms before I end up in a pile at his feet. Which he'd probably like.

"Thanks," I mumble, humbled by the fact that he saved me from embarrassment.

"Can we call this off for tonight?" he asks.

"Call what off?"

"The fact we dislike each other. I don't really want to be here, and I'm fairly sure you don't either, so why don't we just make the most of it?" He holds my gaze, and I find it hard to look away.

I nod because he's right. We're going to be stuck together all night. Might as well try to make it not completely miserable.

"Good. Now what can I get you to drink?" He places

his hand on the small of my back, guiding me toward the bar.

"I can get my own—"

"What can I get you to drink, Bella?" His words are contrite, as though he's exasperated with me.

"Negroni, please."

He nods. "Done."

I hang back with Annie while Carm squeezes in next to Enzo. The two brothers have a demanding presence with their height and good looks, and it doesn't take them long to be served.

"Want to go out there?" Annie asks.

I glance down at her because I have a few inches on her, especially in my heels. I haven't known her long, but I haven't gotten this vibe from her during office hours.

"Come on. I've got a booth." Carm hands me a drink, and our fingers brush against each other's.

Nothing. No zing. Good.

But then his hand finds my lower back again and electricity flows through my body.

"So what's the word about the Hamptons, Carm? Enzo said you were setting us up." Annie slides into the booth. I half expected her to be on the dance floor already.

"You've given me an impossible task. You should've told me months ago." He sips his drink, leaning back in the circular booth overlooking the dance floor. It's set back enough that we can have a conversation.

"I know, but you know you're my favorite, right?" Annie bats her eyes.

Carm stares blankly at her. "You told Blanca she was your favorite Mancini sibling," he deadpans.

"Ah, but you're my favorite brother." She winks.

"Excuse me?" Enzo asks.

Annie laughs, falling into his chest. "Not including you." She tugs on his hand. "Dance with me," she says with an alluring smile.

He sips his Old-Fashioned and nods, then she drags him out of the booth. Carm and I watch them disappear in the throes of the crowded dance floor.

Who knew all this was happening on a Tuesday night?

"She wants to summer in the Hamptons, huh?" Carm and I can at least talk about real estate. It's what we both know.

"Yeah. Impossible, right?"

I nod. "My friend wants to as well. I searched some rentals, but all that's left are the bigger houses. My friend is all about sharing, but I'm not so sure."

His eyes widen. "You'd spend your weekends in the Hamptons?"

I sip my drink, distracting myself from answering for a moment. He'll just think what he already does—that I'm a slacker. That all I do is take people's money and put their home up on MLS and do nothing else. That I'm not a *real* broker. I know that's half the reason he doesn't like me. He sees me as a sellout.

I shrug. "My friend made a convincing argument."

"I always told myself I'd get big enough one day and I could do it."

"You're still young. There's time."

He takes a sip of his drink, his gaze darting to the dance floor. "It's just—" He looks back my way, a question obviously on the tip of his tongue. He waits a moment before he asks. "Why did you get out of the game?"

My stomach sinks. The last person I'd ever want to have this discussion with is him. So I use the same excuse I tell everyone. "I didn't enjoy it. The constant prospecting for new clients, the long hours, having to be available at a moment's notice if an offer came in. My life was just about work."

He nods before I can finish. He understands. I knew he would.

"I like the money too much." His ego-filled smile shoots in my direction.

I did too. He thinks it's easy money going FSBO, but it's not. Sure, the clients mostly come to me, but there are no huge windfalls when a deal comes together. But it does have its benefits...

"No comeback?" he asks, pushing his half-empty glass into the middle of the table.

"Nope. I get it."

He nods. "Do you think they'd notice if we snuck out?"

Annie and Enzo are on the edge of the dance floor, and she's definitely feeling the alcohol.

"I didn't see her drinking that much at the bowling alley." I take a small sip of my drink, aware that I need to keep my wits about me with this man.

"She's a lightweight, but I'm still not sure why she's drunk as much as she has. She and Enzo are so focused on growing their new ad company, they work all the damn time. I don't understand why she wanted the meet-and-greet in the first place."

"Everyone needs to let off some steam once in a while." I smile, watching her grind her ass into Enzo. His hands are on her hips, but he doesn't seem too into the act—other than watching her movements.

"He fell hard for her," Carm says more to himself than to me, I think.

"What do you mean?"

He looks at me and shakes his head. "Nothing. It's just

my brother seemed to be happily single one minute and ready for the altar the next. It's insane to think how fast life can change."

My breath catches. He has no idea. Has nothing life-changing ever happened to him? I push back the dark thoughts trying to cloud my mind.

"Are you a closet romantic?" I ask, wondering where his comments are coming from.

He makes a sound that says I'm crazy. "I'm too selfish to be into monogamy."

Annie and Enzo disappear toward the bar, while Carm and I are barely sipping our drinks at this point.

"Figures."

"What?" he asks. "I don't have to be ashamed for feeling that way. I don't promise breakfasts and dinner dates and flowers. If I pick you up in a club and go back to your place, you should know I'm not sticking around for cuddle time and breakfast in bed."

I roll my eyes. Just when I thought he was a halfway decent guy. "You're unbelievable."

"Come on. You've never had a one-night stand?"

"Why would I ever tell you that?" I bring my drink back to my lips.

"Because we're here when we'd rather be in bed and we might as well get to know one another." He sips his drink while his gaze remains steady on me over the rim of his glass, waiting for an answer.

"Do you want to play Never Have I Ever or some-thing?" I set my drink on the table and cross my arms.

He shrugs. "Sure. I'm always game for anything."

"You're so juvenile. I'm going to say my goodbyes." I move to slide out of the opposite side of the booth, but Annie and Enzo approach at that exact moment.

Annie's not looking very good. Enzo is practically holding her up. Carm slides out of the booth to help with what he can.

"We're out. Party girl is sleepy," Enzo says.

"Did she get sick?" I ask.

Her pasty complexion screams that if she hasn't, she's going to.

"Not yet." Enzo shakes his head.

"Want help?" Carm asks.

I would've pegged him for the kind of guy to point fingers and laugh at someone who's had too many, but he only seems concerned about his brother's girlfriend.

"Nah. I got her." Enzo sweeps her up and over his shoulder. "Thank God you're wearing pants," he murmurs.

Her hair falls down over her head. I think she might be out cold. She doesn't move at all as Enzo makes his way through the crowd.

"Guess we're off the hook now." I slide out of the booth.

"Wanna share a cab?" Carm asks.

I'd normally say no, but I'd rather not get into a cab by myself at eleven at night. "Sure, but no more talk about one-night stands."

He laughs. "What do I have to do to loosen you up a little?" He waits for me to go first, following right behind me.

When we reach the street, he flags down a cab and I slide in first. I give the driver my address and we sit in silence while the car makes its way through Manhattan.

"I think we should keep this truce going," Carm says out of nowhere.

"I don't hate you. I think *you* hate *me*."

He shifts in his seat to face me. "Just don't steal my clients and we're cool."

"I told you it wasn't intentional."

"But it happened." His eyebrows raise.

"You can't call a truce and then say I'm a liar."

The cab driver chuckles. My gaze shoots to the rearview mirror and we share a look.

"Fine. You didn't steal him. But maybe next time you tell people you can't service them."

"Service them? I'm not a call girl. And I'm not going to turn down business."

The cab driver pulls over to the curb of my condo building, and I move to slide out my side because Carm isn't opening the door to let me out.

He pushes his hand through his hair. "Sorry."

"Are you trying to be nice tonight and it's just not working?"

His attitude has been back and forth all night. One moment he's cool and the next he's hot under the collar.

"No. It's just..." He blows out a breath. "Annie said earlier I was a douche, and I'm not, so I'm trying to show you I'm not. I'm not even sure why I give a shit, but I do." He runs his fingers through his hair again, his eyes cast down. He opens the door and steps out. "I'll be right back," he tells the cabbie through the passenger window.

"I don't need you to walk me," I say, although I like having him with me. It makes me feel safe.

"Listen, I may like variety in my sexual encounters, but I'm a gentleman, and even though I love to hate you, I don't want anything to happen to you." He steps into the small foyer of my condo building.

"Thank you." I open the main door and step into the lobby where the overflowing mailboxes are.

"Do you want me to walk you up?" he asks, holding the glass door.

"No. I got it from here." My mace is in my purse. I'll pull that out once he leaves.

"Okay then. I'll see you tomorrow." He rocks back on his heels but doesn't leave.

"Is there something else?"

He hems and haws for a moment, then his hands come out of his pockets. I've noticed this evening that he uses them to communicate. "It's just... I'm not an asshole, and for some reason it bothers me that you think I am. I enjoyed talking to you tonight. I don't want the animosity between us to stand."

I nod. "Okay. We'll be civil to one another when our paths cross." I turn to head farther into the building but turn and face him again. "And I don't think you're an asshole by the way."

"You don't?" His eyes light up, making them even more irresistible.

Jeez, I would not have thought that was even possible.

I giggle. "No. I understand that our views on dating are different. If the women you're with know the score, then it's mutual. I don't judge them or you."

He chuckles lightly, his eyes falling for a moment before they pierce into mine. "You surprise me, Bella."

Hearing my name off his lips sends tingles across my skin. "Thanks."

"Have a good night," he says, lingering on the other side of the door.

I let the glass door close, effectively locking him out.

"I'm sure I'll be seeing you in my dreams," I mumble, because though I won't admit to it anyone else, I'm very attracted to Carmelo Mancini. I don't judge those women. I'm jealous of them. Much to my own disappointment.

CHAPTER TEN

Bella

I stop applying my mascara, resting my hands on the edge of the bathroom sink. Why is Carm occupying every cell in my brain today? Last night was one thing, but it's a new day. I even put on a shirt I always get compliments about, on the off chance I run into him at the office today.

I'm not naïve. The sexual tension between us last night wasn't my imagination. Since neither of us had enough to drink to give us the illusion that we could sleep together and blame it on the alcohol, I'd left him last night, feeling unfulfilled. If he'd been anyone else, when he walked me into the lobby, I might've asked him upstairs.

I apply a little more powder under my eyes to try to hide the dark circles. Staying up half the night trying to convince myself I'm not attracted to him was a useless endeavor. His lips were the first thing that crossed my mind as my hand slid down past my mound. His hands and eyes came next.

Then the way his biceps tug at his shirt sleeves, followed with me imagining how the scruff on his face would feel scraping against my inner thighs as he teased me. He was who I imagined as I bucked into my hand.

My phone rings, distracting me from the memory. I swipe the screen and put it on speaker. "Hey, Mom."

"Sweetie, I'm so glad I caught you. Instead of dinner, let's do brunch, okay? Greg has somewhere he wants to take me tonight."

I think through my schedule for this morning, but Max can handle anything that comes up. And I can work late anyway. My excuse last night of an early morning meeting was a fib. "Okay."

"I want you to meet him. He has a quick business meeting first, then he's going to join us at our table."

"Oh, it's not necessary if he has business to attend to."

"Don't be silly. I've already told him all about you and how proud I am of the business you're starting. He's dying to meet you."

I highly doubt a man like Greg Throttle, whose reputation in this town is unmatched, is impressed by my measly FSBO company. "Where and what time?"

"Ten thirty at The Cobbler. That way we get some time alone together while he's doing business."

"Perfect. I'll see you there."

That means I won't be fresh-faced and wrinkle-free before seeing Carm, which kind of means the whole hour of getting ready was for nothing.

I know. I know. Stop thinking of him.

If only.

"Can't wait, and oh, I brought you a tin of cookies for Max."

"She'll love hearing that. See you in a bit, Mom."

We say our goodbyes, and I stare at myself in the mirror, grab my mascara, and start applying again. After I'm ready, I send Max a message to say I'll be in this afternoon and to call me if anything important comes up. Otherwise, I'm working from home until brunch.

———————

AT 10:25, I step out of the cab in front of The Cobbler. It's a large restaurant below a condominium building I'm fairly sure is owned by Greg Throttle. Guess I shouldn't be surprised he chose this place, if he really is *the* Greg Throttle.

I head inside, but before I approach the hostess, someone else opens the door behind me and a rush of air tousles my perfect curls that took twenty minutes to get just right. What a waste. By the time I reach the office and the possibility of running into Carm, my red hair will be thrown up into a ponytail.

My mom stands from one of the tables, and I spot Greg Throttle next to her. No one owns a room quite like him. His salt-and-pepper hair and perfectly trimmed beard work with the slacks and polo shirt he's wearing. Both of their skin has the bronze coloring of a Floridan. At least he's not someone pretending to be Greg Throttle. My mom has the real deal at her side.

"I see my party, thank you," I say to the hostess.

Her eyes aren't even on me, but on whoever is behind me. I reflexively glance over my shoulder to see what's grabbed her undivided attention, and I'm greeted with an egocentric smirk so big, all the blood flowing through my body zeroes in between my thighs.

Damn, I dressed to impress, but Carmelo Mancini upped his game this morning too.

I feel confident he didn't do so for my benefit though.

"Good morning." His voice sounds rougher than I've ever heard it. "What are you here for?"

"Um... good morning." I bow. Why am I bowing as though he's some prince or something? I straighten my back. "My mom... she's in..." Jesus, his tailored suit is distracting. Like it covers but shows off his body all at once.

"What?" He chuckles under his breath.

I'm totally giving him the pleasure of knowing he has me tongue-tied.

"Bella! Sweetie!" my mom calls from her table.

I turn to see her and Greg Throttle's eyes are on me.

Carm follows my line of vision and sets his eyes back on me. Questions fill those blue hues instead of the desire I swear I saw when I first turned around. "That's your mom?"

I look back one more time as though I don't recognize the woman who raised me for twenty-eight years. "Yeah."

"With Greg Throttle?"

"Yes." I release a breath. "New relationship. And now I'm meeting the boyfriend."

"Interesting," he says, stepping toward the hostess. "Don't let me keep you."

"Nice seeing you." I wave, almost tripping over my feet as I turn. "I'll see you at the office."

His lips tip up. "I think sooner than that."

I stop. "What?"

His lips turn into a megawatt smile. One that lights up every cell inside my body. But this time, there's something I can't decipher behind that smile. "Nothing. If we finish at the same time, we'll share a cab."

I nod. "Sure."

Man, we totally have this being civil to one another thing down pat.

"Bye." I wave as if he's all the way across the street or something. *Get a grip, Bella. He's not Bradley Cooper.*

"See you soon." He winks.

I circle around, and my mom's up and out of her seat before I can make sense of his words.

"Sweetie, you look beautiful. You're glowing." Her hand lands on my cheek as she takes me in.

It's been less than six months since I saw her over Christmas, but sometimes it feels like a lifetime.

"It's summer in New York. I'm flushed from the humidity. I wouldn't call it glowing."

"It's only May. Wait until July." Greg Throttle stands from his chair. "Are you going to introduce us, Linda?"

"Oh yes, sorry. I just can't believe how good she looks." Her eyes fall over my body once again. Truth is, my mom usually gets the slouch version of me since it's my downtime when I visit her. "Bella, this is Greg Throttle, my..."

"Boyfriend." He holds out his hand. "Pleasure to meet you. I've heard a lot of great things."

I shake his hand and nervousness plagues me. This is *the* Greg Throttle. Real estate mogul. He makes and breaks people's careers. Rumor has it that at one time, you had to go through three of his employees to score a meeting with him. How on Earth did he land in my mom's bakery in Florida asking about a book club?

"Thank you. She does love to brag," I say and smile.

"I'm sure there's a lot to brag about." The male voice comes from behind me.

I still have Greg's hand in mine as I turn around to find Carm standing there. Of course. Carm must be the meeting my mom mentioned on the phone.

"Bella," he says with a nod, ignoring the fact that he knew before I did and didn't warn me. "Mr. Throttle, Carmelo Mancini." He holds out his hand.

Greg slides out of my grasp and into Carm's. "Yes, I saw the two of you over there. You two know one another?"

My mom looks on with intrigue, waiting for answers.

"Not really," I say at the same time Carm says, "Yes."

"Our offices are across the hall from one another," I rush to explain. "I recently relocated my office to the same building as his."

"You're a realtor?" my mom asks. If I only could give her the Cliff's Notes version.

"I am. Good to meet the mother who raised this lovely woman." He puts out his hand, and I roll my eyes. He's laying it on a little thick.

When my eyes manage not to lodge themselves in the back of my head, I notice that Greg saw me. He smirks.

Great first impression I'm making.

"This is the realtor I have the meeting with, Linda," Greg says, placing his hand on the small of her back.

Since my dad's death, I've seen many men do that exact same move. It never gets easier. Whether it was my father's sudden death or the fact that I know how in love they were, it's like a quick slice to my skin every time. I wonder if my dad is up there cursing her for trying to replace him, or does he want her to be happy?

Carm's shoulder bumps mine, and I look at him. What I see isn't gloating or smugness; he appears empathetic. Am I that transparent right now?

"Let's sit," Greg says.

"Oh, I thought..." I say.

"All four of us?" Carm asks.

"Originally I was going to have the meeting with Carm

while Linda and Bella caught up, but I just had an epiphany when we made our introductions."

I look at my mom and she shrugs, smiling more at Carm than me.

We sit around the table and I watch as she pulls out her phone. My phone dings seconds later. I'm pretty sure the other two people at the table know she messaged me. Discretion is not in her vocabulary.

Carm glances at me but swivels his chair so he's more in line with Greg. Go figure. Anything for the deal.

The waitress comes over and goes through the specials then takes our drink orders. I slide my phone out to see what my mom has to say.

Mom: *Are you dating him?*

I type a quick response.

Me: *NO*
Mom: *He's handsome.*

I roll my eyes and drop my phone into my purse where it hangs off the back of the chair. She smiles at me. I unwrap my silverware and place the napkin in my lap.

"I'm just going to cut to the chase. I'm a straight-shoot-er," Greg says.

Carm straightens in his chair. "I'm the same. Tell it like it is."

What a suck-up.

Greg humors him with a smile. "I like you, Carm. I've done my research. My vice president said you did a helluva job moving his penthouse. Got him over asking. Said I should give you a shot. I also heard that you're the new blood who doesn't accept no or the word can't."

I inwardly roll my eyes this time, because I don't want Greg to catch me again.

"Yes, sir. I have some figures from this past year that I think will help convince you I'm the guy for you."

Greg raises his hand. Before he can speak, the waitress brings our coffee and teas. I'm tempted to ask her for a large amount of Bailey's in my coffee.

"You can cool it on selling yourself, Carmelo."

"Carm," he corrects. "Everyone calls me Carm."

I shake my head and roll my eyes, because this is a version of Carm I do not like. I look up from my napkin, and all three of their heads are turned in my direction. "Sorry. I was just thinking about something from earlier this morning. My neighbor and I had it out."

Carm smirks. He knows I got caught. My mom's eyebrows furrow, and Greg smiles as though I just told him my darkest secret.

"That's not like you. You get along with everybody," my mom says.

"Not everyone," I say, looking right at Carm.

"We're getting off track. I've got a building that's going to be ready by the end of the year, and I want every unit sold before it opens. I have a proposal for you both. You each get a floor. We'll do FSBO with you, Bella, and Carm, you do what you have to in order to sell the floor. Whoever sells out the fastest gets the rest of the building."

"I'm sorry. What?" Carm leans forward as if he didn't hear him correctly.

I laugh, manically laugh, because Greg Throttle cannot be serious right now.

CHAPTER ELEVEN

Carm

Someone tell me I never woke up this morning. That I'm in some twisted dream.

I pinch my wrist under my cufflink to be sure I'm actually awake. Yep.

"Greg, you're aware that I'm not a full-service brokerage, right? I only work with FSBOs, so you only get your property listed on MLS, whereas Carmelo would handle everything."

This is definitely a dream. Bella Scott is selling me over herself? Hell *has* frozen over. I glance out the windows to see if pigs are flying too. Nope.

"I'm aware, Bella, and thanks for the disclaimer. I'm sure we have some intern or lower-level employee who can show prospective buyers the units. You're Linda's daughter and I know you're starting out. Don't think of this as a hand-out, but..."

"It is," I say before the words travel through my mind to be stopped by the bullshit filter in my brain.

Greg tilts his head. "Not that I don't think it's an excellent idea. I just had a client this week who'd been toying with going the FSBO route and decided to try things out with Ms. Scott."

I lean back and sip my coffee with the hopes that my outburst is forgotten, but I feel Bella's eyes boring into the side of my head.

"I've always wondered if you brokers really work for your cut."

I smile and set down my coffee. What an asshole he is if he thinks I don't work for my commission. My lack of a social life and the fact that my weekends are like weekdays should give him a clue. I won't even add in the money I spend on advertising and stagers and photographers, or the bullshit I take from clients, prospective buyers, and brokers alike. I'm in the only profession where people pay you for your expertise then fight you on everything you say. No one goes to the mechanic or the doctors and argues with them about how to fix the problem. But my clients don't want a time sheet for hours worked and a record of expenses paid. In the end, they all think brokers make too much money, even when you're making them more money.

"I guess you'll find out in two months," I say with a smile.

"I said three," he says.

"I know." I sip my coffee and let it hang in the air.

A huff leaks out of Bella to my left.

"You're cocky," Linda says across from me.

I wink and smile. "For good reason."

"Oh." She looks at her daughter with wide eyes. "He's dangerous."

Bella rolls her eyes, then straightens her back. Our breakfast arrives and the waitress sets my omelet and fruit in front of me, followed by Bella's yogurt and granola. Greg's eggs Benedict and Linda's quiche are delivered next.

"So it's three months and we each have our own floor? Interaction between the two of us will be minimal?" I ask.

Greg chuckles, holding the dripping egg with hollandaise above his plate. "I wouldn't say no interaction." He slides the eggs Benedict off his fork and sets down the utensil as he chews.

I glance at Bella. She hasn't touched her food.

"This isn't nearly as good as mine. Try this." Linda holds out her fork to Greg.

Surely, he's not going to eat it off her fork in front of us? Bella might be quasi-family, but I came for a business meeting.

But sure as shit, he opens his mouth and allows Linda to feed him.

"You're right," he says. "I told you, let me open you a place here."

Bella coughs, and we all glance in her direction to find her choking on something. Her eyes water and her face is red, but she recovers and swallows a good amount of ice water.

"You okay, sweetie?" Linda asks.

Bella nods, plastering on her fake smile. "You're thinking of moving here?" she asks with concern in her eyes.

Which I don't understand, because it appears that they have a good relationship.

"No, I could never leave Vista Park, but Greg thinks I should expand." Linda smiles at Greg and inches closer to him.

He looks at her fondly, and I suddenly feel as though

I'm interrupting a moment. "Her pastries would do so well up here. Add in some killer coffee and you'd have lines out the door."

"You're a baker?" I ask, trying to steer this conversation anywhere other than the direction it's going because I can tell Bella's upset and the last thing I want is to be part of a family spat.

"I am. Stop by Bella's office this afternoon. I have a basket full of cookies being delivered to Max." She smiles.

"I thought you'd come back with me and we'd give them to her?" Bella interrupts, sounding like a disappointed nine-year-old.

Linda looks at Greg. "We're going to see the sights, so we had a courier pick them up this morning. But I'm all yours tomorrow."

"Until we leave for the Hamptons," Greg reminds her.

"That's right, and I was hoping we could go shopping?" She looks at her daughter.

Bella sighs. "Mom, I have to work."

"Okay, well, let's do lunch," she says with a small frown.

"Breakfast would be better." Greg slides another forkful of eggs Benedict into his mouth.

Linda looks at her daughter.

Bella puts down her fork, a piece of cantaloupe attached, and pushes away her plate. "Sure."

"Perfect."

"Then I'll take you shopping," Greg says, searching for Linda's hand under the table.

Linda smiles as if he's a damn rock star, and I can't help turning toward Bella to see her gaze focused on her teacup.

"You're going to the Hamptons?" I ask, once again trying to move the conversation forward. "My brother's girlfriend has been on me about finding her and my brother a place. Do you own any other properties there?"

I'd do just about anything for my family, and Annie is family now. If she wants the Hamptons summer experience, I'm going to deliver.

"I do. I can give you my guy's number up there, but..." He glances at Linda then at Bella. "I was going to offer my house to Bella this summer since I'll be in Florida with Linda."

I want to raise my hand and ask Linda to adopt me with all the kissing up Greg seems to be doing to Bella.

Bella perks up for the first time this whole meal. "Oh, my friend wanted to go, but I told her I have to work."

Greg chuckles. "I'm all for hard work, but you only live once. It took me a long time to realize that. My fourteen-hour days at the office are over now."

Hello, he's in his late fifties and owns half the city. He has the luxury of sitting on his ass on Florida beaches.

"Take the house. Maybe you guys can come up with some arrangement. It has ten bedrooms and is right on the ocean."

"I'll pay you," Bella says.

I choke on my coffee for a second. Does she have any idea how much that would cost? Greg chuckles. I think we're on the same wavelength.

Bella peeks at me. "Maybe Enzo and Annie wouldn't mind having us as roommates?"

I shrug. As if I would mention this to them.

"When I was your age, I rented a house with my friends. It was the best summer of my life," Greg says, smiling.

I'm skeptical. The man is a machine. I doubt he took a summer off to fuck randoms and get plastered.

"You should do it," Linda pushes. "The two of you and maybe Max and Evie? Carm's brother and his girlfriend? It would be fun, and you deserve to have some fun." Linda's hand takes her daughter's across the table, and she stares into Bella's eyes.

It feels like the moment is about more than just a mother wanting her daughter to have a fun summer. There's a secret between them.

My eyebrows furrow.

"I'll think about it. Thank you, Greg, but please allow us to pay something."

He thinks it over. "How about half?"

Bella blows out a breath. "We'll see."

Her phone rings and she quickly silences it, stuffing it back into her purse.

"Please, sweetie, take Greg up on his offer. You need to get time away from work."

Bella nods, but her eyes plead for her mom to stop pushing.

I steer the conversation back to business, and before I realize it, I've paid the bill and the four of us are getting up from the table.

Bella and Linda hang back, discussing their plans for tomorrow. I overhear Linda apologize for not being able to spend as much time as she would've liked with her daughter.

We all say our goodbyes outside. Greg's driver pulls up, so he and Linda get in the vehicle, leaving me with Bella.

"I'm going to walk," she says.

It's unusual for it to be so hot in May in the city, but I'm not complaining. I hate the fucking cold. "I'll join you."

She stops at the corner. "I'm good. But thanks."

"We're going to the same place," I say. Our building is at

least ten blocks away, but I can tell she's heading toward Central Park and figure she's cutting through.

Justin's texted me ten times already, probably thinking I'm hungover in bed and forgot my appointment. I should forget Bella and get a jump start on Greg's properties. He said he'll have someone send us all the information before we've returned to the office. But I can tell that Bella's rattled, and something in me feels the need to make sure she's okay.

"I'm going with you. You can choose to talk to me or not." I shrug and she doesn't respond.

Sure enough, she steps off the curb, crosses the street, and concrete and steel are replaced with green grass, lush gardens, and the sounds of musical instruments. We pass a saxophonist, and Bella drops a few dollars into his case. He switches gears into a special tune, and she smiles at him, bowing her head.

We remain side by side, our footsteps in unison for what feels like eternity. I'm a talker, so being next to someone and feeling as though I can't say a word is excruciating.

"She's always like this," she says out of nowhere as we pass a small child with a bag of food for the ducks. Bella's voice is so quiet, I almost think she's talking to him at first.

"Your mom? Like what?"

"Obsessed. He's the center of her universe until he breaks her heart." She stops to stand on a bridge overlooking the stream, staring down as if there's a show to watch. "She just. *Ugh!*" Her fists tighten at her sides. "She believes in all that shit."

"What shit?"

"True love. Soul mates. The entire love story. She spins everything to make her believe he's her prince. He's not a fucking prince. He's a city developer with so much money he could start a whole chain of her bakeries and not give one shit whether they survive or not. Now he wants to throw me this bone and give me a floor to prove myself, not to mention the house in the Hamptons. I'm not twelve. I won't be calling him Daddy if that's what he thinks."

I'm not sure where to go from here. Enzo would give her some solid advice. Dom would stay silent, not wanting to deal with anything resembling feelings. My impulse is to wrap my arms around her and tell her I get it. But I don't. My parents have been happily married for almost forty years.

"Then enjoy it while it lasts. It's his choice to give you this opportunity and the house in the Hamptons."

She swivels away from the water and I match her pose, both our backs resting on the cement bridge. "Watch me succeed and then he loses interest. The men my mom finds always lose interest."

That felt like a knife to the chest. I know she's talking about Greg, but I also know what Bella thinks of me. Maybe she's thinking that he's just like me. Annie's already made it clear that's how she sees me. Why wouldn't Bella?

"I've seen a woman change a man," I say.

"Who?"

"My brother. He wasn't like he is now until he met Annie. No other woman made him as obedient as Annie does."

"Obedient?" She cocks one eyebrow.

"He does whatever she says." I shrug. It's the truth.

She pushes off the cement and heads down the walkway. "It's called love. You want to make the other person happy."

I shrug. "Maybe Greg will fall in love with your mom."

She rolls her eyes and keeps walking. "My friend Evie is

all over me about this Hamptons thing, and the more I think about it, I just need to get out of this city. One thing he said that stuck with me is that life is short. Talk to Annie. If she and Enzo are cool with sharing, they're more than welcome. And... if you want in too, I'm sure the house is big enough for the both of us."

Yeah, that's not going to happen.

But I nod anyway.

I might as well sign myself up for an experiment to discover how long a guy can live with blue balls. Just the thought of Bella Scott in a bikini makes me hard.

"Thanks for the offer," I say and leave it at that.

It's not like she actually wants me there.

CHAPTER TWELVE

Bella

The next morning, after breakfast with my mom, I arrive outside 15 Bond St. The building is still undergoing heavy construction, and a part of me doubts Greg Throttle can get this completed in time. But then again, he's mega powerful, which makes just about anything possible.

I walk into the small showroom on the ground level, where a scale model of the building, along with the layouts of the three different floor plans, are showcased in the center of the room.

"Hi, I'm Helena." A blonde woman, who's taller than me, walks out from behind a desk, dressed in a cream-colored pantsuit. Her makeup is flawless, and her hair has not one strand in disarray. She's beautiful. Like model stunning.

"Hello, I'm Bella Scott."

She smiles, but it doesn't come close to reaching her eyes. "Yes, Mr. Throttle told me to expect you."

When she doesn't say anything else, I look over the model to busy myself.

"We're just waiting for the other broker, then we'll begin," she eventually says.

What is she talking about?

"I'm here." Carm's voice rings out behind me.

"Oh, I didn't know you'd be here," I say.

His eyes shift from Helena to me before he stretches out his hand and moves his gaze back to Helena. "Carmelo Mancini."

This time her smile does reach her eyes. Hell, I'd say it reaches her pussy with the way she's practically purring. "Very nice to meet you. I recognize your name..." Her gaze tracks back my way for a millisecond.

"Probably my billboards." He shrugs.

Her gaze slips down his body as though she's mentally tracking what he looks like naked. "Oh yes, I remember now." She doesn't even bother trying to hide the appreciation in her voice.

I inwardly roll my eyes, knowing I can't be unprofessional in this setting.

"So this is the model?" Carm switches into business mode, releasing her hand and coming up next to me.

Whatever, buddy. Maybe I should give them fifteen minutes alone so we can move on to what we're really here for.

"Yes. There are three different floorplans..." She continues on her spiel.

I take in all the information even though she never glances at me once. Her manicured nail—with nude polish —points to various places on the floorplan while she explains the features. Carm's "uh-huhs" and "interestings" as though she's the most fascinating woman on earth aggravate me to no end.

My body is hot all over and you'd think I was about to start my period or something. Even I can feel myself getting pissed off with very little poking. Well, Helena's poking me by wanting Carm to poke her.

Jesus, I need to get this guy out of my head.

"I'll take you up to show you the space now." Helena disappears into an office, presumably letting whoever's in there know that she's stepping out.

Whoever the other person is, they discuss lunch, and I step toward the door to flee this situation as soon as I can.

"How was breakfast?" Carm asks me as if we're friends.

We're not friends.

Right now, we have competing interests. If I can sell out an entire development as an FSBO broker, there are no limits to how successful I can make my company.

"Breakfast was fine."

"That's it?"

"I'm not sure what you're looking for?" Yes, I'm being a bitch because of the woman whose heels I hear clicking on the floor as she approaches. Sue me.

"Okay, let's go." She uses a key to open the elevator door.

Carm motions for me to step in first, so I do. We pack into a small elevator that, if I'm honest, I'm a little afraid of.

Carm talks with Helena about her work history with Greg and the building, as well as what development projects the company has coming up next. She practically trips over her tongue to spill secrets I'm sure she's not supposed to give. I swear good looks and a little charm can get a guy anywhere in life. It's ridiculous.

Finally we arrive and step off on the thirty-third floor. Helena turns to me. "This floor will be yours, Miss Scott. Go ahead and get yourself acquainted. I'll take Mr. Mancini to the floor above and we'll come back and grab you on our way down."

She's kidding, right? The place is practically empty, with only framing giving a basic outline of the units. But I'm not about to argue since being alone is better than dealing with Helena's desperate attempts at flirting with Carm.

"Sure. Have fun." I step forward, looking side to side, thankful there aren't a bunch of construction workers on this floor.

"Let's go through them all together." Carm follows me, not waiting for an answer from Helena.

I hate that him staying eases the tension in my body. "You don't have—"

"Yeah, I do. Ma would kill me."

Helena huffs. "Okay then." She takes the lead, going through the space as though she was the architect of the property. "There are eight units on each floor, and you have views of the river from most."

We're back by the elevator before I can blink or ask a question.

"Um." I stop her hand before she pushes the elevator button. "Are they all the same price?"

"I'll give you the pricing downstairs."

"Are the buyers allowed to change anything as far as layout, since it's still under construction?"

She presses the button and I'm growing more irritated with her by the minute.

"What's the rush, Helena? She has to sell this property with nothing but an artist's concept video and a floor plan."

I hate the fact that Carm has to come to my defense.

I walk away from the elevator and back into the space. "This unit, for instance." I step over the entrance. "How will my client know the views they're getting? I'm going to have to have someone come and take pictures unless you supply them."

Helena huffs and joins me.

"They'll be overlooking the garden and pool of the building next door." I point below us.

"Yes, but look out there." Her arms widen.

"But then look down," I say.

"A pool could be inviting," Carm remarks, and irritation pricks my neck.

"Not when the guy lounging on a chair is naked."

They look harder and gasp.

"Well, it's New York, what can you do?" Helena shrugs.

"If that man happens to be out there when clients come to view the unit, it will not sell."

"Let's cross that bridge when we get there."

I stop her before she can turn around and I catch Carm smiling, but he diverts his gaze out the window again.

"Can my client change the layout if that's an issue? I'm not talking major construction here. I'm talking about moving some walls. Is there flexibility?"

"Maybe you should ask Greg. I'm sure he'll consider it, what with him being so chummy with your mom," she says.

Carm's head rears back and he steps away as though instinct tells him I'm going to launch us into a fight. But I'm not a fighter.

I walk away. "Maybe I will."

What can I really say? She's right. I have this opportunity because Greg is nailing my mom. So I might as well make her fearful that I'll use my connection against her.

"I'll also be sure to let him know how helpful you've been." My snide tone tells her I have no intention of giving a favorable report.

I step into the elevator. A quiet Carm follows, and Helena eventually joins us and presses the button for the thirty-fourth floor.

I mostly look around by myself while the two of them go through each unit. I loathe women like Helena who flirt with a man while conducting business. How are we supposed to get ahead in this world if women keep letting men get their way because they're good-looking?

Her giggles are like acupuncture pins digging into my skin, and her hand seems to be drawn like a magnet to his forearm until it's almost permanently stuck there. He doesn't once try to get out of her way or remove it.

Annoyance drowns me like quicksand—slowly and painfully.

When they round the corner to the elevator, I step in before them just to get this over with. I wish I would've brought Max. She always knows how to handle these things.

Helena talks to Carm about where he works out on the way down to street level. Does she not see how transparent she is?

I stay as far away from them as I can the entire ride down, finally able to breathe once the doors open.

"Let me grab you guys the flash drives with the pricing and promo stuff." She disappears.

I scour the model again. I won't be able to bring customers here like Carm will because that's not how I do business. Which leaves me at a disadvantage.

"Want to come with me to the Trading Post?" Carm asks. "I have lunch there with my brothers every Thursday, but you could be my Wednesday date. The food is good."

I eye him, wondering what his angle is. "Wanting to delay me so I can't get my listings up before you?"

He chuckles. "Never."

But I'm fairly sure I'm right.

"What do the Mancini men talk about anyway? The women in their beds and the dollars in their bank accounts?"

His smile only grows.

Helena interrupts us, handing us each a business card and the flash drive, but the card she gives Carm is turned over and there's a phone number scribbled on the back in ink.

"Any time. I'm here to help." Her eyes are solely on Carm.

"Yeah. Have a great day. Thanks." I walk out, annoyed that I don't seem to be on equal playing ground. She'll probably send any of my clients straight to Carm.

She holds Carm back as I'm heading out the door. Thank goodness. I can make my exit quickly.

A cab stops outside, and I slide in, thankful the driver has the air conditioning on. This heat wave is killing me. This weather is typical for July, but that's more than a month away still. The weatherman said it'll be the hottest summer in years.

Before I can shut the door, Carm jogs out of the building and puts his hand on my door. "I'm heading back to the office, too. Have an appointment I forgot about."

He slides in without permission.

"By all means, please."

His cocky smirk is his only response as he slides in and grabs his phone from the breast pocket of his suit.

My eyes slide over his body. I can't blame Helena. I mean, she's a woman and Carm is... well... Carm. He's like the quarterback of the high school football team, all grown-up and successful.

We ride in silence while his fingers fly over the screen of his phone.

"I have to go to dinner with my cousin on Friday night." He groans, hammering out another text message. "This is the first time he's been in town since he got engaged. The wedding isn't too far off and I'm hoping his bachelor party will be in Vegas."

"Surprise, surprise." I cross my legs.

Carm's eyes leave his screen for a second, eyeing my movements.

"Vegas. Every bride's nightmare."

He pockets his cell phone. "So you'd have a problem with your husband-to-be celebrating his last nights of freedom in Vegas?"

The cab is now stopped in traffic. Great. Extra minutes with Carm.

I shift to face him. "If my soon-to-be-husband thinks he needs to refer to the days before he marries me as freedom, then I'd prefer he doesn't show up at the altar."

He runs his hand over his scruff while he watches me. It only adds to his sex appeal. My chest heats and his eyes deepen. He's gauging my reaction and I can't help but like what's reflected back at me.

Want.

He clears his throat. "What I meant is that you're a self-confident woman, right?"

"It has nothing to do with the woman. It's the man's problem."

"How so?" He extends his arm along the back of the

seat, and the energy from his fingertips so close to my neck makes it hard to concentrate.

"You have to be willing to bring to the table the same thing you expect. Which means, I doubt any guy is okay with his bride spending her 'last days of freedom,' as you call it, being shitfaced drunk, dancing with different guys, watching men stripping, and making out with strangers. Because I understand how guys like you think, and kissing is cheating." My eyes widen as I realize how much I just unloaded on him.

"Whoa. Were you cheated on?"

"No." I scowl.

"Are you sure? You seem really sensitive about the whole topic."

I slide across the bench seat of the taxi and twirl my finger up in his tie. His eyes shoot to the rearview mirror and back to me.

"Tell me, Carmelo, why is it so much easier for a woman to seduce a man?" My other hand lands on his hard thigh. That was a big mistake, but I need to prove how easy it is to get a man to flip.

"Because women are the devil," he says, his hand falling from the top of the bench seat to my waist, locking me in place. "But don't make me prove you wrong," he whispers, leaning closer. "It'd be easy for me to have you melting against this vinyl right now."

Our faces draw together until his lips hover over mine. I feel his breath on my face and a tingle shoots up my spine.

"Just imagine it. My lips on yours. My tongue searching for entrance. The two of us lost in lust in this cab, trying to hide what we're doing," he whispers. His gaze dips and his other hand joins the torment, sliding up my bare thigh. "I'd inch closer and closer, and you'd nudge your legs open for me. Tell me, Bella, how wet are you right now?"

I tug at his tie. One kiss—one long, sultry kiss—wouldn't do any harm, right?

A lone finger glides up under the hem of my skirt. I glance down and see the prominent bulge in his slacks.

"You tell me first, Carm, how hard are you?"

"Like granite. I'm not embarrassed to admit I want you."

All the girly parts inside me puddle. Carmelo Mancini wants me.

"But that doesn't mean I'll have you, because contrary to what you think, I have self-control." He squeezes my thigh and smirks.

I release his tie, slide out of his grip, and shift over to the other side of the cab.

The player just got played. Why did I ever think I'd beat him in a game of temptation?

CHAPTER THIRTEEN

Carm

W hen the cab pulls up outside our building and I step out, my hard-on is only slightly deflated. I wanted to tell that cab driver to take a detour to my condo, but no way can I have filthy sex with a woman like Bella Scott.

"So you'll talk to Annie?" she asks, apparently completely unfazed that I almost smashed my lips to hers minutes ago.

Was it really a game to her? Can she turn her arousal off and on like a light switch?

"About?" I open the door to our office building and let her walk in first. She must've said something while my mind was drifting off, imagining the taste of her.

"The Hamptons." She presses the elevator button.

"I haven't yet, but I will. You're going?"

She shrugs and steps into the elevator. "Yeah. I mean,

life is too short. I'm going to allow myself this one summer to enjoy."

"Oh."

She's trying to get a business off the ground, and we have this whole competition with Greg now. I can't believe she's going to leave the city every Friday through Sunday. I'm kind of jealous.

"What?" she asks, her eyes on me as we position ourselves on opposite sides of the elevator.

It's only the two of us, and the arousing scent of her perfume surrounds me.

"Nothing. Just thought you were a go-getter." I shrug.

The look she shoots back isn't a nice one. "I am, but like I said, I'm doing this for myself without apology."

The elevator doors open, and we step out. "Don't be upset when I beat you then."

She stops in her tracks then walks up to me. I back up against the wall. "You think just because Helena wants you, it's in the bag. Well, you have no idea what I'm capable of, and spending my weekends in the Hamptons isn't going to ruin anything."

"If I cared to give it any thought, I'd have to say you're jealous of Helena."

Her gaze falls to my pocket, where Helena's business card with her personal cell number rests. I don't plan on using it, but I love the rush of pink ravishing Bella's skin. She *is* jealous.

"Figures. You probably think every woman is jealous of the woman of the moment on your arm." She shakes her head.

The door to my office opens and out steps Margo Gregory, my A-list client from Los Angeles.

"Am I interrupting?" Margo asks. She tucks her designer purse under her arm.

Everything about Margo is high class. She has money from a makeup company she started at twenty-one. Her high-end fashion and shoes cost more than some people's rent. Success looks good on her. She's in her late forties but looks like she's thirty. No husband or kids. Loves the younger guys. I should know. In other words, the ideal client for a guy like me.

"Margo." I smile then step away from Bella and do the whole kiss-on-each-cheek thing Margo loves. "Come. I found a new place I want to show you on the computer."

"It looked like I was interrupting?" She eyes Bella like a spiteful twenty-year-old cat inspecting the new kitten her owner brought home.

"This is Bella Scott. We were discussing some issues we've been having with a shared client."

"You're a realtor too?" Margo asks.

"No. Bella does FSBOs," I say.

Bella's eyes narrow into small slits. "I better get going on that." She smiles at Margo and turns on her heels.

As she walks into her office, I admire her ass and consider how well my hands would mold around her flesh before Margo hits me in the stomach with her purse.

I laugh, looking at the five-foot-three woman. "What?"

"I sense trouble." She raises her eyebrows.

"Come on. Let me grab that listing. Sorry I was late getting back."

She waves off my concern. "I was going to head down to the corner and check out a new shop that just opened up. You saved me from buying something I don't need."

I chuckle. "Always at your service." I grip the door handle. "I'm sure Justin was excited to see you."

"Of course he was. He always likes to glance down my blouse. That boy needs to get laid."

I open the door for her, and she walks in first. I follow, remembering how lucky I was to get Margo's business in the first place. She's referred so many of her rich friends to me that she's one of the launching points of my career.

I decide to ignore her comment about Justin because even though Margo loves to talk about sex, I'd prefer to keep our conversation today on neutral ground.

I'm still dealing with the aftereffects of having Bella's body pressed to mine.

ON FRIDAY, I walk into the restaurant Enzo booked, and the hostess walks me to a private room. I'm not surprised Enzo picked this place—it's where he used to take all of his big clients when he worked at Jacobson and Earl.

I open the curtains and jump into the room, trying to startle whoever's in there.

Sadly, it's only Dom, a drink in one hand, his phone in the other, thumb scrolling.

"Whatcha doin'?" I ask, taking the seat next to him. We're the only two flying solo here tonight. Even Blanca is bringing her new guy, who I've yet to meet. He'll be my fun for tonight though.

Dom stops scrolling and tucks his phone into the breast pocket of his suit jacket.

"Were you playing a game?"

He glances at me. "I have more important shit to do than to put a ball into a hole."

"What about a dick?" I ask.

A smile tips his lips but quickly falls.

"So your regular hook-up thing ended? You had a nice little arrangement going on there the past year," I say.

"Yeah." His voice is low, and he downs half of his drink.

"And you're upset?" I ask in disbelief.

"Hell no. She was a hookup. That's all."

Fuck. I haven't seen a Mancini man this down since... well, a long fucking time. Minus Enzo with Annie when things went in the shitter, but they're together now, so I tend to forget all about that. "You're not acting like she was just a hookup."

The waiter comes in and I order Stella with a glass.

Dom picks up his near empty glass before the waiter can leave. "Another."

Once the waiter is gone, I slide my chair so I'm facing him. "You liked her." My words aren't a question, they're an accusation.

Dom's finger smooths out the tablecloth. "I liked her pussy. Especially when my dick was in it."

Whoa. This is serious, folks.

"Then what happened?"

"Just didn't work out." He finishes his drink, the ice cubes clinking inside the empty glass.

"Want to talk about it?"

"No." His voice is curt and authoritative. "I want to fucking forget her. All I'm upset about is that now I have to find someone else who's willing to give me sex on a regular basis without wanting anything else. Stop treating me like I need a tub of ice cream and a spoon."

I hold up my hands. "Okay. Okay."

We sit in silence for what feels like forever before Annie and Enzo walk in through the curtains. Thank God for new blood and a distraction from my brooding brother.

But as soon as she spots me, Annie's finger points in my direction. "*You!*"

Oh fuck, what did I do now?

"*You* never told me about the Hamptons. I had to find out from Bella." She sits down next to me. Great. Now I'll probably have to bear witness while she gives Enzo a hand job under the table during dinner.

Just the thought of hand jobs has my mind moving in Bella's direction. Even after giving myself a handy last night, my sexual fever hasn't gone away. I still want Bella Scott, and no one can fulfill that need. Not even my skilled hand.

I place my napkin in my lap, smiling at the waiter as he enters with our drinks. "Thanks. Just in time."

I pour my bottle into the glass while the waiter takes Enzo and Annie's drink order. Annie doesn't have to tell Enzo what she wants, he just knows.

"What are you talking about?" I ask after the waiter leaves again.

"The Hamptons, jerk. Bella said she has a house at a discounted price if we want to share. Ten bedrooms. A pool. Right on the beach." She punches my upper arm. "Why didn't you tell us?"

"You guys are doing the Hamptons this summer?" Dom peers around me to look at Annie.

"We wanted to and asked the best realtor we know to find us a place, but oh no, Carm Mancini is so threatened by the woman across the hall, he's keeping that information to himself."

"I'm in," Dom says, and all of our heads whip around.

Enzo straightens his back. "You're what?"

"I'll chip in. I might not come every weekend, but I have to get the fuck out of this city."

We all exchange confused expressions.

Annie clears her throat. "Dom, are you okay? I heard—"

"I'm fine. I just need a change of scenery this summer. Don't psychoanalyze me." He sips his drink.

"Then it's settled. We're all going. Now that we have Dom, it's perfect. It'll lower the cost even more." She pulls out her phone.

"You have Bella's phone number?" I ask, glancing over her shoulder.

"Oh no, you don't. You want her number, man up and ask her for it." Annie swivels so she's facing me, and the phone screen is facing Enzo.

"I'm not going," I say.

"Why not?" Enzo asks.

"I have no time for that. I have three months to sell out an entire floor for the biggest developer in New York." I sip my beer, staring at the four other spots and wishing the chairs would fill up so we can move on from this conversation.

"You're going. You're a workaholic who needs a break. Sooner or later, we're all going to have kids and we won't be able to do these things anymore. Let's enjoy it while we can."

I roll my eyes. "Speak for yourself."

She stares at me as though she's exhausted by the words coming out of my mouth. "It's final, Carm. Your mom is really worried about you and she said—"

We're interrupted by the curtain opening, and in walks Mauro with a pretty brunette.

"Mauro!" Enzo says, standing.

Annie follows suit.

Dom nudges me when I'm the only one not standing.

"This is Maddie," our cousin Mauro says. "Maddie, this is Enzo, Carm, Dom, and..."

"Annie," Enzo says, his hand on the small of her back.

The two women shake hands while we all take turns saying hello and hugging Maddie to our chests. We're Italian, enough said.

"Someone message Blanca," Dom says.

But we all sit, no one grabbing their phone. Annie huffs, pulls out hers, and texts.

"So wedding, huh?" I say after we're all seated.

"I can't believe it, but we're more than ready." Mauro grabs Maddie's hand under the table and she smiles at him like Annie does Enzo. I swear my lunch curdles in my stomach.

"That's awesome," I say because I can tell my cousin is happy.

"When's the bachelor party?" Dom asks.

Mauro glances at Maddie, who's smiling as though they've talked about it at length.

"Mine will be low-key in Chicago, but word is Luca's will be in Vegas."

"Love that guy," I say and sip my beer.

"Carm's the youngest of the Mancinis," Mauro says to Maddie.

"Makes sense," she says with a nod.

"Doesn't it?" Annie tucks her phone away, always straddling two conversations at the same time. "They're parking."

"Why wouldn't they valet?" Dom asks.

"Because not everyone has the money." Annie's always ready to remind Dom that not everyone lives in a world with doormen and private elevators.

"I work hard for that money."

She gives him her most innocent look. "I never said you didn't."

Maddie laughs, and we all turn to her. "You guys are funny. I mean, I guess we all have our own banter. I kind of can't wait for you to meet Lauren." She points at me.

Mauro slides his arm behind her chair. "That'll be fun."

"Lauren is...?" Please tell me they aren't going to try the whole fix up thing too.

"Luca's fiancée." Mauro seems to question why I wouldn't know that.

All I keep up with is the tally Ma's doing. One of her boys has settled down but hasn't put a ring on it yet, and the other two are single. Blanca is dating some guy who won't valet in Manhattan. Ma probably looks at the scoreboard and sees how uneven it is.

"She really gave him a fight," Enzo chimes in. He spent a small amount of time with all of them in Chicago when my zia was sick last year.

"How is Zia?" I ask, steering this conversation away from relationships.

"She's really good. Super healthy and walking every day." Maddie answers for Mauro like Annie answers for Enzo when it comes to Ma.

Obviously the same has happened with them—the moms gravitate to the new daughters they acquire. Especially Zia Maria, since she never had a daughter of her own.

"That's great," Annie says, and the two of them fall into a conversation.

Blanca finally comes in with some douchebag wearing a fedora and black T-shirt matched with tight jeans. Total hipster. Where the hell does she find these guys? I haven't liked any guy she's dated since that Jake guy Annie used to work with, but apparently there weren't any "sparks" between them. Now that I think about it, Enzo was the one who set her up with him. It's official—Blanca has the worst track record for picking guys.

She doesn't miss a beat, sliding Enzo away so she can sit next to the girls. Enzo ends up between Mauro and Dom. At least now I won't have to feign interest in wedding plans all night.

CHAPTER FOURTEEN

Bella

The next Monday, I walk into The Mancini Ad Agency and stop at the receptionist's desk.

I had dinner last night with my mom and Greg before they boarded a flight back to Florida, and Greg gave me the keys to the Hamptons house and instructions to follow.

The receptionist is a cute auburn-haired girl with a friendly smile. "Can I help you?"

"Yes, I'm here to see Annie Stewart," I say. "I'm Bella Scott from down the hall."

"Oh, it's you!" she exclaims, her smile growing.

"I'm sorry?"

She's busy pressing buttons on her phone, the receiver in hand, but glances up at me. "I've heard about you. I couldn't go to the meet-and-greet thing, but I heard you're really giving Carm a run for his money."

"Excuse me?"

She puts a finger in the air. "Mr. Mancini, Bella Scott is here for Miss Stewart." She covers the receiver. "She's usually in his office or vice versa."

"I don't want to interrupt."

She almost rolls her eyes but catches herself. "Oh, you're not. Actually, I think Carm—"

"Tracking me down?" a guy's voice says in my ear from behind me. A voice I recognize.

I spin around to face Carm. "No. But while you're here, I heard you decided to do the Hamptons?"

He's wearing what is now my favorite suit of his. It's a dark grey pinstripe with a white shirt and a blue tie. He looks so put-together that I want to unravel him.

"Yeah. Turns out my ma is worried about me working too hard."

"You don't seem like a guy who cares what other people think?" I cock a hip out to the side.

"Except for his mom," the receptionist offers.

I turn her way, having forgotten that she's right there.

"Right. Except for my ma. She's the only one I take instructions from." His tongue slides out of his mouth and across his bottom lip.

"Mama's boy. Didn't peg you for that." I ignore the ache between my thighs and dig out the envelope I made for him. "Here's your key and all the instructions. Maybe try to keep your lady guests to a minimum."

"There's that jealous tone you get when we talk about me with other women." A cocky smirk tilts the corners of his mouth.

"You can imagine whatever you want."

"It's not my imagination." He steps forward. "It's fact." His eyes dip to my lips. "Don't worry, the feeling is mutual."

"You're misreading the entire situation."

"Am I?" He raises an eyebrow in challenge.

"Um..." the receptionist says.

I step back, grabbing whatever willpower I have left to be a safe distance from him. Why is he doing this in front of witnesses? If we were alone... then it dawns on me. He's doing it now because he knows I'd never do anything with him in front of others.

Two can play this game. Be prepared to be schooled, Mr. Mancini.

I step forward so we're almost chest to chest. "Maybe we should set some ground rules, so we don't fall into bed together. The temptation in the Hamptons will be strong. What with my very revealing bikini. Me putting suntan lotion on my long legs, lying under the sun while sweat puddles between my breasts. I'd hate for you to be sporting a permanent erection the whole time."

Amusement and intrigue sparkle in his eyes. "You might have trouble of your own when I air dry after my shower, droplets of water dripping down my abs, disappearing below the towel. I'd hate for you to be rubbing yourself off just to dull the ache."

Touché.

"Bree!" Enzo's voice calls from across the office.

My gaze moves to the receptionist, who I assume is Bree. The phone dangles in her hand, eyes fixated on us.

"Damn," she whispers.

"*Bree!*" Annie makes her way out of Enzo's office toward us. "Hang up the phone." She takes it from Bree and hangs up.

Bree snaps out of it. "Sorry."

"Thank you for making our receptionist unable to function," Enzo remarks from the doorway of his office.

I glance at Carm. Are my cheeks as flushed as his? I'm torturing myself with this man.

Swiveling in the other direction, I pull another envelope out of my bag. "Here's your keys for the Hamptons."

Annie takes it. I'd imagined her hugging me when I delivered her the key to her summer dream, but she's still gauging what just happened.

"Carm, can I talk to you?" Enzo asks, nodding into his office. "It's about Ma."

I'm pretty sure that's brother talk for get-your-ass-in-here.

"I also have Dom's key. Not sure what I should do with it?" I pull the envelope out of my purse and hold it between us. "Thanks for finding him by the way. It really helped with the cost, which was nice."

Annie watches as Carm heads over to Enzo's office while I stick to my tactic of ignorance is bliss. If I keep acting like nothing happened, maybe people will forget it. Hell, if I'm lucky, maybe I will too.

"I can take it. We were all surprised he agreed to it. He's a total workaholic, but between us, I think he's heartbroken." She eyes the two brothers as they disappear into Enzo's office. "The guys say I'm wrong, but I know the signs a helluva lot better than them. My guess is he won't be great company, but he'll pay and he's always willing to help with anything. You two will probably get along well."

I nod.

"I'm not suggesting—I mean, you and Carm, well..."

"There's nothing between us."

"There's something," she counters, a smile playing on her lips.

My eyes betray me and glance at the office where I can

see Carm sitting on the couch, arm stretched along the back as though he hasn't a care in the world.

Yeah, Annie, you're right. There's something, but we're going to act like there isn't. It's best for everyone.

"It's just the head-to-head competition getting to us."

"When we get to the Hamptons this weekend, remind me to tell you about Enzo and me over a glass of wine." She's smiling as though there's some reason I'd be interested besides just getting to know her better. I'd love to hear her story, but if she thinks it's going to change my mind about Carm, she's wrong.

"When are you guys heading there?"

"Oh!" Her eyes widen. I love how excited she gets. She's the total opposite of Evie. "We should start a group chat. My phone's at my desk. I'll start it, but your friend Evie, you can add her?"

"Sure." I adjust the strap to my purse on my shoulder.

"Maybe my friend Mae and I could ride with you and your friend?" she asks.

"Sure." I don't mind as long as I don't have to spend three long hours in a car with Carm.

"Perfect." She leans forward. "Enzo might get pissed, but you know that makes the sex that much better." Her eyebrows shoot up and her body shivers as though she's thinking about it right now.

"Make-up sex for the win?" I chuckle.

"Oh, we won't really fight over it, but he's going to argue with me about it and I might put up a small fight because he loves it when our debates turn into hot sex. Just think, if you and Carm ever..." My hand covers her mouth and she stops talking, so I let it go. "Your secret is safe with me." She winks.

I shake my head. "Nothing will ever happen between

Carm and me. You can get that thought out of your head right now." I point at her then spin and leave the office, Annie's giggle trailing behind me.

———————

TWENTY MINUTES LATER, the door of my main office opens.

"Look who finally decided to cross the line... I guess it's not true what they say. Salt won't keep demons out." Max pushes her chair out from her desk and crosses her arms.

I pick up my bottle of water from our small break station and turn around to watch the show.

"Max, I presume?" His gaze veers to mine for a moment.

"Carm, I presume?" she says in a fake excited tone. "I knew your ads were airbrushed."

His nostrils flare and I giggle. He swivels toward me. "We need to talk."

"Do we?"

"You have to make an appointment," Max chimes in.

"When is she available?" he asks through gritted teeth.

"She's on her break now. Would you like to have a seat?" She picks up the basket of cookies my mom sent. She gives him a saccharine smile. "Cookie while you wait?"

I have no idea how Max does it, but I'm biting my lip to keep from laughing.

He turns to look at me again and throws up his arms. "Seriously?"

My laugh bubbles out. "Grab a cookie to calm down." I nod toward my office. "Come on in."

"Sugar are my favorite, so I wouldn't take one of those if I were you." Max eyes his hand in the basket.

"I like to live dangerously." He snags a sugar cookie, unwraps it, and takes a big bite right in front of her.

"*Ugh...* disgusting."

He smiles as he chews and rounds her desk to my office.

"I don't suggest pissing off Max," I say, shutting the door after he enters.

"Justin will calm her down later," he says, sitting in the chair in front of my desk.

My forehead wrinkles and I take a seat. "What?"

"Justin, my assistant. I think they're fucking." He crunches the cellophane into a ball and shoots it into my trash can.

Cocky bastard makes it too.

"They are not. Justin is far from Max's type."

He shrugs as though he doesn't really care either way. "Opposites attract."

"That's like opposite species."

"Hey, my boy has game." He swallows his cookie and rests his ankle on his knee.

I shake my head. "What do you need?"

"This." He wags a finger between us. "Let's figure out how we're going to live together in the same house for forty-eight hours every weekend."

I lean back in my office chair. "I figure like everyone else. It'll be an adjustment, but we'll figure it out."

He shakes his head. "I say we agree that we won't bring other people back."

"I highly doubt I'm the one who will make that a problem."

"I'll go to the chick's house." He shrugs.

"Why would you feel the need to sneak around? I'm fine if you bring someone back." My chest squeezes painfully as the words leave my mouth, but if I keep lying, I'll be good.

"Believe me, crazy shit happens out of jealousy all the time and I'll admit right now, if you show up with some guy, I might lose my shit."

That's almost sweet. It kind of makes me want to bring someone home to see what he'd do.

"Why would you lose your shit?" I shake my head. "Never mind."

He looks behind him through the glass then back at me, leaning forward in his chair. "Listen, I'm gonna shoot straight right now. I want you. I want you under me, above me, next to me. I want your ass in the air, on all fours, pussy wet."

My eyes widen to the point that I probably resemble a Dollify character.

"But I'm not the love 'em and stick with 'em kind of guy, so that means we have to remain platonic."

I sip my water, hoping it soothes my suddenly dry mouth. "You assume I wouldn't say no to you?"

He stares at me long and hard, his thumb trailing across his bottom lip.

God, why is that so damn sexy? I try to keep a shiver from revealing my desire.

"You know you feel the same."

I lean back in my chair, the picture of relaxation. I hope. "I don't."

"Come on. It's just us."

I could be an adult and admit that he's right—I want him to take me however the hell he wants—but I can't give him that satisfaction. "I'm just joking around. It's a game."

His gaze dips to my breasts, probably doing a nipple

check. Ha ha, I have a bra, a cami, and a blouse on. You'll see nothing today, buck-o.

"Okay then, you're cool if I bring a girl home?" His expression is a challenge.

"For sure." I shrug. "You're paying rent too. I can't dictate the rules."

He stands from his chair and presses his hands on the back. Those long fingers that could reach so far into me I'd be writhing.

"Then I'll see you Friday." He winks, heading to the door.

"Can't wait."

He nods, trying to appear as though he knows I'm lying, but he really has no idea. I might be getting good at this game after all.

CHAPTER FIFTEEN

Carm

I sit in the back of Enzo's rented SUV, still trying to figure out whether Bella is lying about this attraction between us being one-sided. I'm almost positive she's lying, but I can't be sure.

"You're quiet for the first time ever in your life," Dom says from the shotgun position. Asshole called it first.

"How's Ma feel about us canceling Sunday dinners for the entire summer?" I ask. There's no way we'll make it back to the city in time.

"She told Annie she's okay with it, but that Blanca is now her favorite." Enzo looks at me in the rearview mirror.

"I think she's always been Ma's favorite. Hell, even Annie might have surpassed me," Dom says. To my surprise, he hasn't had his phone out the entire ride.

I groan when I see the brake lights on the girls' car.

"Why are they stopping again? Is there another damn wind-mill? A three-hour trip is going to take us five."

Thankfully, they just slow down before speeding up again and taking the next right turn.

Enzo laughs. "Someone's pissy. Maybe you need to get laid."

"I plan on it. This weekend."

"Just remember it'll be a long summer for all of us if you and Bella can't coexist," Dom warns.

"What do you know? You've never even met her," I grumble.

"I know she gets under your skin. If you're planning on getting laid and it's not Bella, it's only going to cause the rest of us a headache. I'm half-tempted to fuck her so you can't and the whole thing will be over."

Bile rushes up my throat. The thought of my brother's hands on her, touching her like I envisioned doing as I stroked myself every night this week, makes me physically ill. Maybe I can't have her now, but after this whole Bond Street competition is over, perhaps it's a possibility.

Enzo raises his eyebrows at Dom, and Dom chuckles, rolling down his window. The breeze coming in helps settle the nausea swirling in my gut.

After a few more turns, we pull into the driveway of a house that is mad money. The house is surrounded by trees, secluding it from nosey neighbors, and the ocean is its backyard.

The girls get out of the car and take a second to gawk at the place.

Bella drove. Of course she did. Control freak can't not have her hands leading the way. She bends over the trunk and the headlights from our vehicle light up her ass that is presently in a pair of tight shorts showcasing its perfection.

"You're fucked," Dom says, glancing back and opening the door. "Wipe the drool off your chin before you get out."

I wish I could fight my brother this once, but I can't. He's right. I'm not sure how to get Bella Scott out of my system—other than screwing her out of it and thereby screwing myself out of a very lucrative contract. Sleeping with Bella would be distracting, to say the least and I don't think I could trust myself to do everything in my power to win if I had her in my bed.

AFTER WE'VE TOURED the house, we all pick our bedrooms. On the plus side, mine is on an entirely different floor than Bella's. On the bad side, I got stuck next to the lovebirds.

"No moaning all night, you two, and my brother is not God, so I'd appreciate you not referring to him as such." I point at Annie, who's already on her second glass of wine, her arms wrapped around Enzo's waist.

"I can't promise that. To me, he is God." She looks up at him.

Enzo leans down and gives her a chaste kiss. "That's right. Let's go see how hard that headboard can hit his wall." Enzo pretends to escort her out of the room, but they stop short, laughing with one another.

"Stop being a buzzkill, Carm. I thought it was going to be him." Mae, Annie's sidekick, points at Dom, who's nursing a beer while he scrolls through his phone.

The room laughs, and Dom picks up his head. "Some of us need to make money."

He up and leaves the room. Too bad my big bad older brother isn't in touch with his feelings.

"Let's go out," Evie says.

Evie's platinum hair is cut to her chin. She's cute, but she's Bella's friend and the evil eye I keep getting from her tells me she's not going to be joining my fan club any time soon. She's obviously not the one to help me get Bella off my mind.

Hey, give me a break. I'm desperate for options in this unchartered ocean.

Mae instantly agrees. She and Evie are practically the same person. "I'll go get ready."

Bella sighs, still sipping her wine.

"We're out," Enzo says.

He and Annie head outside. Probably going to have sex on the beach. God knows how many sexual positions and places they'll knock off their bucket lists this summer.

And yes, that is jealousy.

"What about you?" I ask Bella, who looks much like Dom did, her thumb scrolling down her phone screen.

"I'm tired. Long week," she says to her phone, not me.

"Want a back rub?"

She looks up from her phone. *Success.* "No."

"I tried. Come on. It's our first night here." I'm urging her to go out because if she stays, I'll be tempted to stay as well, and that'll only give me blue balls. At least this way I can maybe find someone who looks like her and bring her home.

Yes, I've decided to bring a girl back home with me at some point. Do I want to make Bella jealous? Hell fucking yes. I'm fully aware it's a dick move, but I know deep in my gut that she wants me like I want her. Why can't she admit it? We're adults. Even if we're not going to act on our feelings, she can still be truthful about them.

She places the phone on the counter. "You're going?"

"I'll go if you go."

"And if I don't?" She crosses her arms. The low-cut shirt she's wearing only shows me the exact spot I'd like my face to be.

"I can think of a lot of things we could do if we stay." I step closer.

She slides off her stool. "Fine, I'll go."

See how she never said it won't happen? As if she might give in to me if we did stay in...

"Perfect." I head in the other direction to get dressed.

An hour later—because Evie and Mae are obviously not the low-key girls I thought they were—Dom, who I coerced into coming, and I are sitting in the living room.

"Car's here," Dom yells.

He's snippy because I told him I'm going to screw Bella tonight if he doesn't come out with us. The thing about my older brother is that he's kind of the one who keeps the Mancini boys in line. I'm not sure if it's Mama's doing from when we were younger or not, but he's hell-bent on making sure we don't mess up. And let's be real, if I mess with Bella, this whole Hamptons summer house thing will be screwed by my screwing.

Regardless, he's here, which will do him good. Whatever's been up his ass lately can maybe wiggle itself out while he's dancing with some chick.

"Coming."

"Coming."

"One sec."

Heels click against the hardwood stairs before the three women present themselves. They're all done up in skimpy outfits, but my eyes are only on the redhead.

What can I say? I fixate on the things I like.

Bella's wearing a silky tank top that ties around her

neck, blocking any view of her cleavage, but the way it clings to her highlights the round shape of her breasts in an elegant way that's still sexy as fuck. Her shorty shorts show off her long legs, and her heels cause saliva to pool inside my mouth. Big Carm just grew a couple inches.

"Let's go." Dom stands from the couch.

I follow.

"Aren't you going to say anything?" Evie asks, spinning around.

"You all look good…" My eyes zero in on Bella, who catches me soaking her in.

"Huh. And here I thought you knew how to sweet-talk a woman." Evie is the first one out the door.

Mae follows, leaving Bella, and I press my hand to the small of her back, getting close enough that no one else hears. "You're stunning, and if you were trying to get me to not notice you, you wore the wrong outfit."

Her back straightens and her body trembles.

Now tell me she doesn't feel something.

"Stop taunting," Dom says from behind me.

Bella catches up with her friends, and just as I'm about to climb in next to her, Dom yanks me back by the collar of my shirt.

"You can ride shotgun." He slides in next to Bella.

I release a frustrated sigh, taking the seat next to the Uber driver of the seven-seater SUV.

Evie and Mae talk non-stop about how excited they are, and I wonder how much they drank while getting ready. Bella is quiet, and Dom doesn't say anything other than directing the driver where we're going.

The music is thumping at the outside bar when we arrive. The girls pile out, Evie leading the way. She sweet-talks the bouncer and they walk in. We approach only to have the asshole put up his hand. Dom slips him a hundred and he steps aside. Money can buy everything.

"Thanks, big bro!" I slap him on the back while trying to find the girls. They obviously don't care if they party with us.

"Next time, you're up. I'm going to the bar." He winds through the throngs of people while my eyes scour the crowd for the redhead who's quickly becoming my obsession.

By the time I spot her, the three girls are on the deck that overlooks the ocean. Two guys have found their way to them, one looking like he's purchasing their drinks.

Fuck this. What the hell am I doing? Chasing some chick to try to get her out of my mind? There are lots of women who can do that.

Instead of heading to the deck, I follow Dom to the bar.

"Two shots of whiskey." Dom raises his fingers in case the bartender can't hear how many.

"Shots?" I ask.

Dom isn't a get-drunk-quick kind of guy. Whenever he does lose control, it's at a wedding or a bachelor party. Where the day is long and one drink spills into the next and before you know it, eight hours have passed. He's never been the one who drinks as much as possible to get loaded.

"What do you want?" he asks.

"I thought one of the shots—"

"No."

The bartender places both shot glasses in front of him and pours the alcohol. As I'm ordering my beer, Dom downs the shots. I look quizzically to my left.

"Another two," Dom says.

The bartender removes the cap from my bottle of beer

then pours another two shots of whiskey. Dom downs them and stalks off without a word.

"Hey!" the bartender calls after him.

"I got it." I pull my cash out of my pocket and tip him generously with the hope that next time he sees me, he'll come my way first.

Taking my beer, I search for Dom, but he's nowhere in sight. Did he really just ditch me? What happened to being each other's wingmen?

I head toward the deck, figuring that maybe he joined the girls, when a woman approaches me.

"Hey, I know you," she says, brushing her blonde hair off her shoulder.

"You do?" I analyze her face for any recognition but come up empty.

"Yeah, you're the one with the billboards." She points at me and stumbles to the side. Laughter pours out of her as a friend of hers comes over and steadies her.

"Sorry," the woman says, holding her friend by the waist.

"It's okay. Excuse me." I slide by them, not in the mood to deal with a drunk girl all over me because of my billboards. I normally enjoy that, but as much as I try to stay away from Bella, I keep being drawn to her.

The women are still outside, Evie and Mae talking with the two guys while Bella is farther down the railing, all by herself, staring at the ocean with an empty glass in her hand.

I close the distance between us, always wanting what I shouldn't.

CHAPTER SIXTEEN

Bella

"I thought the point of coming here was to have fun?" Carm sidles up next to me, resting his forearms on the wooden deck railing and staring out at the ocean.

The man is gorgeous in fluorescent lighting, but with the moonlight shining on his features? My stomach and my thighs clench.

"I told you I wasn't much for going out tonight."

"Why not?" he asks.

I sip my drink, but only ice cubes hit my top lip. Carm offers his beer, but I shake my head. "The pressure of this Bond Street deal is weighing on me. How on Earth do I find a way to sell them for sale by owner without wining and dining? Let's be serious for a moment—what client is going to spend millions when I don't even show them the unit myself or run through the contract with them?"

He chuckles, sips his beer, and holds it out in front of him. "It's definitely a disadvantage."

"New builds are different than existing properties with homeowners living there. I have to rely on Helena to walk them through the place, and I can't afford to do all the things you can to fish for buyers."

He nods. He's been in the game longer than me. He knows the score and can't really offer me much advice.

"I shouldn't even be telling you this."

"I don't want us to be that way. I get that we're pitted against one another here, but it doesn't mean we can't try to be friends."

I nod, wishing I could've met him under different circumstances. Carm isn't the forever guy, but I bet he'd be a pretty good one-night stand and maybe even a better booty call.

As if he can hear my thoughts, he bumps me with his shoulder. "You're thinking really hard. Let's blow off some steam. That's what these weekends are for, aren't they?"

I raise my eyebrows. "I think you just want in my pants."

He laughs, his ego-driven smirk on display. "You know me well, but I'll keep my hands to myself. No need to complicate things further."

I narrow my eyes. "Are you sure you can handle that?"

"I'm a grown man. I can control myself no matter how tempting you are."

Why does my body react when he says things like that? Every time he compliments me, my stomach zings as though I'm at the top of a roller coaster, staring over the edge, waiting for the drop.

"Let's get another drink." I turn around and head to the bar.

Evie and Mae are flirting with the two British guys who approached us when we first arrived. Feeling like the fifth wheel, I slowly ventured away from them. No one bothered me after that until Carm found me, as if he's a K-9 with my scent and can locate me anywhere.

Carm slides money toward the bartender. "It's on me."

Once we have our drinks, we head to a table tucked into the corner. The heat wave has passed, and the nights aren't super hot yet.

"Have you sold a unit yet?" I've been dying to know. He's had an entire week, and this is Carmelo Mancini. There's a reason he's so well-known in New York real estate, and it's not just his billboards.

He sips his beer. "No."

A huge breath leaves my throat.

"But I'm close. I have a client in from Los Angeles. She's been looking for a long time and I think a unit on Bond Street will suit her needs. She's just a slow decision-maker."

"The woman from the elevator?" I ask.

Truthfully, that woman gave me the vibe I was stepping on her territory just because I was talking to Carm in the hallway.

He nods. "Yeah, that's her." His gaze moves to the dance floor.

"Can I ask you a personal question?" I lean closer to him. My second margarita on the rocks has done wonders to relax me.

"That could be dangerous." His smile. A man shouldn't be allowed to have those white teeth and such a perfect grin. He winks and puts his finger in the air. "One question."

"What made you go into real estate?"

His entire body seems to lose some of the tension. "I wanted to be in charge of my own destiny. Real estate is a good biz for that. I work hard and I get paid for the work I do. The harder I work, the more money I make. I love the art of the deal and every client, every property, is different. It keeps it interesting."

"So it's not about the clients?"

"That's two questions." He raises his perfectly shaped eyebrows.

I bet he manscapes.

"Consider it an amendment to the original question."

He grins. "No, it's not about the clients. I mean, I like to make them happy when I get the price they want or find them the perfect space to move into, but as far as lasting relationships, I have to admit, that's not what makes me tick. I do what I need to in order to get the job done. But I'd never screw anyone over." He takes a long pull of his beer.

"Have you ever slept with a client?" I laugh to play off my question, but the woman in the hallway comes to mind.

His eyes meet mine. "No." Then he drinks his beer.

I sip my margarita, thinking I may have crossed the line. "Did I offend you?"

"Listen, I get what my billboards represent, but it's just to stand out and be different. To entice potential clients to call me rather than the other way around."

"Use what you can, huh?"

He's smiling and seems not at all upset, so maybe I didn't ruin our conversation by asking. "What about you?"

My body clams up and I down the rest of my margarita, pushing my bad memories to the back of my mind. "No."

He tilts his head, studying me as though he heard something in my answer. "Did I touch a nerve?"

"I'm going to get another drink."

"Bella?" He grasps my elbow, stopping me from sliding off the stool.

I plaster on my usual smile and turn around to face him. "Of course you didn't. We said we were going to have fun and blow off steam. I need another drink to do that."

His gaze doesn't leave mine, and for a moment, my nose tickles and I think he'll call my bluff. But he gets off his stool. "I get the drinks when you're with me. Sit down."

I watch longingly as he ventures to the bar. A woman approaches him, but he doesn't bite, which shouldn't relieve me as much as it does. Looking at all the sweaty bodies on the dance floor, I remember when I couldn't stand to be at a place like this because anxiety and fear crippled me.

"Here you go." He slides my drink over to me and gets back onto the stool across from me. "There's Dom."

He's easy to find, dancing with some brunette. The two of them are more making out than dancing.

"She's cute," I say.

"How can you tell? He's attached to her." He laughs. "There's something about her that seems familiar though."

"You can only see her back," I say.

He shrugs. "I never forget a face. Or an ass." He winks and I shake my head and sip my drink.

Dom and his mystery woman disappear shortly after and "One Dance" by Drake comes on and my body responds, bobbing to the beat. My eyes close as I mouth the words. I love this song.

"You like this song?" Carm asks.

I open my eyes to find his on me. There's heat there. Heat that could burn me if I admit to myself how badly I want him.

"I do." I consciously try to stop my shoulders and hips from moving.

"Come on." He downs the rest of his beer and places the empty on the table.

"What about my drink?" I ask.

"Either down it or I'll buy you another after." He waits next to me at the table.

It's clear he won't take no for an answer, so I down the rest of my drink, take his hand to help me down, and he leads me to the dance floor. His hands land on my hips as we sway, getting the feel of one another. He swivels me around so that my ass is positioned in front of his groin, and his hands move me the way he wants.

"Just go with it," he whispers in my ear, his chest pressed to my back.

I'm not sure if it's his words or being in a throng of people and having the safety of him near, but I do let myself go. I move my hips and my shoulders, my head falling back and landing on his chest.

Sweat trickles between my breasts, and my ass grinds into his crotch. His hands venture places I'd never allow if we weren't dancing, skimming down the sides of my ribcage. The DJ does a great job of shifting into one catchy song after another.

Carm's eyes watch me as he turns me around to face him, stepping into my personal space, but I welcome him with my arms around his neck. My hips swing, and I push out my breasts. Couples around us are just as into it, and I lose myself for a moment, becoming the girl I was once so familiar with but lost somewhere in the abyss.

By the time we finish, we're both sweaty and Carm's T-shirt is just about drenched. We head off the dance floor.

"Another drink?" he asks.

"Sure."

He buys us another set of drinks, and since our table is

now taken, he takes my hand and leads me down to the beach.

"How did I never do this before?" I sip my drink, but it does nothing to cool my body down.

"I know. First night and I already regret the last eight years my friends have asked me to join them and I declined."

He sits in the sand a fair distance from the ocean, and I sit down, right next to him.

"Thank you," I say, stirring the ice cubes in my drink.

"For what?" He props his elbows on his knees, his beer bottle tucked between his thumb and forefinger, hanging in the air.

"For distracting me tonight. Reminding me why I came here."

"I could say the same. I would've stayed in and worked otherwise. Probably would have had to listen to Annie and Enzo banging all night."

"You're still thanking me even though you won't be getting lucky?" I raise my eyebrows.

He chuckles. "You mean I did all this foreplay for nothing?" His smile says he's messing with me.

"You thought a few drinks and a half hour of dancing would do the job?"

"Definitely not. I know you're a game-changer." His eyes find mine in the moonlight, and the casual vibe between us evaporates.

The waves slowly crest on the beach, and a soft breeze ruffles my hair. I lick my lips because I want him to kiss me. I want to confess that he did get me with the dancing. He granted me the security to do what I love.

"What does that mean?" I whisper.

He shifts his weight. One arm extends behind him and

his other hand brushes a piece of sweaty hair behind my ear. "You're not really the type of girl who's happy with a one-night stand."

He's right, but I desperately wish he was wrong. I've never wanted to be that carefree girl who can take what she wants when she wants it and never be invested. But I've learned the hard way that I'm not that girl. I'm the girl who will anticipate his call the next day. The girl who will want to get to know more about him. The girl who ends up heart-broken in the end.

"Sorry, I guess?"

He shakes his head, and his finger trails down the side of my neck and over my shoulder. My goose bumps chase his touch, begging him to not stop, but sadly, his finger falls from my skin before he reaches my hand. "Never be sorry for that. You demand respect. It's one of the best things about you."

I lick my lips again and his gaze casts down, watching my tongue skate over my bottom lip.

"Come on. We need to get the hell out of here before I screw this up for both of us." He stands, brushes off his ass, and holds his hand out for mine.

Together we walk off the beach, platonic and sexually frustrated.

CHAPTER SEVENTEEN

Carm

I deserve a gold medal for keeping my dick in my pants this past weekend.

As if Friday night wasn't bad enough, on Saturday, we all hung out at the beach. If I was a factor in Bella's decision-making when she bought her swimsuit, I commend her on a job well done. I sported a half chub the entire fucking day. The only time I didn't was when I got into a competitive game of beach volleyball with Enzo and Dom.

Now it's Sunday night and the Hamptons are behind us for the next five days as I gear up for my broker party at Bond Street tomorrow night.

After clicking on the Mets game, I toss the remote on the couch and grab my beer from the table next to me. My laptop is shut on the coffee table. I'd usually be working, but my mind is too preoccupied. The never-ending wheel of events from this weekend plays on a loop in my head.

Mistake number one. Feeling her body against mine.

Mistake number two. Taking her to the beach after drinking and memorizing the curves of her body.

Mistake number three. Seeing Bella in a swimsuit, because if ever there were a cock tease, that's it.

At least I had the decency not to act on my want for her. How different is that from when I was first headed there? I was hellbent on getting her to sleep with me just to rid myself of my obsession, but the crystal ball is clear now—I'd fuck everything up for a lot of people I love if I act on my impulses.

My phone vibrates next to me. Needing any distraction I can get, I answer without looking at the number. "Hello?"

"Hey, Carm."

Perfect. Nothing better to dampen my sexual fire than a conversation with my little sister. "Blanca, what's up?"

"The fact that you jerks got a house in the Hamptons and no one told me. I might not have a dick, but I'm a Mancini too."

Whoa. She's pissed and I'm thankful she's on the phone and not on my doorstep. Believe me, all three of us have been kneed in the nuts by Blanca on way too many occasions. The verdict is still out on if we'll be able to father children.

"I thought Enzo was going to tell you."

He lost the rock, paper, scissors on who had to give her the news.

"Yeah, he sent me an email just now. Conveniently he's not answering his phone."

"Because he's screwing Annie probably." I roll my eyes and relax into the couch.

"Ew... I don't need to picture that in my head."

Truth is, Blanca can't afford to join us. I would've loved

to foot the bill for her, but Blanca has a tendency not to look too kindly on her brothers' gifts. She would've felt like she owed us. On top of that, she's starting a new job and wouldn't be able to get the time off work.

"I'm sorry, but you know how pricey the Hamptons are. We're sharing with a bunch of people." I lower the volume on the television after another run scores for the Mets.

"Why do I have to be the youngest? I always get left out. And on top of everything else, I broke up with Carter."

"Are you upset about it?" Good riddance, I say. That guy wasn't good enough for her.

"Yeah, no one likes a break-up. He's nice and all, but I have to figure out what I'm going to do with the rest of my life." The aggravation in her tone is clear. I wish I could guide her, but this is something she needs to do on her own.

"And he can't be part of it because...?"

"Because he's too wrapped up in being the next big thing down at his accounting firm. The man works non-stop. I get it. I mean, I have three brothers who put their social life on the back burner, but I'm not the kind of girl who will wait for him to pencil me into his calendar. I want the type of guy who says screw it to work because he can't bear to be away from me another minute."

Her words worm their way into my head, and I'm left wondering if I'll ever meet a girl like that. One who makes me want to reduce my workload because I'd rather be with her than chase the next deal.

"You deserve the best," I say, because she does.

"Yeah. Yeah. I've always found it funny that my three brothers think I should have a guy who puts me first, but they never put a woman first themselves."

"Put the stones down. I'm sorry about the Hamptons,

but no need to attack us." I take a sip of my beer and place it back on the table.

"I'm only really talking about you and Dom now. Enzo seems to have figured out what's most important in life."

"Anything else besides the passive-aggressive comments tonight?" I up the volume on my television.

"Nothing, but I'm coming up in a few weeks, and after making me spend every Sunday at the family dinner table with just Mom and Dad, you boys owe me."

"I'll make sure a couch at the Hamptons has your name on it."

"Bed, Carm. Your bed. Without you in it."

"Goes without saying. Why me? The other two left you high and dry too." She'll figure out when she gets there that there's an extra bedroom for her.

"I gotta go call Dom now. You know, make the rounds so you all know you're on my shit list."

Thank God I'm not the only one getting reprimanded tonight by mini Ma. "Night, Blanca."

"Night."

She hangs up, and I chuckle while tossing the phone onto the cushion next to me, situating myself on my couch for the rest of the night to get Bella out of my head.

ON THE WAY into the office Monday morning, I stop next to my billboard ad. On the other side of the street is the redhead I can't stop picturing underneath me—her own billboard advertising her FSBO services. She might be fully dressed, but she's totally putting off the same vibe as my billboards do.

"She wants to play this way?" I grumble, opening the building door.

I jam my finger on the elevator button, tapping my shoe until it arrives, then I jam my finger on the button for my floor. As I walk down the hall toward my office, I know I should just go into my own so I can cool down, but I turn left into hers.

The unicorn-colored-hair girl with dark-rimmed glasses smile falters when she sees me. She pushes up her glasses and her fingers hammer away on her keyboard. "The cookies are gone."

"I'm here for your boss." Through the glass of her office, I see Bella on the phone. Probably ordering another billboard.

"She's on a call. If you'd like to have a seat and wait..." Max extends her arm out in front of her, a fake smile on display.

"How long do you expect her to be?" But before she can answer, I see Bella hang up. "Never mind. I see she's off." I round her desk.

"Hey, you can't just go in there!" She chases after me, but I open the door of Bella's office.

Alarm momentarily flashes across her face until she sees that it's me. "Carm? Why are you bursting into my office?"

Instead of standing, she slides her chair under her desk, hiding any glimpse of her long, toned legs.

"The billboard across the street... I thought we had an agreement?"

"And your billboard is allowed?" Max steps into the office, arms crossed, and slams her foot on the floor.

"I think Justin was looking for you," I toss back over my shoulder.

She narrows her eyes. "I'm not dating your assistant. He's the enemy as far as I'm concerned."

Liar. But I won't call her out on it in front of her boss because I'm nice like that.

"Excuse us, Max. I can handle this," Bella says.

Max huffs. I'm surprised she doesn't stick out her tongue like a toddler before closing the door behind her.

"You get all pissed off saying I use my looks for my ads and look at yours." I point in the direction her billboard ad sits. If we had x-ray vision, we'd see it.

"I'm fully clothed. Are you?" She's so poised, and for some reason, that pushes me over the edge.

"Your legs aren't covered. Your skirt is too short. Your necklace dips down between your tits. Any man who sees that will beat off to that image for the next week. You're a hypocrite."

"Oh please." She slides her chair out and stands. Her tight waist is accentuated by the flair of her pants falling over her strappy sandals. "I'm fully clothed and dressed in a professional outfit. I never knocked you for the sexual flair your ads portray."

"You accused me of using a body double, and the insinuation was clear that you think my body is my biggest sales technique, for which you had no problem judging me."

She grabs her hair and sweeps it across the back of her neck to lay on one side. Obviously trying to use her sexual appeal to win this argument, but it won't work.

"Let's go have a look." She saunters out of her office and past Max—who I'm surprised doesn't follow us, considering she's Bella's five-foot-two bodyguard.

We leave her office, and her manicured nail presses the elevator button. The door opens a second later as if she called it up with some voodoo magic. We're both silent on the ride down until we exit through the front door.

She shields her eyes from the sun while staring at her billboard then shifting her gaze to my ad. Okay, maybe she has a point. Mine is definitely more sexual than hers.

"What are we looking at?" Justin sidles up to me, his eyes ping-ponging between the two. "Very nice, Ms. Scott."

"Justin." Bella slides between us, knocking me with her hip. "Does one of these scream sexual to you?"

Justin is my boy and he will not throw me under the bus.

"Your stance looks a little sexual." I want to high-five him behind her back. "But Carm sells sex."

"What?" I whip my head in his direction.

"I mean, that's your MO. It's what you're known for. Your ad copy alone implies sex."

"Do you remember who pays you? And aren't you coming in a little late?" I ask and glance at my watch.

Sex appeal might be what gets them in the door, but it's my skill that's made my name in this business.

Bella laughs and squeezes Justin's shoulder. "Thanks, Justin." She turns to me. "I'd say that's case closed." Her heels click on the concrete on her way back into the building.

"We still have the issue of your ad being outside the office. We said no ads."

"Yours is still there."

Justin opens the door of the building, sliding in before we have a chance to ask his opinion again.

"Mine was grandfathered in." Yes, I'm fully aware this is a dick move and that I'm being a sore loser, and no, I don't care.

"If you'd like to take down your ad, I'll gladly take down

mine." She crosses her arms so they're resting right under her breasts. My eyes zero in, and she must notice because by the time my gaze reaches hers, she huffs.

"What?" I ask as if I wasn't just imagining her nipples through the silk of her cami.

"Would you like me to stare at your dick?"

An older woman and her husband walking by glance at us but continue walking. They're New Yorkers; surely, they've heard worse.

"Have you imagined how huge it is already?" I step forward. "I bet you have. Just like how I've wondered whether you're shaved or not when you slip your hands into your panties at night while you're trying to sleep and can't get me off your mind."

She inhales a deep breath. "I sleep naked. There are no panties."

I barely suppress a groan.

She rushes into the building and onto the elevator, but I'm hot on her heels.

"So you admit that you're attracted to me then?"

"I admit nothing. I simply stated a fact." She jams her finger on the button once we're in the elevator.

"You want an admission from me?" I ask, gripping the railing behind me in an effort to keep from reaching for her.

Her cheeks turn pink and I can't help but wonder if that happens after an orgasm too. "No."

"Too bad. I've beat off to the vision of you every night for the past week."

She swallows, her eyes focused on the numbers above. "Well, I hope the fictional version of me can rock your world."

The elevator dings that we're on our floor, but I quickly press the 'Doors Closed' button.

"I'm dying here, Bella. I keep convincing myself to stay away, but you're all I think about."

She steps back from me and closes her eyes for a second. "We can't. I can't. You. Me. It can't happen. It's just..."

"What?" I'm aware of the million reasons not to cross the line with her. Our list of cons versus pros is crazy outnumbered. But when she's right here and I see that desire racing through her veins like mine, I can't help but think we're stupid for denying ourselves.

"We're too different. We're competitors. And for the summer, we're roommates." She steps forward, nudges my arm down so I'm no longer pressing the button, and when the doors spring open, she flies out.

I mentally prepare myself for the defeat I have to admit when it comes to Bella, but I've never been one to lose gracefully. I'm not sure that's going to change now.

CHAPTER EIGHTEEN

Bella

It's been two weeks since I almost attached myself like Velcro to Carm in the elevator. We've managed to be nice to one another while we're sharing the Hamptons house, though he's working a lot while he's here. I try to gravitate toward the girls, except Mae and Evie have fallen in love with the British guys we met our first night, which leaves me with either Dom, who comes and goes at all times of the day and night, or the lovebirds, who are so wrapped up in one another it reminds me that I don't want just a night of hot sex with Carm. I want what Enzo and Annie have. The solid foundation of a best friend and lover.

It's thundering and lightning outside, which the weatherman did not predict. I'm nestled on the covered deck, watching the rain pelt the ocean and the pool and sipping a cup of tea.

Evie and Mae are off with their new boy toys. Annie

and Enzo went to the store. Dom is wherever it is that Dom goes when we're up here. Which leaves me alone with Carm somewhere in this house.

When the sliding glass door behind me opens, my heart rate increases. He's coming out of hiding. Great.

"Shitty day. I should've stayed in the city." The chair sliding from the table sounds like nails on a chalkboard. Or impending doom. Something like that.

I glance over to find him taking a seat with a beer in hand. He's wearing shorts and an NYU sweatshirt.

"You went to NYU?" I ask. Anything to distract me from his tan, muscular legs lightly covered in dark hair. How opposite are we? I have to lather on coats of sunblock so I don't burn, and this man looks as though he's spent a lifetime in the Mediterranean and it's only been a few weeks since we've gotten the house.

He glances at his sweatshirt. "Yeah. What about you?"

I shrug. "Columbia."

He laughs and shakes his head.

"What?" I bring the mug to my lips.

"Figures. We've been rivals from the start."

I nod, taking his word for it. I never did keep up with the sports teams.

"Where is everyone?" He looks around as though they'd be out playing in puddles like children.

"Out. Mae and Evie are with the Brits. No clue where Dom is, and Enzo and Annie went to the grocery store." I sip my tea, and he pulls from his beer again.

The discomfort between us grows and I'm not even sure why it's there. We've coexisted these last couple of weeks without any problems. But then again, we've both done our best to ignore one another.

"You're going to find out anyway, so I wanted you to hear it from me..."

He doesn't even have to finish his sentence for me to know he should be holding a glass of champagne instead of a bottle of beer. He's been holed up in his room all day, and I overheard him schmoozing a client. The selfish part of me hoped it was for a property other than Bond Street.

"I sold one of the units." Again, his beer bottle tips back and his gaze diverts out to the ocean beyond the pool and yard.

"Congratulations," I mumble.

He shrugs. "I usually love competition. I thought I'd really enjoy competing against you, but it turns out not so much."

I stand from the table and tuck in my chair. "It's fine. Go ahead and gloat. I probably would if the roles were reversed."

Taking my teacup, I open the screen door, but as I'm turning to shut it, Carm stands from the table and stalks over. His tall figure is almost intimidating. He's so powerful, so in control of himself, but no part of me feels any real fear. "I'm not going to gloat or brag. It's one unit out of eight. You could come back with two sold next week. It's a marathon, not a sprint."

I turn away from him and head into the kitchen, where I grab the kettle and set it on the stove again. Maybe I should do what Carm is doing and drink. Take a shot and calm this anxiety and anticipation that's suddenly hijacked my body.

"I've had no inquiries. Do you know how much I've spent on advertising so far?" I shouldn't give him the details, it'll only increase his advantage over me.

"Tell me again why you chose FSBO?" He sits at the

breakfast bar, taking a banana out of the fruit basket and opening it.

"I told you, I was sick of the game."

He nods. "I ran into a buddy of mine. I guess the two of you used to work at the same office?"

My stomach clenches. What has he heard? "Oh. Who?" I try to keep my voice casual.

"Gerald McCoy? We started around the same time. We were working on putting a deal together on one of his listings last week."

I grab a tea bag and put it into my mug to distract myself, my hands shaking. "I know who he is, but other than some morning meetings we sat in together, I didn't really *know* him."

He bites the banana and leans back on his stool. "He said you were at the top of your game. That you'd just beat your previous year's earnings when you quit."

I glance up, and what a big mistake that is. His eyes pierce into mine, and those question-filled blue hues could almost force me to reveal my secret. Only a few people know the real reason why I left the brokerage for FSBO.

"Money isn't everything."

He bites another chunk off the banana and waits for me to fill him in. The kettle whistles and I turn my attention to the stove, feeling his gaze on my back the entire time.

"Do you think it was worth it?"

Please, Annie and Enzo, come home. Now. Someone save me from this line of questioning. The safety that consumes me when Carm is near is way too dangerous, and I almost feel the need to pour out my heart.

"You're prying." I pour my cup of tea, steam rising into my face.

"We're having a conversation. We're in the same line of

work. What do you wanna talk about? The weather? It's raining and the storm isn't supposed to let up until tomorrow."

Just then his phone vibrates in his pocket. *Thank god.* He stands as if on autopilot, but instead of walking out of the room, he halts at the archway.

"Yeah?" Without the rehearsed spiel of "this is Carmelo Mancini," I assume it's personal.

I pick up my cup of tea and head back out to the deck because the gloomy sky and rain match my mood. Especially since Carm's sold the first unit and is prying into my past, picking at old wounds.

A few minutes later, the sliding door opens again and Carm returns. I inwardly roll my eyes, though I shouldn't care. I'm not big on being alone anyway.

"Enzo and Annie are heading back to the city." He slides out the chair and the legs scrape against the concrete again. Once he's taken a seat, he places his phone on the table next to mine.

"Oh?"

"Yeah, they just got word about a client who might want to jump ship from the firm they used to work at, so..."

I smile. "They work well together."

He nods. "They do. My brother was always so self-involved. I was surprised how much Annie has changed him."

"It's rare that you actually see that happen in real life. It's what movies and books are made of."

"What?"

"The whole reformed playboy thing."

He chuckles. "Scares the crap out of me."

"Go figure." I shake my head in disgust.

He takes another drink of his beer. "What does that mean?"

"You're probably so scared of commitment that you could never imagine being in your brother's situation." I sip my tea.

"I'm not scared of commitment. My schedule doesn't allow for it. I can't very well give a girlfriend the attention she would deserve. My weekends are treated like workdays for the most part. If a client calls, I'm off on an appointment or on my computer or phone. This job doesn't make it feasible to have someone as a permanent fixture in my life."

"You're here. It's the weekend." I raise my eyebrows.

His gaze moves to the pool, where the unicorn raft Evie bought the first day here almost tips over from the wind and rain pelting it. "So I am."

"Your argument doesn't stand?"

His head twists in my direction and I should probably look away before our eyes lock, but stupidly, I don't. "Do you *really* want to know why I'm here?"

My heart hammers and my stomach feels as if it's the cage at the zoo's butterfly exhibit. Is he about to stop with the sexual innuendos and get real? Tell me that I'm his reason for coming up here every weekend? I'm afraid of how I'll react if he does. I'm pretty sure it would involve nakedness.

Which is stupid, because in my head, he's wrapped in "Danger" tape. He's too smooth... too suave... he'll eat me and spit me out after I've fallen for him.

"Sure, tell me why you're here." I pretend to be unfazed when my body is poised on the brink of its flight response.

"I'm here for my ma. She thinks I work too hard and that I need to take some time to enjoy life."

All the excitement that was sparking inside me is

doused with a firefighter's hose. The anticipation of finally crossing the line and hearing him say something more than just that he wants me in bed, that maybe this thing between us could blossom into something more, fizzles. My day's grown shittier and more depressing than the weather.

My shoulders slump and I slide my chair out from the table. "I'm going to go work."

"Yeah, I'll be in right behind you." He never looks at me, his gaze focusing on the pool as if he's running something through his head. Deep in thought.

Whatever. He can sit there all day. It's only further proof that he's not the man I want in my life because the kind of man I want isn't afraid to acknowledge his feelings for me. He'd own them without apology. Just another check mark in the column of reasons why Carm Mancini isn't meant for Bella Scott.

My hand rests on the handle of the sliding door. Anger washes over me like the crashing waves on the beach.

Fuck Carmelo Mancini. If he's not man enough to lay his feelings on the line and admit that we're both here in this house because of one another, that we make sure we're always looking our best in case we run into each other— even when we're lounging around this place—then fuck him. He might be willing to deny it, but I can't continue to live this way, ping-ponging back and forth between I want you, no, I hate you.

I'm self-aware enough to know that some of my anger may come from the fact that he sold a unit already, but that was just the match that lit the fire burning inside me.

"You know what?" I turn around, and his head slowly circles toward me. I'm not sure if he sees something in my eyes or not, but his eyes flare. "Never mind."

I turn back around, but his chair legs scratch on the

concrete and before I have time to escape, his chest presses against my back while his arm rests on the side of the house, caging me in. I could leave if I wanted to, but I don't.

"What is it?" His voice is low but confident, like he wants to push me as much as I want to push him right now.

"You," I spit out.

His finger runs down the length of my arm, goose bumps marring the smoothness of my skin. "What about me? Are you distressed over the fact that you can't stop thinking about me?" He steps forward and his hard length presses into my lower back. I release a shaky breath. "That we're so drawn to one another that pretty soon one of us is going to combust? Is that the reason you're so hot and bothered right now?"

Shivers run up my spine, and he blows a hot breath against the base of my neck. I yank my hair out its ponytail so it will cover the spot.

"You're playing games." The bite in my tone can't be ignored.

He steps back, seemingly alarmed by it, his hand falling from my arm. "I thought we both were?"

I turn and there he is. So close. So kissable. So desirable. So confused looking. I lightly push him just to get some clearance so I can take a breath, and I walk to the edge of the deck where rain is coming down in sheets.

"Talk to me." He comes alongside me but not close enough to touch. Thankfully, his hands remain in his pockets.

"You're a coward," I say.

His head rears back.

"Or you're a liar."

His head tilts.

"Because tell me, this thing between us"—I wave a

finger between us—"do you just want to have sex with me once and have that be the end of it?"

He swallows, his Adam's apple bobbing. "I'm not sure what you're so mad at. We mess around, that's what we do."

"*No!* That's what you do. You constantly toe the line between enemy, friend, and wannabe lover. I have no idea who or what you actually want to be in my life."

"Yes, you do." He steps closer. "I haven't promised you anything."

"Is that what you think? That it all comes down to a promise? I don't want a promise but stop the flirting and touching and digging into my personal life if all you really want to do is fuck me and toss me away."

His eyes widen, then he blinks, appearing shocked by my words. I'm sure girls say filthy shit to him in the bedroom all the time. I don't know why he's so surprised.

When he doesn't say anything, I continue my rant. "Put me in a category and leave me there."

"Category?"

"Yes."

We step closer to one another, but I place my hand on his chest to make sure he doesn't come too close. He clasps his hand over mine. "Truth?"

I sigh, some of the fight leaving me.

"I have no idea where to put you."

I nod and slide my hand out from under his. "This is stupid." Circling around him, I step away.

He grabs my hand and pulls me into his chest. "I do want you. So fucking bad it hurts. But I can't promise you anything."

"I'm not asking for a relationship. I'm asking for more than a one-night stand."

"Is there a difference?"

"Yes, Carm, there is." I give his chest a push and he takes a step back. "Welcome to the adult world where there are shades of grey, not just black and white. It's called dating. We see if we even like each other. If we slept together, it doesn't mean I'm looking for a damn ring, but I'm looking for a guy who won't sneak out at three a.m. and I never hear from him again."

"That's not me. I don't do relationships. I'm sorry."

"You *won't*, you mean." I step forward and push him back again.

He rolls his eyes and blows out a breath. "Can't. I'll hurt you. I'm being a stand-up guy here. Why don't you see that?"

I push my finger into his chest. "You're a coward."

He loses his balance and steps back so he's out from under the covering of the deck. Rain pelts him, but he doesn't step back toward me to seek shelter. Instead of retreating, I follow him out into the rain.

"You think you're being a stand-up guy? Fine. Don't flirt with me. Don't make it appear like you can't get me out of your head." I poke him again and he says nothing, allowing me to do whatever I want. Which somehow infuriates me more.

Truth is, I want him to fight me back. The real truth is, I want him to fight *for* me.

All this aggression is coming from the fact that I allowed myself to be put into a position where I'm developing feelings for the exact type of man who has ruined my mother over the years. The type of man who charms his way into a woman's heart only to brush her aside when he's taken what he wants from her. I've fallen for Carm, and he hasn't fallen nearly as hard for me. That's the real reason I want to rip off someone's head and toss it into the ocean for the sharks to snack on.

"Go to hell, Carm." I push his chest and his feet teeter on the edge of the pool.

His eyes widen with fear and the certainty that he's going in. I almost apologize and reach out to save him—until his cocky grin surfaces and he wraps his hand around my wrist, taking me with him right into the deep end of the pool.

CHAPTER NINETEEN

Carm

M y body sinks in the water, Bella's slim body above mine. Her hip bone jabs me in the stomach, but I hold her to me, not wanting to let her go. I know once we rise above the waterline, her armor will be back up. So instead of giving in to my constricting lungs, I turn her around and secure her to me by wrapping my arms around her middle.

Both our eyes open under water. Hers are full of shock over what I'm doing. My hand mindlessly moves up her back until it's lost in her flowing red hair. Our legs slide along one another's, my thigh making its way between hers.

For the first time, she doesn't pull away from me. I wish we were sea creatures who could survive without air.

Sadly, just as I'm enjoying her pressed against me, neither of us has a choice but to kick to the surface. Just as I predicted, once we've sucked in the air needed to stay alive, her eyes burn with flames.

She hollows out her palm and slaps water into my face. "You're an asshole." Her arms extend as she swims to the side.

I grab her ankle and pull her back. I can't even explain my actions other than I want her warm body on mine again. It's a selfish act. There's no way I can give her what she wants. I'm not ready for a wife and kids and a scheduled dinner-and-movie night.

Her feet flail and she fights me, but I'm stronger, which only pisses her off more.

"Just stop," I say, wrangling her enough to follow me to the shallow end where my feet can touch.

"Why? Why do you keep doing this?" There's a desperation in her voice that sends a chill down my spine, and I release her immediately.

She treads water before realizing she can stand too, then she beelines to the steps to climb out.

"Wait." Rain pings on the surface, creating ripples and indents along the top of the water. My clothes are like a second skin now.

She spins around. "What?"

I slowly walk through the water toward her. "I lied."

"About what?" Exhaustion takes over her body and her shoulders sag.

"I'm not here because of my ma. I'm here because of you. Because I can't get you out of my head."

She fights the smile teasing her lips. "Really?"

"You're the one thing I'm telling myself I can't have."

Her hands slide through the water. "Why? I mean, I get that I'm the unofficial enemy, me being a FSBO brokerage and you being a traditional broker. I know Greg has us working against one another, but what's the real reason you haven't taken what you want from me?"

Hearing the word *take* from her mouth almost makes my dick overrule my brain. I'd take her in every damn room of this house. I'd spend fifteen minutes wrangling her wet clothes off her body right now for a moment of bliss with her warm skin touching mine.

I place my finger over her lips. "It's not that. You scare me. What happened to Enzo... scares me. Being with you once won't be enough, because every time you yell at me, I want to shut you up with a kiss. Every time I smell your perfume lingering in the elevator, I want to bust into your office and bend you over your desk. Every time you walk ahead of me and I see your ass, I imagine sliding my hand up your skirt to see how wet you are. That's why I beat off to images of you every night and sometimes mid-day—because you consume my every thought. And it's exactly why I shouldn't have you."

"Yet you still have self-control around me." The grin that was starting to appear fades.

I'm not bragging, but I can read women, and Bella's disappointment that I'm not ripping off her clothes is as clear as the water in this pool.

"It's hanging on a thread, especially since you're not wearing a bra and your nipples are poking through your shirt."

She glances at her chest and crosses her arms over her breasts.

"No sense covering up now. I've committed the image to memory and I'm already rock-hard with the thought of licking this water off you. It's pathetic really."

Her cheeks flush. "You think it's pathetic that you're

attracted to me? I'm not sure what game you're playing, but I'm calling the game over now."

She tries to stomp out of the pool, but she's not getting far very fast. She's dead-set on walking instead of swimming and I watch her straightened back and prissy attitude as she thrashes through the water.

"I think the question is, what do you want?"

She stops, her hand on the railing up the stairs to leave the pool. "An adult relationship, but I should've known you can't handle that. Good luck finding what you need, Carm."

I dive through the water and stop her from leaving.

She whips her arm out of my hold. "Seriously? Just stop."

"What exactly do you mean, an adult relationship?"

"I guarantee you it's not what you're thinking. I was stupid for assuming you were someone different, so let's just drop this whole thing. We can go out tonight and you can find some girl to bring home and send back to her own bed in the middle of the night, and maybe I'll score a date with someone who wants a relationship."

The thought of her with another man is as appealing as jarred spaghetti sauce. *Fuck that.*

"Do you really think you can just tap those heels together and forget me while you head to bachelorville?" I brave a step closer to her. I'd do just about anything to have her under me right now. All I want is to spend the rest of this gloomy day in bed with her.

"You're not irreplaceable." She crosses her arms when she catches my vision straying to her chest again.

"You're wrong. You might be with another man, but you'll still be thinking of me." Another step closer and our chests are almost touching. I pull my wet sweater and T-shirt off my body because when I kiss her and her chest is against mine, I want those hard nipples poking into me. The cool rain pelts my bare chest, but it doesn't damper the heat simmering under my skin.

Her eyes widen as she takes in my bare chest. "That's what you think. You'll only pick up redheads, imagining you're with me."

"Damn right." I lean forward, ready to take what's mine. Damn the consequences.

"Don't do this, Carm, unless you've thought it through."

My hands land on her cheeks to keep her in place. "I'm done using my brain for the day and I think you should be too."

Her hands rise to my collarbones but remain clamped into fists. "Carm..."

She sighs as though she's certain she should do anything but what we're about to do. I'm not sure if I convinced her or not, but she leans into my body, allowing my lips to cover hers.

Sweetness. That's the only word that comes to mind as my tongue slides along her mouth, begging entrance. She grants me access, and a small part of me feels a thrill as though it's the first time I've kissed a girl. I've envisioned Bella under me so many times, I worried I might be disappointed if I ever allowed myself to have her. But she tastes like the promise and culmination of everything I didn't know I needed.

I reap the reward of her nipples poking my bare chest, and my erection strains against my soaked shorts. The rain slides down our faces while our mouths are joined and my hands grow tighter, any resolve I had left breaking.

One of her legs rises up my thigh. If my lips could leave hers, I'd get us out of this water, but the last thing I want is to take my lips off hers because a part of me fears she'll start thinking too much again. Counting all the reasons why this won't work or why I'm the wrong guy for her. I couldn't handle that right now. Not with the feel of her against me.

We explore one another tentatively until her fingertips make contact with my face, meaning she's unfurled her fists to touch me. I pick her up and carry her to the edge of the pool with my lips still attached to hers.

Instead of the lazy sliding of our tongues, we're seeking, each swipe becoming deeper. More urgent. More intense.

I prop her up on the edge of the pool, my palms sliding along her inner thighs to situate myself between her long legs. As my hands wind around her waist and drop to her ass, nudging her forward to position her against me, she moans softly—as though I needed any other incentive to take what we both want without apology right now.

As our lips lock once more and her soft skin is under my palms, it's decided—I'm not going to worry about all the reasons why we shouldn't be together. She wants this. I want this. We're adults. We can handle the aftermath like civilized people.

"Carm," she sighs as my mouth slides off hers and travels down her jaw.

"Here or the bedroom?" It might take everything inside me to walk her into the house, but if she wants seclusion, I'll give it to her.

"I'll never make it to the bed," she says as she tips her head back, granting me the opportunity to run my tongue down her neck.

My hands snake up her wet T-shirt, thankful there's no hindrance of a bra. "My kind of girl."

For once, she doesn't argue with me. The only sound she makes is a gasp when I tweak her nipple.

Damn, this is going to be fun.

CHAPTER TWENTY

Bella

H is lips are perfection. His hands are magic. I'm drowning—not in the pool he's still waist-deep in, but in him. All of him. Every cocky, self-assured, stubborn, sexy, competitive part of him. I knew he would destroy me, but not within the first five minutes of having his sole attention on my bare skin.

Grabbing the hem of my shirt, he slides it up my body, having to pluck away the fabric that's suctioned to my skin. Anyone who thinks this is sexy hasn't tried to rip wet clothes off a body they've been craving for months.

My hands dip along the grooves of his abs. "So no body double then."

"Or airbrushing," he murmurs, his lips moving down my neck. "After seeing your body, I suggest you try my tactic too."

He skips past my collarbones, latching his teeth onto a

nipple. My hands slide to the back of his head and I desperately want to collapse back onto the concrete, but then he couldn't reach me. So I use all my energy to stay upright and watch him devour my breasts while he looks up at me through those long, dark lashes of his.

He's so damn gorgeous, it's unfair. I expected him to have a go-to set of moves for what works with the women he's been with. But he watches me to see what I enjoy, cataloging it and putting the knowledge to good use. His tongue swirls like my tightened peak is an ice cream cone. His teeth scrape, bite, and suck, his eyes on my face the entire time.

This is not who I thought Carm would be. I thought he was a taker—turns out he gives as good as he takes.

God, I'm going to be knee-deep in Kleenex one day when this all crashes down, but I'll enjoy it for the moment.

"Let's move to the lounger." He doesn't wait for an answer but picks me up and trudges through the water, up the stairs, then lays me down on the large lounger by the corner of the pool so that we face the ocean.

He straddles me as my fingers continue to memorize his chest—the strong pecs and biceps, the thin trail of hair below his belly button, and the deep V carved above his hip bones. He pulls the built-in canopy up from behind the lounger to block our view of the house. Thankfully, no one should be out on the beach right now with the storms, even if the thunder and lightning has abated for now.

His hands slide down my body, and I raise my ass to help him strip me down.

"I can't wait to finally find out," he says as he pulls my underwear down my legs.

My brows draw together, and he laughs. Once I'm fully naked, he stands at the foot of the lounger, a satisfactory grin on his face while he stares between my legs.

"Did you think I dyed my hair?"

"No, but I wanted to know for sure. A real redhead."

I giggle, my head falling back into the wet cushions. "Surprise."

But when he takes off his pants and boxer briefs, I lick my lips, needing him inside me. He's thick and long and hard. If I'm honest, I've never been a huge fan of the male anatomy, but if every guy was built like Carm, I might become the founding member of the "I love cock" fan club.

I'm desperate to feel the weight of him over me, but he positions himself between my legs, his palms skimming along my inner thighs and parting them.

"Carm," I sigh for what feels like the millionth time since his lips landed on mine.

"I've waited a long time for this." He kneels at the end of the lounger, pulling me down to him, and positions my legs over his shoulders.

He leans in, and his tongue swipes over my slit and up to my clit.

"Ohhh.... ahhhh..." My fingers dig into his thick dark hair.

I was wrong before. It's his tongue that's magical. It can do things I never even imagined. I squirm a few times and he chuckles into my center, knowing he's tormenting me with small bites to my clit before sucking it into his mouth. When his hand leaves my hip, I anticipate his fingers inside me, but he makes me wait for it. It's unbearable, and maybe that's why it seems like a lifetime later before he thrusts one finger into me, quickly adding another.

I scream, grinding my center along his face. I prop up on my elbows, needing to see him, and there he is watching me again, judging and appraising his performance. The lust and the desire in his eyes unglues any resolve I had, and my fingers grip whatever hair I can get my hands on. I buck forward, screaming his name as I come.

He slows his movements, removes one finger then another while stars line my vision and my head falls back to the cushions again.

It's not until my body and my mind come back to Earth that I'm aware of the rain pelting my skin.

He climbs on top of me and stares at me. "Damn, that's the way I like to hear you say my name." He laughs, his tip poised at my center.

I circle my hips, wanting his girth deep inside me. "Wait!" I press my hand on his chest. "Condom?"

His head falls to my shoulder and a groan rumbles out of him. "Shit. In the house."

Rising on his elbows, he stares at me with a look that says, "Tell me you're on something." I am and I don't regret what we're doing, but I don't know Carm well enough to know his history.

"Sorry." I shake my head, and his chin tips down, his eyes squeezed shut.

"Let's go then." He slides off my body, drags me by my feet until I'm at the edge of the canopy, then picks me up firefighter style.

My yelp turns into a laugh as he heads to the sliding door that leads inside. "You have a great ass." I slap it.

"I know I do."

I giggle. "You're so cocky."

"I'm confident. There's a difference."

Without climbing the stairs, we head through the kitchen, past Annie and Enzo's room, and into Carm's. He deposits me on the bed, digs through his nightstand drawer, unwraps a condom, and pushes it down his rigid length before anything else is said.

"You're in a rush," I say, sliding up the bed.

"You're the one thing I've ever waited this long to have. I need to be quick before you change your mind."

"Well, don't be too quick," I say with some sass.

He grins, parting my legs with his knees. "Don't you worry about that."

He's back where he was moments ago. The rain pelts against the window, and the room is dark even though it's not nighttime. With Carm's warmth above me, this might be the most perfect day ever.

Late at night, when I imagined having Carm, I always figured he'd be the flip-me-over-and-do-me-doggie-style or insist-I-ride-him kind of guy. But real-life Carm holds his weight on his elbows, his hands fiddling with my hair, his eyes locked with mine as he slides inside me.

We both moan once he's fully seated inside me. He's a perfect fit, as if I was Cinderella looking for her glass cock. He rocks and circles his hips instead of thrusting. The Carm in my mind was a thruster and a groaner, a man more worried about himself. Real-life Carm kisses me while my wetness grows. He arches when my nails trail down his spine and growls when my hands squeeze his ass. He builds a rhythm and a pulse for our sex that's ours alone. I don't know how I know that, I just do.

His circles turn to small thrusts, his lips continuing to land on mine between kisses scattered down my neck, along my jaw, sometimes to my earlobe. His breathing and moans make me clench around him.

"We waited so long for this. Why did we wait for this?" His fingers brush a wet piece of hair off my forehead.

"Because you're an egotistical—"

He shuts me up with a kiss and swallows my laughter when he sucks on my tongue. His tongue dives deeper and his elbows move in closer to my head so that I'm caged in by him. He's all I see, feel, hear, taste, and smell. His muscles contract as he thrusts deeper, draws out, and grinds into me again. So unlike my masturbation version of Carm. He buries his face in my neck, the panting and heavy breathing bringing my orgasm to the surface.

"Jesus, Carm. Please."

I don't even know what I'm pleading for, but he takes my words and increases his speed. His moans turn to grunts. My fingers dig into his shoulder blades and my legs lock around him.

I launch into orbit and Carm follows me, pumping then stilling inside me. My limbs feel numb and I'm panting beneath him when he brushes another piece of hair off my face and tucks it behind my ear.

"Hi," he says.

"Hi." My hands fall off his back and my legs open for him to escape should he wish.

But he doesn't. He stays inside me for a second and gives me a kiss that pushes my back into the soft mattress and builds another round of desire to have him again.

My mom was partially right. He's not just dangerous—he's deadly.

"HERE." Carm slides a plate my way.

"Do you think the girls and Dom are coming home?" I prop one foot up on the breakfast stool and take a bite of the turkey sandwich he made me.

He glances out the window to where a big streak of lightning lights up the sky. "Doubtful. I think they're all probably staying wherever they are." He walks around the island and kisses me. Something he hasn't seemed to be able to stop doing.

The gloomy sky turned dark sometime after we finished and fell asleep, only to wake up two hours later and do it all over again. Still the same Carm, slow and steady and the purveyor of earth-shattering orgasms.

"I'm not complaining. An entire night here without them..." He sits next to me, cracking open his soda. "What should we do?" I smile, and he hooks his foot on the rung of my stool and pulls it closer to him. "Yeah, I agree."

I shake my head with a chuckle. "You have no idea what I'm thinking."

He glances at my shirt, where he can probably see my peaked nipples. "I can read you." He touches the messy bun on top of my head. "I love this look."

"Why?" I touch the loose hairs falling down around my head and tuck them into place. The rain washed off any makeup I had on. I can't imagine what I look like, but somehow, when Carm's looking at me, I feel stunning and beautiful, like a natural model.

"It makes me want to bury us under the covers and explore your body."

A huge grin spreads on my lips. "I think you've explored quite a lot already."

He puts down his sandwich. "I've only found two of your erogenous zones, and they were easy to find. I intend to find all of them."

"Maybe they're endless," I bait him, enjoying this version of Carm way too much. I know I'll be disappointed when I lose it, but I push those doubts aside for at least tonight. Tomorrow I can think rationally.

"All the better." He winks, picking up his sandwich and taking a huge bite.

A rush of shivers runs through my body like an electrical current. "You sure are forthcoming with how many more times you're going to have sex with me." I prop my chin in my palm and look at him. "I thought you were a one-and-done kind of guy."

The corners of his lips dip. "Maybe you typecast me."

I shake my head, and he nods that I'm wrong.

"What's the girl's name who scorned you?" I ask.

He focuses on his sandwich but doesn't take a bite, and I know my inkling is correct. There's no way he's a bachelor just because of his schedule.

When he snuggled next to me after our first time having sex, he thought he'd wake up and I wouldn't be there. It was clear to me then that he doesn't fear commitment; he fears abandonment.

I'm not sure which one is harder to overcome.

CHAPTER TWENTY-ONE

Carm

I knew she'd figure me out. I tried to convince myself in the bathroom while throwing out the condom, that I'd get dressed and go watch television. Give her the feeling that I was done with her for now. But I walked out, and she had the sheet around her chest, her head on the pillow. The look in her eyes asked me if she should leave, and I knew I wanted her to stay because I didn't want to hurt her. And now I'm making her a sandwich, sliding her stool closer, and kissing her every time I pass her.

To an outsider, you'd think I was done, stamp me with taken. We need to clear this up right now. I can tell her about Kami and also square things away with what's going on between us. Easy.

"Kami Johnson. Senior year of high school." In my peripheral vision, I see her nod.

"I'm sorry," she says, touching my arm.

My fingers curl into a fist. "I'm not wounded from it if that's what you're thinking. It's just a big reason why I'm the way I am."

"And what way is that?" She leans back on the stool, pushing aside her plate.

I side-eye her. "You know exactly what I'm talking about. You think I'm a commitment-phobe now because I got hurt at seventeen."

"I never said that."

"You didn't have to."

She laughs. "What happened?"

Let's just get this over with. "I fell hard... fast. I thought she did too. But about six months in, she started saying that I was cheating on her. Always looking at my phone. Telling me I was flirting with every girl."

She gives me that look that says I probably was.

"It's who I am. I can be talkative, and I'm friendly. I'm Italian."

She quirks an eyebrow.

"I'll tell you right now, I might be a flirt and I might sleep around when I'm single, but I would never cheat on someone."

She touches my arm again, and warmth spreads into my flesh. "Okay. I believe you."

"Anyway, the relationship deteriorated fast, but I still wanted her, still wanted to be with her. But one night, I had to hang back after the game at my football coach's request, and she headed to a party with her friends. We made plans to meet up there. When I arrived, I couldn't find her, and she wasn't answering her phone. Her group of friends were all uncomfortable when I asked them where she was. You know when you know someone's lying?"

She nods.

God, it sucks reliving that night. The way everyone at that party knew. Everyone but me. Me walking in there after getting my ass chewed out for not having my head in the game. Coach lecturing me about toxic relationships and how I was too young to be so serious. The entire school had seen or heard us fight by our lockers, our cars, or at parties. We were *that* couple, but I loved Kami. I did.

Bella's head tilts in sympathy as she waits for what I'm going to tell her.

"Kami was in the shed in the back of the house with a college guy who'd graduated a year before us. An old teammate of mine. The one I replaced as quarterback. She'd dated him before me, and they broke up the summer before we got together. I was an idiot for not seeing how fast she jumped to me. She wasn't in the drama club but turns out she was one helluva actress."

"Young love can be hard. I didn't have one, but when you're so young..."

I nod, remembering Kami straddling him and his cocky smirk over her shoulder when the stream of light fell across the room from the open door. Her widened eyes. Climbing off him and trying to apologize. As if you can apologize when you're bouncing on someone else's dick.

"She was the only one I'd ever been really honest with and let in. My senior year, I had no idea what the hell I wanted to do. Some small schools had looked at me, but I didn't think college was for me. It seemed like she got me and understood me when no one else did. Enzo told me I was being fucking stupid, that she just wanted popularity and I was the person she was using after I made first string. I didn't listen. Told him he was jealous..." I feel like a fucking pussy sharing this. "Anyway, it was years ago, and it only has a little bit to do with why I am the way I am. I told you, it's my schedule."

"Uh-huh." She sips her soda, a smile playing at her lips.

"It is." I refrain from saying partly. That there's always that feeling like I don't know when I'm being played. I loved her so much that I took her back for a week after that, before finally figuring out she would only ever bring me misery.

"So this?" she asks, waving a finger between us. "What's your game plan?"

I chuckle into my soda, not sure how to answer. "Screw you as long as you'll let me?"

She smacks my shoulder. "How about we just go with it? Have fun and don't put a label on what we are?"

She's got to be shitting me. That's all she's asking for? We can keep sleeping together and not give each other a classification? This isn't what I expected from Bella at all.

"But..."

I point at her. "I knew there was a but coming."

She nods like *of course you did*. "No other people. I'm willing to have fun in and out of the bedroom, but I'm not cool with you sleeping with someone else then hopping into my bed the next night. I'm not saying we're exclusive. If you want to sleep with someone else, go ahead, but be honest with me first and we'll end this." She pulls her knees up to her chest and locks her arms around them. Protecting herself in case I tell her we can't practice monogamy.

I grab her arms and pull them apart, letting her legs fall to the floor. "Done."

I honestly have no yearning to sleep with anyone but her at the moment.

"Really?" I lean forward, but she puts her hand on my chest. "I'm serious. No other women."

I lean in and give her a chaste kiss. "And I said done.

Case closed. Just me and you having sex, having fun, and not having a relationship." I swoop her up off the stool and into my arms. She squeals and her head falls to my shoulder. "I have one stipulation. You sleep in my bed tonight."

"I'm not sure—"

I shut her up with a kiss because if it's only tonight that we have this place to ourselves, I want to get as much time with her as I can.

"And what do we tell the others?" she asks.

"Do you want to sneak around or be honest?" I'll leave the decision to her because my brothers will figure it out and give me shit either way.

"Let's just go one day at a time. I'm not sure how to navigate it with us sharing a house this summer."

I drop her onto my bed, and she slides in under the covers.

"Best view since we've gotten here." I slide in after her.

Pulling the covers over us, I do exactly what I told her. I explore her body and am rewarded with two more zones that drive her crazy. The back of her neck and between her breasts.

I SHUT THE DRAPES. Bella's red hair is sprawled across the bed, a pillow tucked under her arm. Her lips are swollen from a night of sex. She's gorgeous. I should've woken up this morning feeling done with her, but as much as I want to crawl back into bed with her, I force myself to put on my basketball shorts and quietly leave the room because I'm not going to be that loser.

The noises in the kitchen alert me that we're not the only ones in the house anymore. So either the girls or Dom have returned. I cross my fingers it's the girls, but when I cross the archway, there's a big body in the fridge.

"You just come here to eat?" I pop a K-Cup in the coffee maker and wait for the water to heat and brew.

"At least I keep my extracurriculars out of the communal house." He glances over his shoulder at me.

He's wearing the same suit he had on Friday when he arrived, his tie hanging open around his neck. I rack my brain, trying to remember if I've seen him since then. No, I don't think I have.

"What does that mean?" I cross my arms and lean against the counter, waiting for the brew to be done because I need some fucking caffeine.

"The clothes all over the pool deck. What the hell? You brought some girl back here? It's going to be a disaster." He settles on an apple and closes the fridge door then takes a big bite and sits on the counter. Dom's always the one to sit on a counter or somewhere higher than everyone else. I think it's an ego thing.

"I didn't bring anyone home," I say, grabbing the creamer from the fridge.

"I saw the clothes, shithead."

"Yeah, so what? Who's to say they're from me? They could be Mae or Evie's. What about Annie's?"

"I'm not an idiot. Your door is the only one that's shut. Speaking of which, where are the girls?"

"Mae and Evie stayed out last night."

This is where I suck. I can't keep a straight face. And it's not because I'm bragging that I got Bella in bed. But I'm happy it happened, and I can't hide my smile.

"Fuck, Carm, can you rationalize *anything* in that head of yours?" He hops down from the counter. "What do you think is gonna happen now? You're going to turn this house into a war zone." He yanks the fridge open again, the apple not satisfying him. "Think about the parties and two nights a week the two of you have to coexist..." His words trail off as his head dives into the fridge.

Bella comes to the door in a pair of my boxer shorts and a V-neck T-shirt she's tied at her side. My brother can't see her like that. Just as I'm about to tell her to leave, Dom shuts the fridge and turns toward the doorway.

"Shit!" He covers his eyes as if she's naked.

"Morning, Dom," Bella says in a sing-song voice.

"Bella," he bites out, continuing to cover his eyes as he walks away from the room. "I'm taking a shower and heading back to Manhattan. *Carm?*" he yells from the stairway, probably expecting me to follow so he can give me shit.

I don't answer because Bella is strutting toward me with that teasing smile that says she wants me to do dirty things to her again. Who am I to refuse? I aim to please.

"No banging where I eat," Dom calls. "If you two are gonna ruin this summer, at least do me the courtesy of not messing with my food."

Bella giggles and her forehead rests on my shoulder. My arms entwine around her, resting on her hips.

"One down already?" Her eyebrows rise, silently asking if I'm okay with it.

Surprisingly, I don't really care. It's hard to keep a secret from my brothers, so I knew they'd find out. I just don't want word spreading to Ma. That's when problems will arise. She'd love Bella, and everyone knows I hate disappointing Ma.

CHAPTER TWENTY-TWO

Bella

Monday morning, I'm not at my desk for more than a minute before my phone dings.

Carmelo Mancini: *Come to my office and I'll shut the blinds.*

I didn't run into him this morning. We're both doing great at this new having-fun non-relationship—neither of us asked the other to spend the night after he dropped me off at the end of the weekend. See? I knew we could handle this dynamic.

Me: *And what will you do to me?*
Carmelo Mancini: *If I tell you, you won't come.*
Me: *I'm not coming either way.*

Carmelo Mancini: *You'll be coming if you get that sweet ass in here.*

I quickly change his name to just Carm. For some reason, having his full name makes it seem weird that I've seen him naked. The entire weekend.

Me: *As great as that sounds, you're one condo ahead of me, so I have work to do.*
Carm: *Damn, if the fact that you're a fellow workaholic didn't turn me on so much, I'd stomp across the hall and kidnap you for the day.*
Me: *Well, Godzilla, keep those big hands in your pockets for the day.*
Carm: Dinner tonight? No one likes to cook on a Monday.

I laugh, and Max peeks over her shoulder at me.

Me: *Do you cook all the other days of the week?*
Carm: *Not the point.*
Me: *What exactly are you asking me?*
Carm: *Can I entice you with takeout and an orgasm?*
Me: *Doesn't sound that appealing.*
Carm: *Fine. Would you like to go out with me tonight? I'll even let you pick which hole my dick goes into. ;)*

I cough out the coffee I just sipped, and it lands all over my papers. I rush to grab a napkin from my drawer, and when I look up, Max is leaning on the doorway with her arms crossed.

Me: *I'll check my calendar. Bye.*

I put my phone on my desk, screen-side down.

"You got laid, and if you tell me it was by that egomaniac Carmelo Mancini from across the hall, I might lock you in here until you come to your senses."

"What? No!" It should be noted that I am a terrible liar. Horrible. The worst. Total fail. I can't even get it by a six-year-old when I let them win at a game.

"Oh my God, you did sleep with him." She shakes her head and rolls her eyes. "He's so your type. Though I thought the fact that he doesn't want a relationship would keep you away." She takes the seat in front of me.

"Maybe I don't want a relationship?"

She studies me for a second, waiting for me to accept defeat, but the hell if I'm going to. Carm might crumble easily under his brothers' stare, but Max has made it clear she doesn't like Carm.

"Not to mention, it's not him." Maybe I can convince her that I got laid, but by someone else?

She puts her finger to her lips, tapping it while her eyes scrutinize me. "I'll catch you. No way you can keep me from figuring it out." She eyes my phone. "But whoever it is, I do like the blush he gives you. And the smile." She walks out of the room.

I pick up my phone, turn on my camera, and reverse it so it's on me. Yep, I look like America's Most Beautiful Man just kissed me. Damn Carm.

Five minutes later, my phone buzzes and I fully expect it to be Carm again. The man doesn't understand the word no. To my surprise, it's someone interested in the Bond Street project. Hallelujah.

"Can I arrange for you to show me the unit?" the woman asks.

I chew on my lip. That isn't part of my job. I mean, it's

supposed to be the owner who meets them, which in this case is Helena's job. "There's someone at the development. Let me contact them, and I'll call you back."

"Sounds great." The woman hangs up.

I scroll through my contacts and press on Helena's name. This might be my first sale and I'm not going to let it slip away even if I have to go above and beyond what I'm supposed to do. Everyone knows that after the first one sells, every sale in a development project gets easier. It's snagging that first fish that's important.

"You've reached the voicemail of Helena..."

I wait for her rehearsed and yes, professional but annoying message to finish. After the beep, I leave a quick message about a client who wants to see the property and ask her to call me back.

Having no other choice, I call Carm.

"Are you reconsidering my offer?" he answers. That shouldn't make my heart pitter-patter like a teenage girl's, but sadly, it does.

"Helena? Do you happen to know where she is?"

"Why would I know where Helena is? Your request was clear, Bel—"

"No, I had someone call and she wants to see one of the units and technically..."

Thankfully, I don't have to finish. One of the best things is that we each understand each other's jobs.

"Well, I'm going over there in about an hour to show a unit. I'll gladly take your client off your hands." He chuckles because we both know that's not going to happen.

"Yeah, nice try."

"Sorry, I haven't had much contact with Helena since I have my own set of keys to get in and out." Muffled voices push our conversation to the back burner. I hear Justin talking, but I can't hear what he's saying. "Give me a minute." A door shuts on his end and the background noise dies off. "Now, what color are your panties today?"

"I'm serious, Carm. This might be my first sale." I sit up straighter, silently willing my phone to ring with Helena's return call. What good is she? If Carm was calling, she'd probably answer. Wait. "Didn't she give you her personal phone number?"

Dead silence fills the line. Out of all things, me calling him out on getting Helena's phone number shuts him up?

"Yeah, but..."

"Please? I'll come over to your office and give you my panties for that number." I laugh, but he doesn't.

"I wouldn't want your panties for some woman's number who gave it to me without asking." His tone is serious. Why does he sound pissed off?

"So you'll just give it to me then?"

"No, because I threw it out when I got back to the office that day."

"Oh."

My shoulders slump, but I'm happy he didn't keep it. We were only flirting then, but I can't help but wonder if I'm the reason he threw it away. *Ugh*. No labels or classifications mean you don't give a shit what a guy does with a phone number some random woman gives him.

"And that's why I wouldn't mind you giving me your panties. You knowing it's only your panties that make me—"

A rush of energy travels through me, landing right between my legs. This man could make me his slave if he wanted. "Let's stay on task. I'll just book the appointment with the hopes that Helena gets back to me. If I have to, I'll show it myself."

"Hmm... that goes against the FSBO philosophy, doesn't it?"

"I promise to stand by the door and not point out the naked guy on the pool deck below, is that okay?"

He laughs, an honest one that spurs tingles across my skin. "I think it's only allowed if you point out the naked guy below and mention that from one floor up, he's much blurrier."

"Is that so?" I chuckle.

"Otherwise I'd say you're in breach of contract."

I hear the tapping of his pen or something, and I'm desperate to know if he's leaned back with his legs propped up on the edge of his desk or if his legs are wide open. What's he looking at? Because it feels as if I have one hundred percent of his attention right now.

"And what do you plan on doing?" I ask. "Reporting me to Mr. Throttle?"

"Oh no, Miss Scott, I like to handle these kinds of situations on my own. I might just have to demand you come home with me tonight so I can discipline you."

I shake my head, but I can't hide the smile that's going to make my cheeks hurt. Max glances into my office on the way to her chair and stops, staring at me with disbelief. She shakes her head and sits down.

"Hopefully Helena will call me back. I better go now."

"You're leaving me with blue balls. Just commit to coming over tonight. I haven't showed you my place. There's a great Thai place—"

"Sorry, but we're not exactly fuck buddies, remember?" I'm not sure what I'm looking for, but it's not a hit-it-and-quit-it. I hope Carm realizes that, because he's far from out of my system.

"Ah, yes. So I still have to wine and dine?"

"Maybe."

"Five-star level dining?"

"I'm not going to tell you what to do. What fun is it if I say how far you have to go to get me into bed?" I twirl my hair with my finger, unable to care that I should be calling back the potential buyer.

"All I had to do the first time was mention your nipples and kiss you."

"Yeah, you caught me in a weak moment."

"You know you shouldn't challenge me, right?" The tapping in the background stops and I hear his keyboard keys instead. "When I have a mission, I don't detour until I've accomplished the task."

"Then I'm excited to see where this goes, Mr. Mancini."

"Keep calling me that and I'm bursting into your office to show you the color of my boxer briefs."

"Bye," I manage to squeeze out between my giggles. I click off the line before he distracts me further.

I call back the woman to work out the showing details, wishing I didn't feel as though I'm cheating. Carm might be joking, but FSBO agents don't do showings. It's one of the reasons I got out of the broker business.

She answers immediately, which is a good way to judge how badly she might want the condo.

"I can't get a hold of the lady at the development, but I can meet you at a time of your choosing," I say, my gut twisting into a bigger knot.

"Oh great. I just got word about a meeting I have this afternoon. Is six too late?"

Six? The developmental office will be closed then anyway, so Helena is kind of a moot detail at this point.

"Six is great. I'll meet you outside."

"Perfect. Thanks for being so accommodating."

"Of course," I respond.

We say our pleasantries and hang up.

I push my chair back from my desk and walk out into the main area. "Max, I have to go to Bond Street at six o'clock tonight to show a unit."

She circles around in her chair like a zombie, her face as pale as one. "Okay, I'll mark it on both of our schedules."

I smile, one of gratitude. The last thing I want is to go to a construction site with a stranger, no matter how many self-defense classes I've taken.

My cell phone vibrates on my desk, and I see his name before picking up, which pulls a smile from me. He's texted me an address and a wink-face emoji.

CHAPTER TWENTY-THREE

Carm

I'm sitting at the restaurant and it's well past seven thirty. I pulled so many damn strings to get in here tonight. The waiter gives me a look as I order another scotch on the rocks.

"Sorry, she's a realtor and you know how it is. Sometimes clients take a while to make up their mind."

He nods with a "whatever, dude, you're getting stood up" look. I think he might be right.

Me: *Where are you? Still with the client?*

It's odd for me to be on the other side of this situation. Usually it's my brothers or my parents or friends whining about me getting held up with a client.

Bella: *Five minutes. Order me a red wine. After what you pulled, you're lucky I'm coming at all.*

The fact that she responded pulls a grin from me, but I know what I have coming when she gets here. I told Natasha Edens not to mention the fact that she came to me first. I might well get the wine I'm ordering for Bella as my appetizer after she tosses it in my face.

Her cheeks are flushed when the hostess brings her over to the table. I stand to welcome her and help her with her chair, but she shoos me away, sliding into the chair with grace.

"Long meeting?"

She picks up the menu. "I'm going to order the most expensive meal on here because if I don't, I'm going to tell you off and stomp out of here like a thirteen-year-old girl." Her tone displays nothing but sincerity.

The waiter comes over and places down her wine glass. I want to give him the finger and say here she is and yes, be jealous she's mine because you could never land a woman like her. Then I realize I might lose her after this meal and my arrogant inner self quiets down.

"Would you like to order an appetizer?" He pulls out his tablet.

"Give us a minute, please," I say, and he blows out a breath.

Bella must notice because she closes her menu. "I'm sorry about keeping you waiting. I had a meeting, and my client just went back and forth making a decision." Her hand touches his forearm, and he inches toward her. "I do apologize, but I guarantee you Mr. Mancini"—she eyes me in case he can't figure out that's me—"and I will compensate you for the extra time. I'll make sure of it."

My teeth grind, but I force a smile. Yeah, damn Natasha Edens sold me down the river.

"Take your time. I'll be back in a bit." The smug early-twenty-something leaves the table with the first grin I've seen on his face all night.

Bella places her menu on the side of the table and grabs a piece of bread. "We need to be clear about a few things if we're going to move forward." She takes the butter knife and spreads some on her bread. "First off, there's no giving me clients."

"I was—"

She raises her hand with the butter knife in it. She looks angry enough that it could be a weapon of choice for her. "Nope. My turn to talk. You sit and listen."

I lean back, my pants growing tight. I love when she's angry and assertive like this. Total turn-on. I hold up my hands in a placating gesture.

"She went to you for the property. You should've sold it to her and gotten paid your commission. Just because I'm your bed buddy doesn't mean you take pity on me and throw favors my way. I can sink or swim on my own."

All I can think of is what's going to happen tomorrow morning. She could fight Kevin Henderbrook on his contract, but it'd be wasted money. The problem I've debated since this afternoon rears its head—do I tell her or not? It's not why I sent Natasha her way, but when Kevin called me, I was thankful I did. He didn't even give her three weeks to accomplish the sale.

Screw it. I can't let her be blindsided. "Okay, you stand on your own, but you need to know that Kevin Hender-brook is going to call you tomorrow and cancel his contract."

Her face pales.

Unlike me, she gets paid up front, so it's not about the

money. It's about her pride. Not to mention having a property like his sell FSBO would be a big feather in her cap when she's courting other clients.

This isn't what I wanted for our first dinner together. I wanted flirtatious banter. Maybe I'd get her to discreetly slide her foot up my leg. Not business talk.

"I'm sorry. He called me this afternoon. After I gave Natasha your information. I wasn't expecting it, but he was my client and I can't turn him down."

"What did he say? Did he tell you that he got greedy and upped the price one hundred fifty grand when he was already saving money on realtor fees? I'm not sure what he expected by pricing himself out of the market."

Okay, so now her talking business *and* her being pissed off is turning me on.

"I saw what he did. He sunk you before you had a chance. I'm sorry. He's an unrealistic seller. He's a pain in my ass in the buying market as well." I sip my drink while she stares out the window.

"Sometimes I... maybe I should've stayed in the game. What I'm trying to do is stupid." She sips her wine.

I straighten in my chair, placing my drink down. "Don't say that. You're doing awesome. I see you everywhere. FSBO is so hot right now..." My words fade as she stares at me as if I'm a talking rat that hopped on her dinner plate.

"Just don't do it again. Don't hand me things that aren't mine. It only makes me feel like less of a professional, okay? I'm not looking for a prince to ride in on his white horse. I just need the damn sword."

"What about a prince with an amazing condo and a king-size bed?"

Finally I yank a smile from her. Not her inviting one.

Not the one I got blessed with this weekend post-orgasm. But it's a start.

"Do you ever *not* think about sex?" she asks.

I contemplate for a moment and wink. "I thought about you when I gave you the client."

"Was that so I'd be happy and maybe go back to your place tonight?" She crosses her arms and leans back in her chair with a knowing look.

The waiter approaches and I wish Bella had just let me order us takeout, but after the crappy job I've done on day one of being her... well, whatever I am, I owe her a dinner at a five-star restaurant.

"Nah. I have a feeling you want me as bad as I want you. So let's eat and have dessert at my place."

She doesn't argue but picks up her menu and blocks her face from me.

The waiter takes our order, and we share an entire meal, talking about nightmare clients and their unrealistic expectations.

***

"OPEN THE DOOR," she pants, pressed against the wall outside my condo door. Her hands dig into the back of my slacks.

My lips are on hers while I'm trying to fit the key into the lock on the door.

"Are you struggling to find the hole?" She giggles.

I found out a new fact about her tonight. Two glasses of good red wine and she's as happy as a client with the keys to their new home.

"I never have a problem finding the hole." I grin at her.

Her hands fiddle with my belt and she unbuttons my slacks. "Jesus, I never would have imagined you'd be so..."

"What?" She retracts her hand, and my dick twitches with an unbearable ache to get her to touch me again.

"Nothing. Please continue." I sigh when the key fits in the hole and I open up my condo.

"What are you so surprised about?" She slides under my arm and enters my condo, her eyes inspecting every surface.

It's an open floor plan. Kitchen into family room into dining room. A small hallway with two bedrooms and two baths. Nothing terribly impressive besides the view, except maybe that I own it free and clear.

"This is exactly what I imagined." She twirls with her arms out. I drop my keys on the table, toe out of my shoes, and stop her mid-twirl with my arms around her middle. "It's gorgeous, of course."

"You're gorgeous," I whisper, brushing her hair off her neck, nuzzling my face there.

"You're cliché when you're horny," she says, but her fingers push through my hair and my hands pull her blouse out from the waist of her pants. "I'm still mad about you trying to get me a sale."

I murmur a "uh-huh" between casting kisses down the hollow of her neck.

"Then you make that comment in the hall. Did you think I was a prude or something?"

I glance at her face as I unbutton her blouse, one painful button at a time. "Not after you let me feast on your pussy beachside."

She shakes her head and rolls her eyes, but her smile gives away that she likes it when I say things like that. The fact she might've gone to her knees outside my apartment door because she wanted me so badly is the best example of how compatible we are. I was willing to get her off in the back of the taxi.

Once her blouse is open, I splay it wide, pushing it down and off her shoulders. It floats to the floor behind her and she steps out of her heels. Her black lace bra crumbles my resolve, and my dick pops up in my boxer briefs, pleading to be played with.

Bella looks down, a smirk on her lips, and gently nudges me back until I reach the couch. My hands grab the edge as I sit, and she falls to her knees.

She blew me in the Hamptons last weekend, but I wanted to be in her so badly that I stopped it short.

From the look on her face, she's not going to take no for an answer now, and who am I to try to change her mind? I just hope that the fact that she's still pissed about Natasha doesn't mean she'll take it out on Big Carm.

My pants drop to the floor, and she gently pulls me out of my boxer briefs, sliding them down my thighs. Her eyes glued to mine, she slides her tongue up the rigid length, her hand resting at the base and pumping me slowly.

I remove my hands from the leather couch to dig into her thick strands of red, but her mouth leaves my dick with a pop and she shakes her head.

"No?" I ask, my hands mid-air.

"Hands on the couch, cowboy," she says, a twinkle in her eye telling me she wants to be in charge tonight.

My hands fall back to the couch, my fingers sliding along the leather unable to get a good grip.

She licks, she strokes, she sucks, she plays with my balls. All with the cadence of a talented performer who's done it a million times before, though I highly doubt that's the case. When our eyes catch and I watch her take me into her mouth, I buck forward. She moans and groans, the vibration funneling down to my balls. I beg, curse, and grit my teeth over and over until I can no longer control myself.

"I'm gonna come."

She smiles over my dick, her eyes glistening with hunger for me. She stays in place as my dick pulses and twitches, filling her mouth. Darkness takes over my vision for a second before I open my eyes to find her licking me clean. I pick her up under her arms, step out of my slacks, and carry her down the hall.

"I need you in my bed—now."

I'm not sure I want her to ever leave.

CHAPTER TWENTY-FOUR

Bella

"I've got the s'mores stuff." Annie comes down to the beach with a tray full of graham crackers, marshmallows, and chocolate.

"Yum!" Mae grabs a metal stick and slides a marshmallow on it before sitting in the chair next to me. The marshmallow ignites when she sticks it in the fire.

"You're supposed to hold it above the fire, not in," Dom says, his legs open, a beer bottle dangling from his fingertips. He's been staring silently at the bonfire most of the night.

"How nice of you to join us for once," Mae says. "What would I have done without you being here to lend your advice?"

Enzo can't fight his grin, glancing at his brother to see what he'll come back with.

Meanwhile, Carm is next to me, purposely finding reasons to get closer. The only one who knows about us is

Dom, as far as I know. Of course, I assume Enzo might have an inkling. Hell, Evie cornered me this morning when she almost walked in on Carm kissing me good morning. It's just a matter of time before they all know, but for some reason, I feel like if we tell other people and are open about it, it'll put pressure on what's happening between us.

"We need more wood." Enzo throws the last of the logs into the fire. "I saw some dry wood down the way on my run this morning, but I don't think I can carry it all myself." He sets his beer in the sand and places his hand in his palm.

All three brothers pound their fists and Annie rolls her eyes.

"What's going on?" Evie asks.

"Oh, they settle everything with a game of rock, paper, scissors." Annie takes her perfectly-done marshmallow and slides it onto her already-prepared graham cracker and chocolate.

Enzo shoots paper.

Carm shoots rock.

Dom shoots rock.

"Annie!" Enzo looks at her with wide eyes.

She bites into her s'more, chocolate gathering at the corner of her lips. "What's up?"

"I won!"

She glances at the brothers, who all nod and look as if someone sucker-punched them. "Really?"

"Babe," Enzo says.

"He did," Carm admits begrudgingly.

"What am I missing?" Evie nibbles on a piece of chocolate.

"Enzo always loses," Dom says.

"Not always," Enzo argues.

"Enough that it's this exciting when you win?" Evie's smile teases her lips.

"He's been on a bad streak, that's all," Annie sticks up for her man.

Enzo bites a piece of her s'more and tackles Annie to the ground.

"That's mine," she says with a laugh.

"I'll share."

And then they're making out and the s'more ends up in the sand, Enzo's knee between Annie's legs.

"This is getting awkward," Mae says.

"Let's go, Dom." Carm stands and brushes the sand off his delectable ass.

"You should go too. Brother bonding," Annie whispers.

Enzo rolls off her with a groan.

After the guys leave, all of the girls' heads turn to look at me.

"Can I have a stick?" I ask, but no one hands me one.

Evie picks up a metal stick and puts a marshmallow on it for me. I hold my hand out for it, but she purposely keeps it away.

"Talk," she says.

"What?"

"Tell us why you and Carm are doing the horizontal mambo but still trying to act like you hate each other." Leave it to Evie to call me out on my shit.

"We're not. No. What are you guys smoking?" I stretch my arm past Mae to Evie, but she holds the stick farther from my grasp.

"Come on. We're all on your side," Evie continues to pry.

"I get it. I wasn't a huge Enzo fan at first either, but these Mancini boys are hard to resist." Annie smiles like the lovesick woman she is. "Carm is a good guy underneath the multiple layers of ego."

I stop trying to get the metal stick thing and wrap my arms around my legs, staring into the fire. Evie, I can trust. Annie and Mae seem cool, but I don't know for sure. Evie's been spending a lot of time with Mae. If she can trust Mae, I should be able to too, I guess.

"Fine. We're sleeping together." I sigh, waiting for the onslaught of questions I know are coming.

"Fuck buddies?" Mae asks, no judgment in her tone.

"Not really. We're not classifying it."

All of their perfectly arched eyebrows rise.

"So you're pretending there's nothing going on, but sleeping together behind closed doors? And you don't go out at all together?" Of course Evie has to overanalyze it. She's nursed me through heartaches before.

But I'm not her, sleeping with the Brit on the weekend and someone else during the week. She makes no apology and she shouldn't; it's her business. But we're different. She could handle Carm, while I'm still unsure if I can. She probably knows that.

I shrug. "He took me to dinner last week."

"Where?" Annie asks, preparing a new s'more.

"Eleven Madison Park." I bite my lip.

They all "ohhh" and "ahhh", looking at one another.

"I need to up my fuck buddies. The most I've gotten was Thai takeout on a guy's couch." Evie's gaze shifts to the girls, clearly wanting them to agree with her.

"I just told him that I didn't want to be fuck buddies and we're exclusive. No other partners while we're together."

Evie laughs, her marshmallow falling into the fire. The one she put on the stick for me. "Only you."

Mae's hand lands on my thigh. "I get it. Keep that wall half up."

"I'm not. It's not…" Then I realize deep down it is. It's a relationship without putting a label on it. "He's free to do what he wants if he finds someone else. He just has to tell me first."

Annie studies her marshmallow, purposely dodging eye contact. Mae smiles politely but she's calling bullshit, and Evie… well, Evie is staring at me, waiting for me to clue in.

"You're dating and not getting all the benefits of it, like snuggling by the bonfire with him and spending the entire night in his bed. You should just own it."

"But—"

"But nothing. Don't sell yourself short. Whose idea was this? His?" Evie's voice raises. She's gone from concerned to pissed off. Do not pass Go. Do not collect two hundred dollars. She's cast Carm as the villain in this situation.

"It was both of ours." I shrug. "He doesn't do relationships, and to be honest, if we don't label it, there's less of a chance that someone gets hurt in the end."

"Why do you assume someone is going to get hurt?" Mae asks. "Maybe you're meant for him."

I smirk at her and she smiles, nodding. She's single in New York. She understands most guys are Peter Pans.

"You're holding yourself back," Evie says. "The real you wants a relationship, not some magical cock that's only around when the sun dips down."

"Relax," I say.

"You're fooling yourself." She shakes her head at me.

"Maybe she only wants Carm for the summer. A summer fling," Annie offers, but something tells me she wasn't so casual with Enzo.

"She's not us." Evie waggles her finger between her and Mae. "Bella doesn't do unconnected sex."

"There's always a first," Mae offers, smiling at me like she understands.

My best friend sure doesn't.

"Don't worry, Evie. I won't come crying to you should this thing go south, okay?"

She sighs. "That's not what I'm saying. I'm just—"

"Here we come. Your big strong men with the fire-wood," Carm interrupts, approaching with stacks of wood. He looks around at all of us. "What's going on?"

"I'm going out." Evie storms up to the house.

Mae's hand is on my thigh, rubbing up and down and alerting Carm that I have something to do with Evie's mood.

"What happened?" Enzo asks Annie, but she shakes her head. He sits and snags another bite of her s'more, which spurs another make-out session.

My throat locks for a moment because Evie's right. But this time, I'm taking what I want for however long I can have it. And I want Carmelo Mancini in my bed, to hell with future heartbreak.

"You okay?" he whispers in my ear, his finger running down my arm.

I nod, but from the length of time he stares at me, I know he doesn't believe me.

THE SUN STREAMS in and a hand travels up my thigh, a big body rolling up next to me.

"I love having you in my bed when I wake up," Carm whispers, casting kisses along my shoulders.

"Shit." I bolt up, and he rolls over. "What time is it?"

"It's eight. I let you sleep in since we got back from the Hamptons so late last night."

I climb out of his bed, his white sheets pooled at the end of the mattress.

He's on his back, one arm draped over his forehead, while I scramble for my clothes like a trail of breadcrumbs between the door and his bed. Having to pretend nothing's going on all weekend turned into us hungry beasts the minute he put the key in the door.

He comes out of the bedroom fully naked. If he was trying to tease me, it's working. "I'll make you some coffee."

Grabbing my suitcase, I stop him. "I have to go. Raincheck."

He locks me to him with an arm around my waist, pulling me to his chest. "Tomorrow then. If I can't spend the weekend with you, I want to negotiate a few days during the week."

An ounce of hope sprouts, and I push it down with a bucket of dry soil. He only wants me for the sex, I need to remember that. *No, don't listen to Evie.*

"That seems reckless," I say, not moving away from him, allowing his now-hard length to press into my stomach.

"Reckless because we might get an injury from over-doing it?" He chuckles, brushing my hair off my shoulder and nibbling on my collarbone.

"No, reckless in that one of us will get attached," I say honestly, wondering how he'll take it.

"Is this the whole take-me-to-dinner-first thing again?" His tongue slides up my throat and hovers over my mouth. "I'll make reservations."

"No. How about some takeout tonight? I have a feeling it's going to be a helluva day since I already feel hungover."

"Done." He smacks my ass and rubs his hands over my

cheek before sliding under my yoga pants. "Now come back to bed with me."

"I can't." I wiggle out of his hold. "Let's remember I'm down by four condos. You're about to sell out and I'm sitting at two sold."

He nods as though he understands and releases me. "Tonight then. Takeout naked in bed." He points at me, heading into the kitchen.

"Deal. Bye."

"Happy Monday," he says.

I shut the door to his condo and rest my back along the wall, sucking in a breath.

I hate Evie right now. Why does she always have to be right?

CHAPTER TWENTY-FIVE

Carm

"I find it funny that you tagged along." Enzo sits on the bench next to me in the antique store with a bag of popcorn he bought from a vendor down the street.

"I find it funny that you're doing the exact thing you stated was the sole reason for not being in a relationship. You're spending your Saturday looking for the perfect throw pillows." I put my hand in the bag of popcorn, but he moves it out of my grasp.

"Those who cast stones don't get popcorn. At least I'm doing it for love. What are you doing it for?" He waits for me to answer and glances over to where Annie and Bella have just popped out of an aisle.

I blow out a breath and people-watch for a moment. I like Bella, and I like spending time with her, but I'm not going to admit that to my brother.

"I just want some quality time with my older brother," I end up saying and ruffle his hair as if he's the youngest.

He throws a kernel of popcorn at me. "Bullshit. We both know why you're here."

"No way, Annie, they were so expensive," I catch Bella saying. It couldn't be a better time to interrupt me and my brother.

"They were beautiful, and they'd look stunning on you," Annie says, digging into Enzo's bag of popcorn and taking a seat on his lap. She feeds him a kernel. It's disgusting really.

"What are we talking about?" I ask, sliding toward the PDA couple to make room for Bella.

"There were these emerald earrings," Annie says.

"I don't even think they were real," Bella adds, shaking her head at me when I look for a reaction.

"They made your eyes sparkle," Annie presses.

Bella must've really liked them if Annie's still going on about them.

I stand up from the bench, holding out my hand. "Show me."

"No."

Bella shakes her head, but I grab her hand and pull her up. She stumbles forward, but I catch her.

"We'll be back," I say to Enzo and Annie.

Annie smiles, kind of slyly, as if this is exactly how she hoped this would play out.

We weave through some other patrons, and as we approach, the man behind the jewelry case pulls out a pair of emerald earrings. She must've looked *very* interested.

"Carm, I'm not going to buy them," Bella whisper-shouts.

"May I?" I look at them then at the man.

He nods.

I take one out and hold it up to her ear. "Annie's right. Your eyes pop with these."

She bites her lip. "And they'll be a perfect reward when I win the Bond Street account."

"Let's get them early then." I signal to the man that we'll be buying them.

"*No!*" She puts her hand over the box, and the man looks up, apparently surprised that this beautiful woman won't accept my gift. "Carm, we're friends or whatever, but we are not at a place where you buy me expensive jewelry."

She's right of course. I'm not even sure exactly why I want to buy her them, but I do. It feels like the right thing to do.

"Please? I want you to have them and—"

She presses her finger to my lips, and the man slides the box from under my palm. From my peripheral, I see him putting them back. He must be familiar with this scenario and know that I'm going to listen to her and lose this fight.

"It'd mean a lot to me if I bought them for myself."

My shoulders sag, but I nod. She smiles, and to see that grin, I'd decline purchasing her a gift all over again.

"Okay."

"Thank you." She glances around, checking to make sure Enzo and Annie aren't anywhere around, and raises on her tiptoes, replacing her finger with her lips. "I'll let you buy me an ice cream though."

"Double scoop?"

"Triple." She winks.

I follow her out the door of the antique store, disappointed she fought me on the purchase. I've never had a woman tell me no before. And I didn't even mind being told what to do.

Shit, maybe Enzo has a point.

AFTER A FULL DAY of shopping in the Hamptons, I'm ready for a nap, but the other three have made plans for a cook-out.

"I'm going to make my mom's famous chocolate chip cookies, then we'll pair them with ice cream." Bella places all the ingredients we bought at the store on the counter and searches for something on her phone.

"How about I just eat you?"

It's been a whole day since I've been able to really be with her. I sneaked in some kisses and touches here and there, but Bella's not about the PDA in front of our friends and family even though I'm pretty sure everyone has figured out what's going on between us. Which is anybody's guess really.

"How about you help now and then tonight you can eat me?"

I slide my hand up her shorts, push her underwear to the side, and hook my finger into her depths. She raises onto her tiptoes, and I swallow her surprise with a kiss. Her head falls back and circles when I add another finger.

"Want to renegotiate?" I arch an eyebrow.

"Do you want help with the cookies?" Annie barrels in.

Bella pushes me off her so fast, I spin around and almost fall to the floor. "Nope. Carm is going to help me as soon as he washes his hands."

I take the hint and turn to the sink to do as she says, my back to them.

"Okay, then I think I'm going to join Enzo for a short nap. I texted Mae and she said she and Evie are staying with the Brits. And Dom? Who knows?" I hear the annoy-ance in Annie's tone. She doesn't like to be out of the loop, and whatever or whoever Dom's doing while he's in the Hamptons, he's not telling a soul.

"Sounds good," Bella says.

Annie disappears and I dry my hands, coming up behind Bella at the counter.

"What do you need me to do?" I unbutton her shorts and lower the zipper.

"Carm," she sighs. Not a great plan on her part because she should know that when she says my name like that, I'm instantly hard. "Hands to yourself." She smacks my hands but turns around. "Let me teach you how to make these, then maybe you'll get lucky and can give me a massage."

"What about you giving me a massage?"

She's adding ingredients into a big bowl and hands me the wooden spoon. "You can do the muscle work."

"I do like to use my muscles. One in particular."

She hip-checks me and dumps a big pile of flour in with the butter, sugar, and eggs. "Do you ever cook or bake?"

"Not really. Ma really took care of all that when I was growing up, but now we all find somewhere to help in the kitchen during our Sunday dinners. Annie's influence." I mix the flour, my forearms straining as she continues to toss in other ingredients.

"What's it like to have such a big family?"

She dumps chocolate chips into a measuring cup, and I laugh. I would've put the entire bag in there with the excuse that there's no such thing as too much chocolate. But Bella, she's precise, even in her baking. Maybe that's why her demeanor in the bedroom surprised me so much. She's not rigid or traditional. She's wild and exploratory.

"It's annoying as all hell, but awesome at the same time.

When my cousins get together with us, it's a killer Thanksgiving football game. Poor Blanca's the only girl, but she learned quick that if she wanted in, she had to be tough. I hate to admit this, but it's nice coming to the Hamptons and having a break from Sunday dinners."

"Why?" She drops the chocolate chips into the bowl, and I pick one out and put it on my tongue. She says nothing.

"Because I'm Italian and male and twenty-eight, which means a lot of pressure to bring someone home. You'd have thought Annie was the Queen of England when Enzo brought her into the fold. Everyone thinks Dom might be gay because he's the oldest and still single. I have some time to relax now with Enzo and Annie being what they are, but they'll be bugging me again soon." I push the bowl away, and she digs out a spoonful of batter and slides it into her mouth. "What are you doing?"

"Tasting the goods." She swallows. "It tastes just like my mom's."

I swipe my finger in the bowl and suck it. She watches me.

"Want some?" I ask, ready for a reenactment of *9 1/2 Weeks* food scene.

"Sure."

See, this is why she keeps me on my toes. I have full faith in myself that I could get her stripped down on this counter with my head between her legs if I wanted.

"Finger or spoon?" I hold up both.

She takes control of my hand, dips it into the batter, and pulls it toward her, then she swirls her tongue around my finger until it's clean.

"And I'm hard," I say.

She laughs. "Okay, let's get these baked and cooling.

Then we can go take a nap of our own." She winks and I capture her lips with mine. She doesn't push away or argue.

She scoops them out onto a cookie sheet, and I put them in the oven and set the timer.

"Do you have other family besides your mom?" I ask.

"No. She was an only child, and although my dad had three siblings, they're spread out, so for holidays, it was always my mom, me, and her latest boyfriend. One year I had to go over to her boyfriend's family home and his ex-wife showed up. We found them in the closet between the meal and dessert. Good times."

"Wow, that's crazy." My chest constricts when I think of a young Bella witnessing something like that. "Have you heard from your mom since she and Greg returned to Florida?"

It's really none of my business. Greg's reputation in Manhattan is somewhat similar to my own. Playboy, bachelor for life, etc. Just on a much larger scale. He goes to Fashion Week with a model on his arm, movie premieres with actresses, and Broadway shows with Tony winners. But after witnessing what happened with my brother, I'm not naïve enough to think that a woman can't change a man anymore.

"A little. They seem good, but he's a charmer, which my mom falls for every time. I always cross my fingers for her, but sadly, she can't find her second love."

"Second love?" I lean back against the counter with my arms crossed.

"My dad was her first love." Her eyes light up for the first time during this conversation, and it reminds me of the sparkle in those earrings she liked. "Sometimes I wonder if people even fall in love like that anymore. Or if I was young and delusional because they were my parents. Or maybe I just remember what a great man he was because he died so young. You know how when people die, they say you only remember the good?" She busies her finger tracing the lines of the granite.

"How old were you?"

"Six."

Shit, that had to have sucked. Her mom seems so well-adjusted though. I think my mom would permanently grieve my dad if something happened. When my dad's sister remarried after losing her husband, Ma told me she saw it as dishonoring his memory. She's old school.

"I'm sorry," I say, and it feels like not enough.

She shrugs. "It's been decades. I'm over the loss. I just hope my mom finds whatever she's looking for." She sets her gaze on me. "Tell me, do you think a playboy can really change?"

My gut constricts and my throat dries. Way to put me on the spot. As I stare into her beautiful face and study her for a moment—those emerald eyes and flushed cheeks from a morning spent in the sun, the braid coming around her shoulder and falling against her freckled skin—all of that makes it so that I can only answer honestly.

"Yeah, I think they can."

CHAPTER TWENTY-SIX

Bella

I run into Carm's condo building, dodging the rain. It feels more like spring today than summer.

"Miss Scott, Mr. Mancini is expecting you." The doorman presses the up button on the elevator for me.

"Thank you." I slide in and he reaches in, pressing Carm's floor number.

"Enjoy your evening," he says as the door slides closed.

On the way up, I debate if I'm spending too much time here. I mean, he rarely comes to my place, but we're usually together a few times a week now. Plus our time in the Hamptons. It's all becoming a cozy routine, which I don't mind, but Evie's words about what exactly we are to one another and whether I'm settling stick in my head.

I step off the elevator and there's Carm in the open door of his condo, in his slacks with bare feet, his button-down untucked as he waits for me. The first time I saw him like this, I tackled him, and we had sex before dinner. It's becoming normal, like I expect to see him like this when I step off the elevator.

"Hey, beautiful, you kept me waiting." His perfect white teeth snap down on something green, which, as I grow closer, I realize is a snap pea. He offers me the other half, and since I'm running on a half sandwich and a pickle, I welcome it. Carm drops it on my tongue and kisses me on my neck. "I should punish you."

"I totally think you should." I giggle and slide around him into his condo.

"Is that your sly way of telling me you'd like me to be rougher in the bedroom?" He walks into his open concept kitchen and stirs whatever is in the pan.

I stop short. "Did you cook for me?"

"You answer my question first." He glances over his shoulder.

"I wouldn't be opposed to some ass slapping or tying me up." I blush just thinking about it as I slide out of my heels and unzip my skirt. "I gotta change. I'll be back."

I head down the hall to his bedroom and strip out of my office suit then into a pair of yoga pants and a T-shirt I keep here now. I leave the room, pulling my hair into a messy bun, and stop in my tracks—again—seeing him plate our meal.

"Did you really cook?" I ask.

He looks up and smirks. "It's one of the fresh meal kits. All I really had to do was put it in a pan and heat up the rice, but it's a meal." He shrugs as though it's no big deal.

Instead of taking a seat at the breakfast bar, I wrap my arms around his stomach, kissing his back. "Thank you. Now all I need is a foot rub and you'll be my prince."

The pan slips from his hand. *Shit.* As soon as the word

prince slipped out, I knew he'd misinterpret my words into thinking I mean happily ever after. Unlatching myself from him, I round the counter and head back to the safe zone of the stool.

He puts down some forks for us and pours two glasses of wine. Then he pulls a file folder off the other counter and slaps it down beside my dish. "I was hoping you could help me. It's a garden unit, and it's getting stale on the market."

"You're asking me for advice?" A part of me feels honored that he'd consult me.

"You were a broker once upon a time, and even though you won't tell me why you got out of the game, I've heard enough to know that you were successful."

He opens the folder and goes over the property with me, the good and the bad features, and we brainstorm the options of what he could do—the demographics of who would love it, some fresh marketing ideas that might get it some attention and whether or not the price needs to be adjusted—all while we eat the stir fry he prepared. The entire thing feels way too similar to a relationship, and I fear we're veering off the course we thought this was headed, his obvious uneasiness when I made the prince joke serving as a giant red flag.

"I LOVE YOGA PANTS." Carm yanks them down my legs as I'm brushing my teeth. "Especially since you never wear panties with them."

I bend over and spit out my toothpaste and he slaps my ass. Hard. I scream, my head almost crashing into the mirror. After I rinse, I cock my eyebrow. "Been waiting all night for that?"

He shrugs, but his big grin says yes, yes, I have.

Stepping out of my yoga pants, I strip off my T-shirt and strut by him. He's still in his slacks, although he's undone his belt, button, and zipper so the fabric hangs open on either side. His shirt is unbuttoned too, revealing his mouth-watering chest. Sometimes I wonder how I caught his eye and kept his attention this entire time.

"I have a question." He throws his shirt in a ball in his closet where I assume his maid picks up his dry cleaning for him. One of my suits was hanging in a nice plastic bag last week and it made me feel as though I should tip the poor woman.

"What could that be?" I set the alarm on my phone and place it on what has lately been my side of the bed.

"You're on birth control, right?"

I put my hand up in the air. "Say no more."

"Well, we're totally monogamous. I'm clean." He winds around the bed and comes up behind me. His smooth chest presses to my back and his hands slide forward, each taking one of my breasts. "When do we get to not use a condom?"

I giggle and my head falls back as his lips zero in on my most potent erogenous zone—where my shoulder and neck meet. "That's risky. You do know that the pill is only ninety-nine percent effective, right?"

I turn in his arms and help him with his pants until they puddle on the floor. His erection bulges in his navy briefs.

"Better than condoms." His hands glide around my backside, playing with my ass cheeks.

"Not more effective than condoms *and* the pill."

"You know I like to live dangerously." He chuckles.

I hook my fingers into the elastic waistband of his boxer briefs and pull them over his thick length and down his legs. He gently shifts me until I'm on the bed and he's over me.

"Why do I have a feeling you're already sold I'm going to say yes?"

He chuckles into my skin. "I could trace the freckles on your body with my tongue." He starts doing so as if I'm a map he needs to memorize.

He's already had me memorized for weeks.

His thigh nudges my legs wider, and he nestles between them. "Have you ever?" he whispers before kissing my eyelids, the tip of my nose, my chin.

"No."

Then he kisses my mouth. "Let me be your first?"

He's asking so nicely, and of course I want nothing between us. It's not even pregnancy that scares me. It's the fact we're getting closer every day. This breaks another barrier that says we're a lot more than what we're not labeling ourselves as.

His lips travel down the valley of my breasts and he nudges my legs farther open, each hand fondling a breast and running his thumb over a nipple.

"Okay," I say before he gets to my belly button.

"Really?" He's back up face-to-face with me.

"Yeah."

He waits a second, looking at me. "I know you want to get kinky, but you cool with some plain old grinding tonight? It's going to be hard enough to be inside of you without anything."

I run my fingers through his hair. "I'm more than okay with that."

As his mouth devours mine and the tip of his cock teases my opening, I push away all the crap about what we are. Why am I trying so hard to shove us into a category? By doing that, I'm ruining what's transpiring organically between us. Because maybe this *is* headed somewhere?

Once my head is out of the equation, all I can do is feel him. His touch, his lips, his muscles. The way he moves... the way we move together. Yeah, we've been together lots of times over the weeks. We know what one another enjoys, what makes us gasp, but this is different.

Our starved kisses turn long and soft, filled with emotion. His fingers graze my skin rather than grab, but he steals my breath anyway. I find myself waiting, trying to anticipate his next move, but he's different tonight. I'm completely lost with him in this bed. I never want it to end, yet I'm eager for it to begin, so I wind my legs around his thighs. He slowly pushes into me and withdraws.

"Carm," I sigh because this feels like... more.

"Bella. My gorgeous Bella." His fingers play with my hair, his lips and tongue exploring my skin. "This feels unreal. You're unreal."

He pumps in and out of me in slow, steady strokes, basking in this newfound feeling.

"More. I need more." I beg him to thrust into me as hard and unwavering as usual. It feels like too much yet not enough right now.

He knows what will get me off and he's always willing to accommodate, but tonight, he doesn't listen to my words. His knuckles track down my ribs, my shivers chasing them, begging him to never stop.

The weight of his body is my shelter, my safe haven.

We find a rhythm that works for both of us, and the sounds of his soft moans and whispered compliments have me bearing down on my orgasm. Somewhere between his "I'll never have enough of you" and my "don't ever stop," I tip over the edge of the cliff. The fall is long and exhilarating, and near the end, it's like someone pulled the parachute and I float back to earth.

He stills inside me and comes, filling me in a way no man ever has before. "God, I love fu..." His words trail off, which I'm thankful for. We both know we didn't just fuck.

After cleaning up, we find our way under the covers and Carm turns off the lights, snuggling in next to me. "Sweet dreams, baby." He kisses the back of my neck.

Goose bumps take over my body as I lie awake while he drifts off to sleep, and I try not to overanalyze what just happened.

The next morning, I wake up to an empty bed. When I grab my phone and turn off the alarm, my hand hits a box instead.

I sit up and wipe my eyes, reaching for the small box. Inside, I find the emerald earrings I tried in the Hamptons that day. I pick up the note and sigh as I read his masculine print.

I know. I know. I know. Don't hate me but these were made for you. ~ Carm.
P.S. Hurry into the office. You're late.

PET NAMES, no condom, a gift. Could I really be lucky enough to tame Carmelo Mancini?

CHAPTER TWENTY-SEVEN

Carm

Ten o'clock in the morning, I step out of my car in front of The Cobbler restaurant. After straightening my tie, I open the door and smile at the same hostess who eye-fucked me a couple months ago, before I started sleeping with Bella. Back when she was only someone to get out of my system and not someone I can't get my fill of, both in and out of the bedroom.

We've done carriage rides through Central Park. We've gone to the zoo. Now that Evie and Mae seem to hang out with the Brits every weekend and Dom's gone more than there, we've practically been double dating with Annie and Enzo every damn weekend. I've somehow become domesticated without signing up for it. Oddly enough, it doesn't bother me like I thought it would.

My phone rings, and when I pull it from my pocket, I

DIRTY FLIRTY ENEMY   217

see that it's Bella, so I hold my finger up to the hostess and accept the call, tucking myself into a corner.

"Want to know what I'm wearing?" I play with her.

"I saw you get dressed after your shower this morning," she says.

I bite my bottom lip, remembering how I took her against the tiled shower wall. What a great way to start the day. "I'll be back at the office in about an hour. Meet me in my office and—"

"No, listen, I have an idea about that property we were discussing the other night. The garden condo you're struggling to sell?" There's excitement in her tone.

Another thing I love about Bella is that she loves real estate as much as I do. Which doesn't explain why she went FSBO, and she's still close-lipped about it. I'm wondering if she'll ever trust me enough to open up.

"Great. I'll stop by on my way in."

"Perfect. Where are you anyway? Did you sell another Bond Street unit? Because I'm only two behind now. I'm on your heels, Mr. Mancini, are you shaking?"

She's teasing, but instead of the warmth that usually spreads through me, I feel dread. If she knew who I was meeting with right now, she'd be upset.

"Just meeting with a client. Wants the best deal in New York." The lie slides off my tongue too easily, but until I find out why he called me, I don't want her to worry.

"Hurry back. I kind of miss—" She stops abruptly.

I've noticed her doing that more over the last couple weeks since we had the bonfire. She and Evie are still hardly talking. Whatever went down while we were grabbing wood has lingered way too long. Bella's holding herself back from saying anything people do in normal relationships. Maybe it's about time we classify this thing.

"I will and... I miss you too."

"You do?" I hear her smile over the phone, and I can't help but smile knowing that those three honest words unglued her a little.

"Yeah. Always when I'm not with you." The hostess taps me on the shoulder and points toward Greg Throttle, who's seated at a table. "Listen, I gotta go, but I'll be back in about an hour or so."

"Okay, bye."

"Bye."

I thank the hostess and walk toward Greg, knowing things are about to change. There's only one reason he'd be calling this meeting, and it's going to mean once again that Bella Scott will end up on the wrong side of this deal.

"Carm." He stands and puts out his hand.

I shake his hand. "Mr. Throttle."

"Thank you for coming, and it's Greg."

Yep, my suspicions were right.

"Sit." He ushers me to sit in the chair across from him.

A waitress comes over and pours me a cup of coffee. I thank her.

"Breakfast?" Greg asks, adding sugar to his coffee.

"No, I'm good. Coffee is perfect."

He slurps his coffee and places it back down. "You know I'm a straight-shooter, so I'll get to the point—you have the deal. Bond Street is yours."

Instead of the elation I thought I'd feel, my stomach rolls over and I feel as though I might vomit. "But it's only been six weeks. There are six weeks left, and I still have to sell one more unit."

Truth is, I don't even have anyone interested in the last unit. Justin has been on the phone with everyone we know and nothing. I told Greg I'd do it in two months but was worried I'd fall short. The fact that Bella is hot on my trail scared me, but I always thought I had it in the bag and wondered what things would be like between us when I won. Maybe that's why I was okay with leaving that one property hanging until push came to shove.

"Between you and me, I did it as a favor to Linda. I'm not a FSBO kind of guy. I like my properties to be exclusively shown with an upscale brokerage with a great reputation, and I like the kind of elaborate ideas you pull off. But you know how it is." He winks. "It made her happy, and when Linda's happy, I'm happy." He winks again and I feel as if he's caked in slime right now.

He played Bella. She never really stood a chance.

"Are you and Linda still...?"

He shrugs.

I've been the man behind that shrug, so why is my hand curling into a fist in my lap? I shouldn't care what he does to Linda. Except if Linda hurts, Bella will hurt, and that means what exactly?

"I'm sure you understand. She refuses to move up here even with her daughter in the city. I've been going back and forth, but Florida is ridiculously hot and humid." The disgusted expression on his face makes me think it's not only the weather. "How are you guys enjoying the house?"

The abrupt subject change takes me a second to respond. "It's a great place. Thanks again for the discount."

I'm one step behind in this conversation, and I need to pull myself up. Stop worrying about Bella and her mom. Take what's mine. I've worked all these years for an opportunity like this. Any broker would give their right nut to work for a mogul like Greg Throttle.

"Happy to do it. Glad you two were able to work it out as easily as you did." His eggs Benedict arrives, and the waitress slides the plate in front of him. He picks up his silverware and I watch the yolk ooze out of the over easy egg. "So what do you say?" I wince at the sound of his teeth scraping along the fork prongs. "You accept, right?"

I nod, sipping my coffee, my mind a world away from this conversation when it should really be the only thing I'm concerned about. "Of course I accept. Thank you for the opportunity. Are you going to have us finish selling the floors we were assigned first?"

At least if I sell that last unit, Bella doesn't have to know that she was the underdog buried in the backyard before the competition was even over. Six weeks ago, I'd have been thrilled by this revelation. Now, not so much.

"Nah. I'll call Bella after this. Honestly, Helena said she's doing most of the selling. That the clients come in and she has to show them the place."

"Well, that's FSBO. But I know for a fact that Bella's showed the building more than once when Helena didn't respond."

His fork pauses halfway to his mouth. "You and Bella are... close?"

I understand his implication. But it's none of his business and I'm not going to talk to him about us. "She called me once to find out if I knew where Helena was since I was on the property a lot."

He nods, eats a bite of breakfast, and wipes his mouth with his napkin before sliding it back onto his lap. "I don't want this to be messy, so I hope it goes smoothly. I almost reconsidered after Linda told me what happened."

I tilt my head, and he studies me.

"Oh, you don't know. I guess that confirms you're not close." He laughs, shaking his coffee cup. Coffee splashes onto the table, staining the white tablecloth.

What is he talking about?

"Then again, I thought all you brokers traveled in the same gossip circles. That you'd have heard why she got out of the business."

"You know rumors. You never know whether to believe them or not." I pretend I'm in the know so maybe he'll throw something my way. A puzzle piece I can fit into place.

I told her about Kami. That took a lot. Is there something big she's hiding from me because... I realize we haven't labeled what we are. She owes me nothing. She's not my girlfriend, no matter how much it feels like she is.

"True, but in this case, it's true. Sad really. Linda said she was doing really well and now she's scraping by. That's why I threw her the chance at the development. Even Linda thought it would make her change her mind and go back to what she used to do."

I lean forward, ready to be direct, but his cell phone rings on the corner of the table. He puts his finger up, and I lean back in my seat. He's talking to someone about a business deal, so I pull out my phone and hammer out a text message.

Me: *I need to talk.*

Three dots appear within seconds.

Enzo: *Come down to my office.*
Me: *I don't want Annie involved.*

The three dots appear and disappear. *Please don't be a codependent douche right now.*

Enzo: *Meet me at the Trading Post. Dom?*
Me: *No. Just us.*
Enzo: *I'll be there in a half hour.*

After I place my phone down, I second-guess myself and pick it back up. I need Dom's opinion too.

Me: *I have a problem. Meet me and Enzo at the Trading Post in a half hour.*
Dom: *It's ten-thirty in the morning. If I'm making it to the Hamptons this weekend, then I have to work.*
Me: *It's an hour and since when do I ask for much?*

I can almost see him sighing at my request.

Dom: *Fine.*

I tuck my phone away as Greg hangs up.

"Sorry about that. Okay, well, I'm going to call Bella and settle that. Linda said she'd follow up with her later this afternoon to make sure she's okay." He pulls out some bills, sets them on the table, and slides out his chair.

I stand as well. "Well, I appreciate the opportunity. I won't let you down." I put out my hand and he shakes it.

"I think we're going to make each other very rich, Carm. Well, I'll just get richer than I already am." He winks and walks away from the table.

Everything runs through my brain at warp speed and I realize what needs to be done. "Greg?" He stops at the hostess station and I walk over to him. "Can you give me an hour before you call Bella?"

The expression of "I knew you were fucking her" crosses his face, but he nods. "Sure."

"Thanks."

As soon as I climb into the cab, I pray I can get this handled so she at least has someone there for her after Greg breaks the news. I'm not the one who should help her when I profited from her loss.

CHAPTER TWENTY-EIGHT

Bella

"I know you're screwing him. Justin told me the two of you travel back and forth to the Hamptons—just the two of you. Why would you do that when you supposedly hate him?" Max deposits my coffee on my desk, crosses her arms, and stands in the same stance she uses when she thinks she's being intimidating.

She doesn't intimidate me.

"It's called getting info on the enemy. Like recon work."

She rolls her eyes. The office door opens and my stomach flips with the hope it might be the man in question. Thankfully, Max turns to see who it is and doesn't catch my disappointment when Evie walks in.

"Nice outfit. And you're successful at your job?" Max asks.

Even I can admit that her t-shirt with 'Not today Satan'

printed on it and her multicolor cheetah print leggings aren't the epitome of professionalism.

Evie puts her hand up in front of Max's face. "I work from home. You're jealous. I understand." She beelines it past Max and sits in the seat on the other side of my desk. "Can we talk for a minute?" she asks me. "Oh, and I'll take a coffee." She gives Max a saccharine smile.

Anyone listening in would think they didn't like each other, but the truth is they just like to have a go at one another. Neither of them ever takes offense.

Max reaches for the door handle. "I can point you to our coffeemaker."

She shuts the door, and the room is silent. Other than a word here or there, Evie and I haven't talked much since that night at the bonfire. She has her opinion about Carm and is somehow disappointed in me for not demanding to be called girlfriend.

"Here, I stopped on the way over." She digs into her purse and pulls out a box that she places in front of me. From the Magnolia Bakery packaging, I know there's a cupcake inside. "I was going to grab Annie a s'mores one, what with her addiction to making them every weekend, but they were out."

"Evie," I sigh, ready to put our argument behind us.

Her head bobs right and left in a mannerism I'm familiar with. The only other time we got into a disagreement and acted like juveniles was right before college when her boyfriend didn't come to graduation and I told her it was grounds for a breakup. I guess we're kind of protective over one another, and maybe I shouldn't have been so mad when she voiced her concerns about Carm.

"I'm sorry, okay? I just felt like you were settling and taking less than what you deserve. You don't need some douche who only wants your pussy and not your brain or your heart."

I smile because she's worried, as I am.

"But I guess he seems okay. I just wish you'd define it as a relationship since it *is* a fucking relationship." Evie props her feet on the edge of my desk.

My landline buzzes. I press the button. "Say I'm in a meeting."

"It's Greg Throttle," Max says over the speaker.

Evie's face falls. She doesn't know who he is. I mean, I might've mentioned him casually, but Evie isn't a clout-chaser and probably doesn't really understand his importance.

"Give me a minute, okay?" I ask her.

She nods and slides out of the office, closing the door behind her. She joins Max at her desk.

I pick up when the call is transferred. "Hi, Mr. Throttle."

"Bella, please it's Greg."

"Okay. Greg." I pick up my pen and poise it over my notepad so I can write down whatever notes he's going to give me. "Is this about one of the deals? Helena's been a great help."

"No. As far as I'm aware, it's all going smoothly. Your buyers have been very easy to deal with, which is helpful since there's no broker to mediate the deal."

My stomach sinks. He knows what FSBO means. "That's the one downfall, but the bonus is your savings on commission. Especially with you not having to pay a percentage like you do to other brokers." I purposely don't throw Carm's name out there. The commission he's making on these condos is huge and we all know it.

"I understand that, but after some consideration and since we're down to the wire now—"

"There's still six weeks and neither one of us has sold all the units." Unless Carm withheld information from me? But I talked to Justin in the elevator this morning and he said they've been looking high and low for their last buyer with no luck.

"Technically yes, but I'm going to adjust the agreement between us and throw a little bonus your way for your trouble."

This is why I hate dealing with men like this. I want to ask if he's screwed over my mom too. Did they break up? Did he find some other hottie to keep him company and that's why I'm being kicked to the curb like an unwelcome stepchild? "Bonus?"

"Yeah, good news is the Hamptons house is yours for the rest of the summer and no more rent. It's a bonus for a job well done."

I roll my eyes and catch Evie and Max staring into my office with concern.

"I don't want a handout." It's the truth, but if he's firing me from the job, it's probably wise to take him up on his offer.

"Please, I insist. I have no use for it and I'll never find anyone else to rent it anyway."

"Okay, well, thank you for that."

"I am taking away the remaining units you haven't sold though. I've given the project to Carm. I apologize for the early termination, but this building needs a flashy sale. Helena's mentioned that it's too much work for her to show the FSBO units and how great Carm's office has been at handling his deals."

I twirl my finger in the air. Screw Helena and her fake

tits she throws in my boy... Carm's face all the time. "I understand. FSBO isn't for everyone."

I should put that as my slogan on my billboard. A warning to potential clients.

"I'm so happy you're good with this. Lin—your mom was worried how you might take the news, but this is just business."

"Of course."

"Well, I better get going. I'm heading down to Florida to see your mom this weekend. You should come down with me sometime. We can take my private plane."

I nod but don't actually answer.

"Bye, Bella. Have a great weekend up in the Hamptons."

"Bye." I hang up and my head falls onto my desk, smashing right into the cupcake box.

The creak of my office door's hinges sound, but I don't move.

"I'm sorry," Evie says. "This was for you to eat away your sorrows, not use as a pillow." She picks up my head and takes the box and lays my head back down on the desk.

She knew. How did she know?

I sit up straight and look at her. The great thing about friendship is that sometimes you don't have to speak the words for the person to understand.

"Carm called me."

My eyes close on a sigh. "He already knew?"

She nods. "I guess I might've been wrong about him." She sits on the edge of my desk, prying open the box. "We can salvage this with a fork." She turns and looks over her shoulder. "Max, your boss needs a fork."

"When did he call you?" I ask.

She shrugs, licking the buttercream frosting off her finger. "Like, half an hour before I came."

I slide out of my desk and stomp across my office. Why didn't he call *me*? He should be the one here, rather than sending my best friend in to save the day.

"Where are we going?" Evie asks, like a kid on a field trip, following on my heels.

"Are we finally going to kick his ass?" Max is two steps behind her.

I fling open the door of Mancini Real Estate. All his little minions stop what they're doing and stare wide-eyed at us.

"Hi," the receptionist—who I never got the name of—greets me, but I spot Justin outside the corner office.

"This is, like, twice our size. What the hell?" Max looks around. "And they have an actual break room, not just a table." She steps over to the door of the break room and points at an array of goodies inside. "Is this all free?"

I ignore her. "Justin!"

He peers up from his computer. His eyes are wide and his face pales.

"How old is this kid? Sixteen?" Evie says from behind me.

"He's twenty-two," Max says.

We both whip around. She looks away, which says that Carm was right, our assistants might be screwing each other.

"Where is he?" I glance at the closed office door.

"Not in. At lunch." His gaze goes to Max.

I step to the side to block his vision of her. "Where? And when is he due back?"

He picks up his phone, but he's flustered, and he drops it, then picks it back up only to drop it on his desk again.

"Um..." He glances at the phone on his desk then the computer.

"It's not that hard of a question." Evie steps forward, trying to peek at his computer.

"He's with his brothers," he says, clearly panicked.

"Oh, that's easy enough." Evie grabs her phone out of her cross-body purse that looks more like a reusable grocery bag than a purse, and she presses a few buttons before bringing the phone to her ear. "Shit, voicemail." She rolls her eyes. "Hey, Annie, it's Evie. Give me a call, girl." She ends the call and tosses the phone back into her purse.

Which leaves us back at square one.

"Okay fine. When is he due back?" I ask nicely, trying to calm Justin. I imagine he's scared, what with being confronted by three women with fire blazing in their eyes.

"He didn't say." He slides to the side to look at Max.

"Stop looking at her. She's not going to save you because she's on my side." I step forward and eye the computer with Carm's schedule on it.

Justin's gaze flickers to the screen and he presses a key on his keyboard and the screen goes black.

Tricky little fucker.

"Where was he this morning?" I want to know how long Carm's known about this. Did he just find out?

"Relax, ladies." Max steps up between us, looking more like our little sister compared to my and Evie's taller stature. Plus, we wear heels and Max... well, that's just not her. "Justin..."

"Max, it's my job. He's my boss, and obviously, she's upset," he says as though I'm not even there.

Evie snickers and we exchange an amused glance.

"I know, that's why I'm going to settle this." She picks up the phone. "Call him."

His eyebrows draw together. "No."

She waves the phone. "Come on. You get him on the phone and Bella will do the rest."

His Adam's apple bobs, but he presses a button and puts the phone to his ear. "If I get fired, you're hiring me at the same rate," he says, looking at me.

"Oh please, you're due for a promotion. He's keeping you down anyway." Max shakes her head.

I think I can safely bet on who holds the power in the bedroom if they really are sleeping together.

"Carm?" Justin says. "It's me... Bella Scott is here asking for you."

I yank the phone out of his hand. "Carmelo Mancini, we need to have some words."

The silence makes me think Justin called the wrong number until his throat clears. "Okay. I think we both have something to say."

CHAPTER TWENTY-NINE

Carm

I 'm first to arrive at the Trading Post, which is a first in all the years we've been meeting here for lunch.

Our usual waitress, Kate, approaches me. "Surprised to see you here so early."

The best I can do is give her a wane smile. I know she's used to seeing us for lunch, but this is an emergency and can't wait a couple of days.

"Stella?" she asks.

"Jack and Coke," I answer without thinking.

Her eyebrows pull together, but she nods and disappears.

My fingers tap on the table while I wait, my mind whirling with the fierceness of a tornado winding up to an F-5 level.

Kate brings over my drink and slides into the seat across

from me. The restaurant isn't busy since it's only ten forty-five and lunch service hasn't started yet. She places the drink in front of me. I stir the straw twice, lick it clean, and place it on my napkin before taking a sip. After I down a third of it, I realize she's still sitting across from me.

"What's up?" I ask.

Her finger follows the grain of the lacquered wood table, her eyes following her finger's path. "I think it's pretty clear, don't you?"

Fuck. Not now.

"What is?" I ask, feigning ignorance.

"The fact that I've been throwing myself at you for the past year. Hell, I cut you deals, I've given you my phone number, I've asked you to share a ride with me. So I'm just going to put it out there... do you want to get together some-time?" Her blue eyes stare at me through her long dark lashes.

I'm going to hurt her. Might as well start a line in front of me of women who want to kick me in the balls at this point. "I'm sorry, Kate, but I'm kind of in a situation right now."

"Situation? You mean relationship?" Her lips are already pulling down at the corners.

I hate causing someone sadness. "I mean... well, I don't know what I mean, but we're in agreement not to be with other people."

"Sounds like a relationship to me." She slides out of the chair.

"I think you're great and I'm sorry if I ever gave you the wrong idea."

But she's already a step away from the table, her eyes on the door where I see Dom entering and heading our way.

"No. It's fine. I should've taken the hints." She smiles at my older brother. "Hey, Dom, I'll be right back with your drink."

"Thanks, Kate, and can you put in an order for mac and cheese? I'm in a hurry."

"Sure thing." She diverts any eye contact away from me and disappears back down the hallway.

"What did you do? She looks like Blanca did when we told her the Easter Bunny wasn't real." Dom takes his usual seat to my right.

"She asked me out and I turned her down." I down another third of my Jack and Coke.

"What are you drinking?" His expression reads, "What the fuck is wrong with you?"

"Jack and Coke."

"Just like college."

I shrug, wanting him to shut up.

"Anyway, why are we here?" He looks toward the door, probably for Enzo.

"I got the Bond Street project." I down the rest of my drink, and when Kate returns with Dom's, she brings me another.

"That's the last for him," Dom says.

Kate diverts her gaze to me and nods before walking away.

"Are we celebrating? Because you don't look like you want to throw confetti," Dom says.

"Sorry, traffic and Annie's twenty questions made it hard for me to get here." Enzo sits down across from me. "I thought you weren't inviting him." He nods at Dom.

"Why would I not be invited?" Dom asks, picking up his drink.

Another waitress I've seen a few times approaches the table. "Hey, boys, I'm going to take over for Kate. She's not feeling well."

"Great. Now you've screwed us over." Dom shakes his head in disgust.

I throw my hands in the air.

"What am I missing?" Enzo turns to the new waitress, whose name I never caught. "I'll have a water and a goat cheese pizza. And I'll be putting in a to-go order before I leave."

I roll my eyes. "God forbid Annie gets her own lunch."

"Strike one." Enzo holds up his finger, his mouth pressed into a thin line.

"What the hell are you talking about?" I ask.

Dom blows out a breath and pulls out his phone, his thumbs scrolling along the screen.

"You keep knocking my relationship with Annie and I'm sick and tired of it. Yes, I love her, okay? Which means I do what she wants to do, and I grab her lunch when I'm out. But guess what, asshole, she does the same for me. When you love someone, you enjoy doing things that make them happy, so get over whatever it is that pisses you off about me doing things for her."

Dom shuts down his phone. Both our mouths are hanging open.

"Well... okay," I say.

"Seriously." Enzo's face is red like when he was thirteen and we teased him about how many showers he took and the nudie magazines in his closet.

"I'm sorry. I was just busting your balls. I didn't know it bothered you so much."

"Now you do."

I eye Dom, and he cringes but distracts himself with his drink. When the waitress sets down Enzo's water, I hope it cools him off. Out of the three of us, he's the least likely to lose his shit. When Dom does, it comes as no surprise—he's always a grump. But Enzo is pretty even-keeled unless something is really pissing him off, which in this case seems to be me.

"Why are we here anyway?" Enzo asks a minute later.

"Carm got that deal on Bond Street," Dom says.

"You called me away from the office to celebrate?" Enzo asks with a tone of displeasure.

"No. I called you down here because with me in, that means Bella is out."

"Ohh," they say in unison, leaning back in their chairs, understanding the hurricane that's about to hit shore.

"And this is going to ruin whatever the hell you two have going on with one another. Which is what exactly?" Dom asks.

"You tell me where you disappear to every weekend and I'll tell you about Bella and me."

Enzo glances at Dom then props his elbows on the table, staring at me. "It's not usually something you'd care about. I mean, normally you'd skip the Hamptons for the rest of the summer, dodge her in the hallway at the office, and hope she goes bankrupt. Why do you care?"

Should've figured that the man who fell first would see right through me.

"Because I like her, and this is going to gut her. I mean, the client she stole from me left her and came back to me. I had a client go to her and she figured out that I'd sent them her way. She's two properties behind me in sales, and Greg Throttle pulled the project out from under her." I start on my next drink.

"When you say like...?" Enzo asks.

Dom remains quiet.

"I like spending time with her," I say, looking into the bottom of my glass.

"What are you guys to one another? You say no labels and all that bullshit, but you're always together. You're spending all weekend in the same bed. Be honest with us." When our new waitress places Dom's meal in front of him, Dom picks up a fork and dives into his mac and cheese.

They wait while my mind runs over the last few weeks. "It feels a lot like she's my good friend and we have sex."

"Come on!" Enzo rolls his eyes, and the table next to us glances over.

"Fine. She's my girlfriend. Although she doesn't want to classify it that way."

"And that word scares you?" Enzo asks.

It was the reason I called him in the first place, wasn't it? I figured my older brother who just went through this could weed through all the bullshit for me. Direct me to the clearing so I could pass through without any pain.

"Of course it scares me."

"Are we talking Kami again? That girl was a bitch from the start. That's why you've been a manwhore your entire adult life?" Dom manages to get a full sentence out between his enormous bites of food.

"No. Yes. She fucked me over, but with Bella, it's different. I know we were supposed to just have a summer of fun, but with all the shit that's happening, I want to be there for her. Help her through this. But how can I when I feel like I'm the reason she's in this situation to begin with? Plus, Greg Throttle said her mom told him why she left the traditional brokerage and went FSBO, said it's not a huge secret, but she's never shared it with me, even after all the times

I've pried. Obviously, she doesn't see me as long-term if she doesn't trust me enough to talk about it."

They both remain quiet, processing what I'm saying.

"And I told her about Kami right after we first slept together. I told her how fucked up I was because of it."

Matching shit-eating grins rise on my brothers' dumbass faces.

"Shit. I never thought I'd see it," Enzo says.

Dom nods. "Out of all of us, I pegged you last."

"What?" I ask.

They share a look and turn back to me.

"You love her," Enzo says. "Welcome to the club. You're screwed." He leans over and pats me on the back. The waitress sets his goat cheese pizza in front of him and he looks at her. "Thanks. Can I also order a club sandwich with fresh fruit to go? No mayo."

The waitress nods and leaves.

"How does it feel?" Enzo gloats.

"Weird and uncomfortable." I twirl my glass in my hand.

"But...?" he keeps prying.

"I kind of like it. That is, if she loves me back." I down the rest of my drink. I could use the liquid courage with this revelation that my happiness is now in the hands of another. "What about the reason why she went FSBO? Do I demand she tell me?"

"Hell no. Even I know that's stupid." Dom wipes his mouth with his napkin and pushes away his plate. To my surprise, he didn't finish his meal.

I pick up my own fork and eat off his dish because now that I've identified that weird feeling in my stomach, I'm starving.

"Wait it out. Give her some time. You've just realized your feelings and we had to tell you what they were. I'm sure once she trusts you and feels safe to tell you, she will," Enzo says.

"When did you become the Yoda of love?" I ask, piling more mac and cheese into my mouth. I see why Dom loves it so much.

"Because I'm the most mature and I'm not afraid of my feelings." Enzo smirks.

My phone vibrates in my pocket. Pulling it out, I see that it's the office calling. "What's up?"

"Carm?" It's Justin.

"The one and only."

Enzo and Dom start their own conversation about how we should maybe throw an end-of-the-year party with all our friends in the Hamptons.

"It's me... Bella Scott is here asking about you."

Then I hear a lot of murmuring behind him.

"Carmelo Mancini, we need to have some words." Bella's voice comes on the line.

As my brothers sit across from me discussing the invite list and whether our parents should be invited or not, I clear my throat and finally man up. "Okay. I think we both have something to say."

"Why didn't you tell me?"

"I'm leaving the Trading Post in a few. Do you want to meet at my condo so we can talk?"

"Fine." She bites it out as if it's a big deal.

"I'll be there in a half hour."

"Okay."

"Have you eaten?" I ask.

"What? I'm not hungry. I'm pissed. Just don't be late. I

have to work, you know, because I just lost a big account."
Click. The phone line dies.

I raise my finger. "I need a to-go order as well," I say to the waitress as she passes our table.

My brothers smirk at one another.

Fuckers.

CHAPTER THIRTY

Bella

Justin's face regains its color once I hang up the phone.

"Thanks," I say, happier now that I know we're about to lay down the law on this relationship.

He cannot send Evie in to console me when business goes his way. We have to separate business and pleasure if we're going to coexist. All this has made me realize that we need to figure out where this is going anyway. I don't need a proposal, but I can't continue to exist in purgatory with him either. The thought of us not being together spurs my stomach to revolt against the only thing I've had this morning—coffee.

"Can we talk before you rush over there?" Evie asks as the three of us head back to my office.

I take a seat at my desk, calculating how long it will take me to get to Carm's condo. But then again, he's the one who should be worried, not me.

"Yeah," I say and signal to my small couch in the corner of the office.

She shuts the door and sits down, crossing her legs so they don't touch the floor. I always admire her "I am who I am and no one or thing will change me" attitude. I get up from my desk and take a seat beside her.

"I'm sorry. I shouldn't have left you out in the cold like that these past weeks. It's wrong of me to judge. It's just that you deserve so much better than a guy who is going to use you for sex and toss you aside."

I cross my legs and lean back into the soft fabric. "It's not really like that. I was on board with the whole thing. We're having fun, and I kind of enjoy the non-label."

She shoots me her look that says, *really?*

"It's true. I can't deny that I've grown to like the egomaniac, but he's not who we thought he was. There's a layer underneath that's kind and sweet and..." I don't finish because I can tell from the way her head slightly falls back and her eyes widen a millimeter, she's taking my compliments to mean I've fallen.

Truth is, I kind of have. Which is why I'm not sure this arrangement of ours can last much longer.

"So it's too late."

"No." I look out my door at Max.

Justin's at the edge of her desk and they're having a heated discussion—probably about how we busted in and attacked him. I smile because she'll own him in and out of the bedroom, I'm sure. They're two dramatically different people. But so are Carm and me.

Evie pats my leg. "I don't like it, but the fact that he was worried enough to beg me to come over here so you wouldn't be alone when that douche Throttle called says that maybe I was wrong about him. Your business is your business. You know I'll be there for you regardless of the outcome—whether I'm the maid of honor or a gravedigger."

I laugh, happy to have my friend back.

"But do me one favor," she says with a crease between her eyebrows.

"What?"

"Don't sell yourself short. You're an amazing woman, and you've been through hell this last year. None of that means you don't deserve a guy to worship your feet. If you want to just have fun and damn the consequences, well, I can't be a hypocrite, but make sure it's not because you're settling."

I nod and debate telling her the truth. She's being upfront with me, so how can I not with her? My head falls into my hands.

"What? Is this about..." I shake my head and she slides over, putting her arm around my shoulders. "What is it then?"

"I think I've fallen," I mumble.

"Come again?" She swipes back the veil of hair blocking her view of me.

I pick up my head. "I've already fallen for him. It's done and over."

"Oh." A smile lights up her eyes.

"What?"

"Then I think it's time for you and Carm to be adults and talk this out, because you might not be alone."

"Something has to give. Maybe I should just end it."

"No." She stands and offers me her hand. "Come on."

My gaze diverts again to Max and Justin. Are they, or aren't they? Justin pulls his phone out of his pocket and answers. He waves goodbye to Max and hurries out the door.

"How did I ever let myself get into this?"

"Because he's like Zeus. Men like Carmelo Mancini were born to be noticed and wanted and craved. Even if he ends up being the asshole we cast him as, you had great sex, right?" She picks up my purse and thrusts it into my chest.

"True. He is great in bed. Not selfish at all."

"Huh... that does surprise me a little."

Oh, the stories I could tell her. How his eyes are always watching, soaking in information. Or how he's perfected the way I like him to play with my clit. He's figured out my body like a genius solves a complicated math problem. Step by step by step.

"I see I've lost you to a recollection of sex with him, so don't forget you're mad at him." Evie chuckles.

"Right." I point at her because I was close to wanting to strip down as soon as I entered his condo. "Very good point."

She laughs and opens my office door. "Now go and be the strong, self-assured woman you are."

Max turns her chair to face us. "Back straight, chin up, Bella."

I nod.

Evie opens the door to the hallway. "Call me after... even if it's tomorrow morning." She winks.

I hope she's right. I hope he feels the same way I do. That whatever this is between us is worth the risk of being hurt if it were to end. Maybe we *can* keep business and personal separate. Maybe Carm has changed his view on relationships.

Maybe, maybe, maybe.

"Thanks," I say.

Evie wraps me up in a big hug, her patchouli perfume

suffocating all my senses. "It's what I should've done in the first place. Love you, chica."

After one more tight squeeze, she pushes me out into the hall—right into Margo Gregory exiting Carm's brokerage office.

"I'M SORRY." I touch her bicep. Damn, she must work out regularly.

She smiles curtly. "You're that FSBO girl, right?"

Girl?

"Yes," I say, making my way to the elevator.

"What's your name again?" she asks.

I press the button for the elevator since she's standing there expecting someone—me, I suppose—to press it. "Bella Scott." I put my hand out between us.

She looks at it, contemplates for a second, then daintily puts her hand in mine. "Nice to meet you. You should use my pore reducer. It does wonders." I'm not sure what my expression says, but she rushes to clear up her meaning. "Not that you're not beautiful."

"Thanks?"

The elevator arrives and we step inside. Again, I'm the one who presses the button even though she stood on the button side of the elevator. I guess with wealth comes immobility. The door closes and the elevator descends.

"So you're fucking Carm, are you?"

My head whips around. She's got that smile in place. A fixed grin women like her have mastered from conniving and manipulating people over a lifetime.

"Um... I'm not sure why you would think that." I glance at the numbers on the elevator. Three floors to go.

"The first time I met you, he stared at your ass until you got into your office. I know men like Carm. Hell, I know Carm—well."

The insinuation is purposeful. She's spun this conversation just so she could tell me.

"Carm is definitely a flirt, but I'm not sure why it matters where Carm and I stand with one another. It's none of your business."

She laughs. The elevator dings when we reach the main floor, but she rushes forward and puts her finger on the Doors Closed button.

Oh, now she can press the buttons.

"The fact you're calling him Carm is one sign. The other one is that he was supposed to show me a condo today, but Justin tells me his lunch is running late. You're leaving the building in a rush, so I assume you must be his lunch." She raises a brow in challenge.

"What's your angle? What is it you want?"

Her gaze falls over my body. "If you can't figure it out, then you're as naïve as I thought you were."

I say nothing because all I want is to end this conversation and get away from her.

"Men like Carmelo Mancini don't change. He's still the man who likes to celebrate with his clients after signing a deal. And I'm not talking about champagne. Consider this a nice way of telling you he'll only crush those sweet, little girl dreams of a happily ever after you have."

My heart rate increases, and my veins feel as if they're pulsating. Warmth spreads up my neck and hits my cheeks. "You have no idea who I am or what I want. Please release the button."

Another laugh escapes her throat. "I know women like

you. Women who think they can change a man. I'm doing you a favor here. Believe me."

I nudge her hand off the button. The door springs open and I rush out. "I don't need any favors from you."

I head to the doors, praying there's a taxi there.

"He's good though, right? The way he knows his way around a woman's body. Did you think he read it in a book?" She laughs, and I raise my hand frantically for a cab. "Maybe I could join you. We could surprise him. I heard he's into that too."

The creamer from my coffee curdles in my stomach and tears spring to my eyes. I blink them back and keep my hand in the air. Thankfully, a taxi pulls alongside the curb and I jump in as she smiles at me with a small wave.

My hands shake in my lap as I rattle off Carm's address. He slept with her? Maybe she's lying.

I pull out my phone and almost call Evie for that pep talk that I'm not some naïve Cinderella looking for my Prince Charming, but that I'm a queen and deserve to be treated as such. I don't need a man who lies and cheats and manipulates to get what he wants.

Was I the fool who let him take everything from me and now I'm just waiting until he drops me after he's stripped me of everything, including my dignity? The rational side of me says to get his side of the story. She might like Carm and be acting out of spite.

But if they have slept together, then he's lied to me.

My phone dings in my purse with a text message I want to ignore because I'm sure it's Carm asking why I'm late. But when I pull it out, I see my mom's name on the screen.

Mom: *I called the office and Max said you're out. I didn't* *want to interrupt in case you're working. I'm sorry about Greg, sweetie. It's just business.*

I clench my phone. It's only a matter of time before Greg breaks my mom's heart. He cut out her daughter before the competition he put into place was over. But I don't have the heart to tell her, so I ignore her text.

The taxi stops in front of Carm's building. I pay and step out, staring at the tall building and telling myself I need to have a spine as strong as that steel.

I can do this. I will not cry.

CHAPTER THIRTY-ONE

Carm

I press warm on my oven and pop the pizza I ordered for Bella inside, then I loosen my tie and unbutton my top button so I can breathe. Right now I feel as if one of my brothers has me in a chokehold.

Do I really love her?

No.

I definitely shouldn't tell her I love her. Right? Then she'll be able to use it against me.

It's been a couple months that I've been in daily contact with her. You have to be with someone for, like, a year before love comes into the equation, don't you? Then there's Enzo and Annie. They fell fast. Hell, even all my cousins. From what Mauro told me, when he was in town, Luca went from hating to loving his new fiancée.

My doorman calls up, and I don't have to answer to

know that Bella has arrived. I already told him she'd be coming.

"She's on her way up, Mr. Mancini."

"Thanks," I say, walking to the front door and unlocking it.

I remain in the doorway to wait for her to get off the elevator, like I always do. Surely, she has to see that this is out of my control. That I can't decide what Greg Throttle does. Up until that meeting, I thought I'd win the contract fair and square after the allotted time.

The elevator dings and she files out, wearing a navy skirt that's tight all the way to above her knees and a tank blouse that's tucked in to show off her incredible figure.

"Hey," I say.

"Hi." Her eyes are rimmed red and there's still wetness pooled in her gorgeous greens.

My hand rises to cup her cheek, but she slides past me into my condo. She stands by my entryway table without putting down her purse or taking off her shoes.

"I got you a pizza," I say, stepping into the kitchen.

She doesn't follow.

"I need to ask you a question," she says, her voice quivering.

On the phone, she sounded mad, but not like it would be the end of us. I've been so wrapped up in my own dissection of my feelings for her that I didn't consider that this could break us up.

How do we break up when we were never really together? At least not formally.

"Come and eat." I take the pizza out of the oven. "I hope you like goat cheese. Enzo swears by it."

"I'm not hungry."

I glance over my shoulder. She's still in the same spot, so

I drop what I'm doing and walk over to her. Grabbing her purse strap, I try to lower it down her shoulder, but she stops me, her hand cold.

"I'm sorry about Greg. If I could change it, I would. I was actually thinking of some ideas where maybe we could—"

"Did you sleep with Margo Gregory?"

Air leaves my lungs in a rush.

Her eyes lock on mine. She wants to see my reaction, to judge if I'm lying or not. Bella does it often. I always thought it was a trust thing.

"Why would you ask me that?"

"It's an easy question, Carm. Did you, or didn't you?" A tear slips down her cheek because whatever happened in the time between that phone call and now, she's decided she already knows the answer.

"What happened? I thought this was about Greg. Why are you bringing up Margo?"

She swallows, and it's so audible that it echoes through the quiet condo. My hands yearn to grab her, to hold her to me and beg her not to leave, because once I admit the truth, she's going to storm out of here.

"I had a little run-in with Margo. She's upset, by the way, what with you canceling on her. So she decided to ambush me in the elevator and tell me about all the times you fucked her after she signed on the dotted line."

I wince at her words. All the times? It was once. I run my hand through my hair, pull my tie from around my neck, and toss it on the entry table. It's stifling in here.

"Answer me," she says, her jaw clenched.

I stare into her eyes as I deliver the truth I know will gut her. "It was once. A long time ago. I was young and naïve and stupid."

She nods, another tear dripping off her eyelash onto her cheek. "You lied."

I think back, trying to remember exactly when we talked about Margo.

"In the Hamptons at the nightclub our first night. I asked you if you'd ever slept with a client and you said no."

"Did I?"

She inhales such a deep breath, the flesh in her collarbone indents until I think she might never release her breath. "Have a nice life."

She reaches for my doorknob, but I sprint there and sprawl in front of it, blocking her exit.

"That was before us. What does it matter? I'll tell you everything you want to know. It was once, and it was years ago. We were drinking after she got the place she wanted, and one thing led to another. She means nothing. But you..."

Her eyes remain on my hand on the doorknob, her head shaking asking me to just stop talking, but I'll keep going if there's any hope in convincing her.

"Bella, what we have..."

Her eyes shoot to mine. "All we have is sex. We fuck. That's all there is between us. Now let me leave." Her hand lands on top of mine on the doorknob.

"No. Listen to me."

"No, you listen to me. Since you've entered my life, I've gained and lost a client. My business is failing, and you seem to be the one benefiting from my downfall. I was willing to put that aside because it's business. But you lied to me. You lied to me when it didn't even matter what the answer was. I wouldn't have cared. I might've thought a little less of you, but we weren't anything then, so what did it matter? If you lie about that, what else are you lying about?"

My hand falls off the knob and I grab hers. "I'm sorry, but this isn't something for us to break up over."

"Break up? We're not even a couple. You made that perfectly clear. You don't do relationships, remember?"

"I know what I said, but the truth is that I want one. With you. When I said that, I was scared that my job would get in the way of us or that you'd hurt me. But I know now that having you in my life is better than not having you at all, even if there's the chance that means future heartbreak. I've fallen for you, Bella."

She stares at me for a minute, and I plead with her with my eyes.

"Too late." She grabs the doorknob.

I push my shoulder against the door. "No, I'm not."

"You are. What else have you lied about?"

"Nothing."

"That you remember." She crosses her arms.

"So that's it? You find out I slept with a client over five years ago and suddenly you're ready to call it quits? Who's the coward here?" I storm away from the door. I'm not going to lie down on the train tracks just for her to plow me over.

"You're a liar. You manipulate people."

I shake my head, opening my fridge and taking out a bottle of beer. "Did I manipulate you to sleep with me? You're going to put our downfall on me?"

"*I* didn't lie. You supposedly want to make us official now, but you don't lie to someone you care about."

I slam the bottle down on the island countertop, my palms resting on either side of it as I lean forward. "You're so goddamn righteous. Some people might say that a lie by omission is still a lie. I've tried for how long to get out of you the real reason you left your old brokerage, and every time I ask, you dodge the question. You were never fully in this relationship, so don't make it seem like I'm the only one who had reservations going in."

"We don't have a relationship, remember? You made that perfectly clear! And my reasons are personal!" She's yelling, but I don't even care at this point.

"We *are* in a relationship. Maybe we didn't say the word and we told ourselves it was just fun, but I don't go antiquing with the women I fuck. I don't take hours exploring their body. I don't take them to five-star restaurants, and I certainly don't leave them texts begging to come over. You're my fucking girlfriend, whether you want to admit it to yourself or not, and we both know it."

"Have you fucked any other clients?"

I shake my head and down the entire beer. "And you still can't trust me."

"I can't trust you because you lied."

We're at a standstill. I'm so aggravated and pissed off, and I'm at a loss of what to say to get her to understand that she's the first woman I've cared about in a decade.

"I'm sorry I lied. I knew you'd think less of me and we'd just gotten over the whole you-hating-me hump. We were talking and we weren't anything yet and it wasn't something I felt you needed to know. I forgot about it as soon as we finished the conversation. Even if I had thought of it after we were together, I don't know if I would have brought it up. If I told you that I'd slept with Margo, you'd go back to thinking what a bad guy I was. That I wasn't the guy you were discovering I was deep down. I wanted you to know the real me, not the person you thought I was. But it was wrong not to answer honestly when you asked."

Her strong stance sways and she stares at the floor.

"Come on, Bella, we can move on from this." I'm halfway to her, and from her appearance, it looks as if I'm getting somewhere with her. "I want to explore this thing with you because I think we're perfect together."

Just as I'm inches away from touching her, she retreats, her eyes back to being two green balls of rage. "I'm sorry, we can't. I can't."

Just like that, she hurries out my door, slamming it. I throw my beer bottle into the back of it, and it smashes into brown shards across my wood floor.

"Fuck!"

This is exactly why I shouldn't do relationships.

CHAPTER THIRTY-TWO

Bella

"Come on, Carm's not coming." Annie sits on the other side of my desk.

It's Friday, and they should've already left for the Hamptons. Evie tried to stay back with me, but I know the British guys are having a huge party and she should be there instead of wallowing in my own personal pity party.

"It doesn't matter. I'll just be a downer, and I really need to work."

Annie leans back into the chair rather than leaving. She clearly has something she wants to get out, but she's worried about how I'll react. "Before I say anything, I want you to know I understand your reasoning. Lying is not a sign of a good man. And he is my boyfriend's brother so I can't really pick sides, but I get why you freaked out."

"Just say it."

She wavers for a moment. "He's a good guy. He lies

about stupid shit sometimes because he worries what people think of him. But with you... it's the first time since I've been in their lives that I've seen the real him. He's himself with you. Even Enzo says so."

"I just need some space."

"He's a mess. Have you seen him? He hasn't shaved. His eyes are sunken in. I stopped over last night, and the condo was a disaster. I listened before I knocked, and he was playing some song and when it stopped, he started it back up again. It was country. I've never heard him listen to country."

I can't say I'm much better than Carm. I have "Be Alright" by Dean Lewis on repeat hoping it'll help things make sense, but Carm didn't cheat on me. He lied. Then a song like "Meant to Be" by Bebe Rexha and Florida Georgia Line will come on and I think that maybe I'm overthinking this whole thing.

"I don't know, Annie, I mean..."

"You like him, don't you?" she asks.

"I do."

A small smile creases her lips. "Do you think you could forgive him?"

I sigh. "Did he ask you to come here?"

She shakes her head. "I'm here on my own. Actually, Enzo's in his office right now, making sure he doesn't come up this weekend in case I'm successful in getting you to join us."

"Oh."

"He'd probably kill me if he knew I was here. He's doing some kind of Bella cleanse."

"Which is what exactly?"

She laughs. "Well, any redhead woman gets a death stare. He makes sure his cabs don't drive by any of your billboards. Even the one outside the office. He'll have the cabbie go around the block to park on the other side of the road, so his back is to it. He calls someone the minute he steps off the elevator to keep him from coming into your office. I think he even told Justin that if he didn't quit sleeping with Max, he was fired. You know Justin. He said okay." She shrugs.

That explains why Max has almost been Team Carm lately. She told me that maybe he isn't so bad and what he did with Evie was thoughtful. The worst was when she told me that I should've been honest with him about why I started the FSBO brokerage.

Traitor.

"Sounds like he's been busy the last few days."

She rolls her eyes. "Carm isn't good with patience. Three days to him is like three months to the rest of us."

I don't say it, but I feel like it's been six months. Every night is lonelier than the one before.

"And you look... beautiful but tired. Enzo and I didn't have a smooth journey, you know. We had some kinks to work out too. It's natural, but if you quit communicating then..." She stops talking, as if she doesn't want to overstep when she's invested in both sides. "Well, I should get going. I just wanted to try to convince you to come to the Hamptons. It seems like a waste not coming."

"Thanks, Annie. Have fun." I give her a small smile.

"Will you come next weekend?" She stops at the door, waiting for my answer.

"Maybe we can be civil and talk about a schedule. I'm not sure you'd want both of us there at the same time."

Her lips tip down, and that's when I see how truly upset she is that Carm and I might not work out. "I'd love for you two to coexist, but I imagine I'm asking too much. Have a great weekend, and don't work too hard." She smiles and opens my office door. "Max."

Annie heads out of my office into the hallway, and Max circles in her chair. "You know I'm usually always on your side, but..."

"Oh stop. Annie just spilled the news. Justin's holding out on you to keep his job."

She rolls her eyes and stands from her chair. "He's being a weasel and I'm annoyed with it, but I would never tell you something for my own gain."

I know she wouldn't, and I was really only kidding.

"I just never saw you as happy as you were. I called you out on it a lot, but it was nice to see you that way. You deserve it."

"Max, are you being sentimental?"

She rolls her eyes again. "Would you rather have me tell you that you're going to blow it with the first man who's ever fucked a glow into you?"

I laugh. "Being good in bed and being good out of bed are two different things."

"I think you're harping too much on this lying thing. Are you sure you're not pissed because you got blindsided by the bitch in the elevator? Or that it's easier for you to blame him when you weren't completely honest with him yourself because opening up to him would make you vulnerable and—"

"I hate you," I say.

"You hate that I'm right." She tips her head and looks at me from under her eyebrows.

"Shut my door."

She stands and starts to shut it. "It's okay, B, I get it. You've spent your entire life proving the fairy tale wrong— that no man is as great as your dad was for your mom. But somewhere, you forgot about yourself. He doesn't have to be a prince to be Mr. Right."

Click.

Silence accosts me, and Max smirks before swiveling in her chair to face her computer again. I look at the clock on my computer. Three o'clock, which means she'll be leaving soon. Maybe tonight I can really think through this thing between Carm and me.

I pick up my cell phone and allow myself to look at the one and only picture I have of us. Annie secretly captured it the night of the bonfire and sent it to me the next morning. I'm beside Carm, leaning into him with my head on his shoulder, and we're smiling at each other. I rub my thumb along the screen.

Am I being an idiot?

I pull up a text message thread with my mom.

Me: *How are things there?*

Three dots appear immediately. She's probably left the bakery already.

Mom: *Just humid and hot. You know, typical summer. Greg is picking me up this evening on his jet and we're heading to Santa Barbara for a long weekend.*

I guess things are still going good there.

Me: *Sounds like fun.*
Mom: *You okay sweetie? Want to talk? I'm just packing my bag, but I have some time*
Me: *No. Just checking in.*

Mom: *Okay... have fun in the Hamptons this weekend.*

No need to tell her what's happening.

Me: *Thanks. Have fun in Santa Barbara.*

I drop my phone on my desk and face my computer. I should try to get some work done before I actually do head across the hall.

CHAPTER THIRTY-THREE

Carm

"I warned you this would happen." Enzo sits across my desk from me, his ankle propped up on his knee, relaxed with a smug expression.

Screw him.

"Thanks for throwing salt in the wound."

He holds up his hands. "I'm just saying. You lie about stupid shit, and now you got caught and ruined what was starting to form between the two of you."

I stare at him then look back at my computer to distract me from punching him in the throat just to shut him up. "You can stop with the lecture. I feel like shit enough. And just so you know, it's not all me. She wasn't all in. She was holding things back from me too."

He blows out an annoyed breath. "Did you ever think that maybe you didn't allow her the safe space to entrust you with whatever happened? When you're dating, it's called discovering each other. You don't write down every fear you have and go through it like a checklist."

I'll give him that one. But it doesn't negate the fact that she didn't feel like she could share whatever it was with me —especially when other people obviously know.

"She's not going to come running back to you with your new look. You out of razors?"

I run my hand down my short beard. "I like it. I'm gonna keep it."

"It looks like shit."

"Thanks. Way to boost me up, brother."

He drops his foot to the floor and leans forward, resting his forearms on his thighs, then he places a small box on my desk.

I stare at it. "Are you crazy? I'm not proposing. I get that you got me to see that I want an actual relationship with her, but a ring?"

"Open the box. It's not for you to give Bella. Jesus, is lack of sleep affecting your intelligence?"

I open the box, and there rests a huge diamond on a silver band. It's round and traditional and somehow fits Annie perfectly.

"I'm asking her this weekend. Mae and Evie are going to the Brits' party. Dom told me he'll make himself scarce. Even though Annie's over at Bella's trying to convince her to come this weekend, I'm telling you not to." He picks up the box and shuts it with a loud clap. "It's funny though." He plays with the box, staring at it. "I can't help but think this moment would've never come if someone didn't give me a piece of advice when I thought I'd lost her."

I lean back in my seat, taking the bait.

"My younger brother told me to fight. That I was Enzo Mancini, and I had to fight for the love of my life if I wanted her back. That sitting on my ass being scared wasn't the right move." He stands and tucks the box into the inside pocket of his suit jacket.

I lace my hands behind my head. "Words of wisdom, huh?"

He shakes his head, his hand on the doorknob. "Just telling you to keep your ass out of the Hamptons this weekend, that's all. Oh, and thank you for kicking my ass when I needed it because otherwise, I would never be what I am today—one lucky bastard." He walks out of my office then peeks back in. "And stop cockblocking your assistant."

Justin returns to his desk with a stack of brochures for a new listing. There's no smile or pep in his step.

Yeah, that was a douche move on my part, I'll give my brother that one.

"*Justin!*" He walks in, and before he can say anything, I say, "Go ahead and bang Max. I don't care. Your job isn't on the line."

"Okkkaaayy," he says.

"Did you really cut her off?" I ask.

"Well, I can't lose my job and Max is wishy-washy sometimes, so I had to make the secure choice and that was the job. But if I really cared and thought she did, I would've told you to fuck yourself."

I chuckle, and the truest smile I've felt all week reaches my eyes. "Good man."

I bury my head in my work for the next few hours, but Enzo's words run on repeat in my head. I'm Carmelo Mancini, the man who takes chances others don't and doesn't admit defeat. I go after what I want until I get it. I'm not afraid to lose because I'm always right.

So at six o'clock, when I'm about to shut down for the

night, I pack up with one intent only—to find Bella and convince her that the two of us belong together.

I step out into the hall and see the light in her office is still on.

I think it's my lucky day.

Until a bloodcurdling scream comes from the other side of her office door. I turn the knob to find it locked.

Another scream echoes out, and my gut sinks. I need to get in there.

I kick the door.

Once.

Twice.

Sweat pours from my face and I strip off my suit jacket, throwing it on the floor.

I kick the door again.

And again.

And again.

"*Bella!*" I yell.

"*Bella!*"

"*Bella!*"

Kick.

Kick.

Kick.

Finally the wood splinters by the doorjamb and the door bursts open, but what I find almost brings me to my knees.

CHAPTER THIRTY-FOUR

Bella

At five thirty, Max finally calls it quits. She tried to stick it out with me, but I'm pulling a long night because I have to get this business in the black. Jess and Brent don't work today, so I'm on my own. I might've gotten sidetracked by Greg Throttle's little experiment between Carm and me, but now's the time to find my client base and build my business.

After a half hour of listening to music from my computer to fill the silence, I get up to grab a soda or a coffee —anything with caffeine that will keep me going.

The office door creaks open and I turn, thinking Max must've forgotten something, but a man walks in. He's wearing black sweatpants and a sweatshirt with some type of writing on it, his hair pulled back into a slick ponytail. A cross earring hangs from his right earlobe.

I know to take down details this time. After that night

over a year ago when I could barely give a height, weight, or ethnicity, I know how crucial details are.

My gut clenches, and I step back since he hasn't seen me yet.

He heads to Max's desk, opening drawers and searching through the contents. I feel a small amount of relief. Robber.

Not a rapist.

This isn't a planned attack... can I hide out until he's done, let him take what he wants, then call the cops? Our office is so small though he's going to see me. Can I make it to the door before he can do anything?

As I take another step back, my right hand hits the stacked coffee mugs Max washed before she left. They all clatter to the floor. The man's head springs up, his eyes finding me, and the color drains from his face. I drop my pop can and it bounces off the counter then falls to the floor, spraying dark liquid all over everything, including my white blouse.

He rounds Max's desk, and relief floods me when he goes for the door. He got caught and now he's going to leave. Thank God.

But instead of leaving, he locks the door. His eyes dip to my now-see-through blouse then back to my eyes. "And here I thought all I'd find was some shit I could sell."

I see now that he's probably on something. His pupils are dilated, and his eyes move rapidly over me. Fear has a vise grip on my throat when he walks toward me. Locks my voice inside when I know I should scream.

I note the small limp with his right leg. I need to alert someone as to what's going on. Scream for help. With any luck, someone is still working nearby. Maybe at one of the Mancini offices.

I throw a mug at him, but he dodges it and lunges toward me. He grabs my hand, and because he's so much stronger, he pulls me to him. I open my mouth to scream, but nothing comes out.

He looks down at my blouse and, in one swift motion, rips it open. I'm transported back to that night a year ago. Except that man dressed the part. He was clean-cut, in an expensive suit. I was there to show him the condo he was sure he would put an offer in on. But that's not why he wanted me there.

I come back to the present when he throws me on Max's desk. I kick at him, missing his balls. If only I still had my heels on, I could do so much more damage.

A stapler jabs into my back, but I ignore the burst of pain.

"Get off me!" I yell, finally finding my voice.

His sour breath hits my nostrils as his grubby hands try to pull up my skirt, and I gag. I wiggle and move, trying to stop him from getting a hold of me. Once he pins me down, I'm out of this game. I've been here before.

I cry out, desperate for help, and reach for anything on the desk to fight back with. When I stab his hand with a pen before he can wrap it around my wrist, it only makes him angrier. I scream, but he tries to cover my mouth. His rancid-smelling hand blocks my only hope for help.

I fight back and manage to wiggle myself to the side, so the stapler is no longer pressing into my back. Once I can grab it, I knock him in the head with it hard enough that he removes his hands from me and holds the spot, stunned.

I race into my office and lock the door behind me, barely able to catch my breath. Before I can get to my desk to call the cops, he takes a paperweight Max has on her desk and throws it into the glass panel beside the door. He reaches in to try to unlock the door and I grab the first thing I see—my letter opener. I stab his hand so he can't get ahold of the lock.

Continuing to scream, I hear Carm on the other side of the outer office door, screaming my name. He's kicking the door. The guy looks back at the door, then at me with fear.

Unless he wants to jump out the window, there's nowhere for him to go.

"Get lost, asshole," I say, stabbing at him again.

He finally retracts his hand and looks hurriedly around the office for another exit before moving toward the door. The door hits him in the face, knocking him down. He's sprawled on the floor by Max's desk, and there stands Carm, with a furious and desperate glint in his eyes.

His face is beet-red, his hands fisted at his sides. He takes in the scene, looks at me through the broken glass beside my door, and his face crumples for a second before he zeroes in on the guy on the floor. Straddling him, he hits the intruder over and over and over. Blood splatters all over Carm's shirt, the floor, and the side of Max's desk.

It takes me a second to unlock my door, my hands are shaking so much, but once I do, I race to him. "Carm!" I reach for his arm. "Stop! Come on! Carm, stop!"

He doesn't stop until the man lies lifeless underneath him. Then he climbs off him and looks at me. "Are you okay? Did he..."

I shake my head, unable to speak. Then I retreat into myself.

CHAPTER THIRTY-FIVE

Carm

"You don't know who this man is?" the police officer asks.

A female police officer is talking to Bella across the hall in my office so they can get her to open up away from the scene.

"No. I don't think he works in the building."

The man is on a stretcher, and the paramedics carry him away with an ice pack over his nose.

"We'll be following him to the hospital and press charges then. And your relation to Miss Scott?" He poises his pen over his pad of paper.

"Boyfriend." I push my bloody hands through my hair.

"Not that I'd blame you, but it's a good thing you didn't kill him." He jots something else on his notepad and walks toward the door. "I'll see you both down at the hospital."

The detective leaves, and I walk away from the guy taking photographs of the scene. When I enter my own office, I see that Bella is still rocking.

The female detective sees me and ushers me back into the hall. "We need to get her to the hospital. Usually we'd drive her, but why don't you? This is common in repeat instances. She's lost somewhere between the first time and this time. She gave me enough to know he didn't penetrate her, so that's a good sign, but we want the DNA from her fingernails and to take pictures of any bruises and lacerations."

"Okay," I croak, since the words *repeat instances* are flashing like a neon sign in my head.

"We're heading to Memorial. Please come soon. Time is of the essence."

I nod and watch her and the other detective leave. Before grabbing Bella, I call down the hall to the officers. "Since her purse is still in her desk drawer, am I allowed to take it and her jacket?"

The officer nods. After I retrieve them, I head back into my office. Bella is still staring at nothing. No tears, no anger, no fear. It's the weirdest thing I've ever seen, and it scares me.

"Bella, we have to go to the hospital," I say in a soft voice.

"Okay." She stands and heads over to me.

She allows me to escort her down the elevator and into the car I called. She's quiet and reserved.

"Do you want me to call your mom or Evie?" I ask once we're secured in the back seat.

"No. I'll be fine."

"Bella?" I reach for her, but she retracts her hand.

"Don't touch me."

I pull back, trying not to show that I'm upset she won't let me comfort her. Her gaze lands on mine, and she must see the pain of wanting to do something there.

"The DNA. I don't want to mess any of it up. Better if I just sit still until they do what they need to." She's so matter-of-fact.

"Bella, the detective..."

Tears fill her eyes. "Can we talk after?"

"Okay."

"Will you take me home after?" she asks.

"Of course." I want to say more, but I have no idea what. I'm so out of my element here.

She nods. "Thanks."

We arrive at the hospital a short while later, and they take Bella into a room. My knee bounces as my mind runs over the vision of Bella with her shirt stained and ripped open. What could've happened if I had arrived any later than I did? I can't even stomach the thought.

More than an hour later she comes out in a set of scrubs, her hair pulled into a ponytail.

"I'm done," she says.

"Can I touch you now?" I ask, standing from my chair.

"No." She walks out of the hospital.

I follow, not knowing what exactly to do to help her through this.

More silence fills our ride back to her apartment.

She walks into the lobby and turns around with her hand up in front of her. "You can go now. Thank you for coming with me."

She has to be kidding me.

"Bella. No." I shake my head. "I'm seeing you upstairs,

and I don't intend to leave tonight. I'll sleep on the couch or in the hallway if you prefer, but I'm not leaving."

She looks at me for so long, I fear she's going to refuse me, but she nods and we both head to the elevator.

Her apartment has a homey factor mine doesn't. Her array of colors brightens the small space, making it more welcoming than my own condo, albeit much smaller.

"I'm going to shower," she says and walks down the hall.

Once I hear the water running, I quickly change into the clothes I grabbed across the street from the hospital while she was with the doctors and the police officer. I was covered in that guy's blood, and I don't want her looking at me to be a visceral reminder of what happened.

I debate calling Evie or Annie or Blanca or Ma. Someone who can give me advice on what to do so that I say the right things instead of the dumb shit that usually comes out of my mouth.

Bella obviously doesn't want to be touched, and all I want to do is hug her and tell her how thankful I am she's in one piece. Tell her what a badass she is for fending off that asshole and how I would've killed him if she hadn't stopped me. Most importantly, I want to tell her that I'm never leaving her and whether or not she accepts my apology, I have no intention of taking no for an answer. That we're meant to be together and we will be.

Now isn't the time for that though. Right now my priority is making sure she's okay. Or as okay as she can be at the moment.

Instead of calling anyone—because it's Bella's business —I look through the cabinets and the fridge so I can at least feed her.

I'm stirring the pasta for the mac and cheese when she

walks down her short hallway with her hair in a high wet bun, a pair of sweats, and Columbia T-shirt. Usually I'd make a remark about her T-shirt, but now isn't the time. She comes over to the stove and I turn toward her, resting the spoon on the counter.

Tears hang off the ends of her lashes. "Now you can touch me."

She falls into my waiting arms, sobs wailing from her lungs. I grip her tightly, my hand running up and down her back. I whisper all the praise I've mentally been giving her all night. Telling her how brave she was and how sorry I am that I wasn't there.

It physically pains me to see her like this, and I wish I could take some of the pain for her. Hell, I'd take all of it if it meant she'd be whole.

The water boils over onto her stovetop, and I turn off the burner and guide her to the couch. We sit there with her wrapped in my arms, the only sound her silent sobs and sniffles. I want to find the bastard and kill him for what she has to go through because of him.

She draws back after a little while and wipes her tears. "About a year ago, a client called me..."

My eyes close. I should've figured this out. This is why she left the business. Because if you're a FSBO broker, you don't have to show properties.

"He wanted to see this property, but he was only in town for a short while. It was eight at night and the property was vacant, but I said okay. He used a fake name and a throwaway phone."

"You don't have to tell me." I squeeze her into my side. For months I've wanted this information, but now that she's giving it to me, it doesn't seem that important. Not if it's going to mess with her head.

She looks at me, the smallest of smiles creasing her lips, and her hand runs down my chin. "I do. If we're going to get past this, you have to know what I've been hiding."

I grab her hand and place it in my lap. "If it's too much…"

"He was dressed in a suit. Clean-cut haircut. Cell phone to his ear when I arrived, like a busy professional. As soon as I opened the door, a chill ran over my body. He didn't do anything unusual, but the energy was off. He let me say my spiel. I walked him over to the windows, pointing out the sliver of the city he'd see at night. At first he came up behind me and pressed into me." She pauses and swallows, the tears stopping. "I'd had clients who made a pass at me before, but this felt different. So I kept my distance, hoping to get us out of there before he tried again."

"But that didn't work?"

She shakes her head. "He was too big. Too strong. He had me cornered. Luckily another agent arrived for a showing. The other woman was so shocked and surprised, she came to my aid and he got away. The police were called, but his DNA didn't show up anywhere. So he's still out there. I couldn't bring myself to show strangers properties anymore. That's why I went FSBO." She falls into my side again.

"You could've trusted me. I would have understood."

"I know that now, but at the time, it made me feel weak and inadequate. I've been through therapy and self-defense classes to get myself together, and it worked for the most part." She looks at me.

"I hate that this happened to you." My jaw flexes as I picture the scene I walked in on.

She nods. "Thank you for being here."

"I wouldn't be anywhere else."

We sit like that. No more words are exchanged, and

eventually she falls asleep. I carry her into her bedroom and slide her under the covers, then I lie on top of the covers in case she needs me.

Somewhere between watching her sleep peacefully and her nuzzling into me, I vow to always keep her safe.

CHAPTER THIRTY-SIX

Bella

Two weeks and six therapy sessions later, a small amount of peace has returned to my life. A lot of it has to do with the fact that my offender has been charged.

Carm has taken it upon himself to be my savior. He's moved my office into his, making us share office space. Not that I've been there. Max is handling it all for me.

I threw myself in therapy after the attack, since that's what helped me last time. Today I'm purposely going back to the office without Carm knowing, because I have to do some of these things by myself.

We haven't even talked about what we are to one another, although I did smile when the detective referred to him as my boyfriend.

I use my key. Besides getting the door fixed, I made everyone promise not to touch anything inside. The detectives just closed the case, so the yellow tape is off, and I step in. The smell of blood is the first thing that hits me. Then the disarray of the desk. The struggle comes back to me. I'm not sure how long I would've lasted without Carm coming to the rescue, though I do feel some satisfaction that I cut him with the letter opener.

"What the hell?" Carm's voice booms from behind me. "What are you doing? You shouldn't be in here." He storms in.

"I'm good. I had to see it."

"Why do you keep torturing yourself?" he asks, desperation lacing his words.

He's questioned it many times. Every time I bring up what happened, he doesn't understand why I want to talk about it. But talking helps. When something pops into my mind, I talk about it. Or when I cut myself shaving and the blood dripped down my leg like it did on the guy's arm when I first pierced his skin, I talk about it. The therapist says it's good that I'm willing to talk about it. That it's a big part of why I'm doing better than last time.

"It helps me put it all behind me." I walk across the broken glass. "What are we going to do with this space? I have to clean it up and—"

"No. I'm putting my foot down on that."

I can't help but grin at his stubbornness. He wants to rule my life right now. Although he hasn't said it, I can feel it in his actions and the words he does say—Carmelo Mancini loves me. And I love him too.

But I don't want those words to be tied to what happened here, so I keep them to myself. I want the memory of us speaking those words for the first time to be untainted. It's why I've decided to go to the Hamptons this weekend. We need to start fresh.

"I'm not talking about moving back in here, but someone has to."

"I told the landlord that I'll pay to get everything fixed up, then he can rent it out." He holds out his arms, and I walk into them. He kisses my forehead.

Another great thing about Carm is that he always has to be touching or hugging me. We haven't slept together or even snuggled in bed since the attack. He's given me distance and comfort—two things I need right now. Who would've ever thought a selfish prick like him would be just what I need?

"Come on. Show me my new place."

"I thought you'd never ask." He grins at me.

We walk across the hall, and I see the shiny new sign on the door.

Mancini Real Estate & Scott FSBO Brokerage.

"My name on the door seems a little permanent," I say as he pushes open the door.

"Because you're a permanent fixture in my life." He shuts the door behind me and meets my gaze. "Tell me I'm a permanent fixture in yours. I haven't wanted to press the issue. I'm sorry about lying, and I swear to you I never will again. You're the one for me, and I'll *never* jeopardize that again."

I laugh as my forehead falls into his chest. "Yeah, we're getting there, but I don't see you going anywhere either."

He wraps me up in his arms, and I feel the tension leave his body.

That weekend in the Hamptons, I take him to the beach as the moon is high in the sky and reflecting off the ocean. I thank him for everything he's done for me. And I start to say I love him, but he presses his finger to my lips. Before I can finish, he says the words, beating me in true Carm fashion.

We seal our new love with a kiss, and that night, he slides in under the covers and cuddles me. I've never felt more safe, secure, and loved.

EPILOGUE

Carm

Almost one year later

"I don't wanna go bungee jumping," I whine, sitting up in the hotel bed and watching Bella throw a sundress over her body, sans bra. She's trying to kill me. I know it.

"You love to do those dangerous things." She climbs across the bed and straddles me, then puts on the emerald earrings I got her. She plays with my hair when she's done.

"That's before I found something to live for." I grab her ass and pull her into me. "I'd stay here all afternoon with you. That's adventurous enough for me."

She leans forward and kisses me.

My girl is so amazing. The work she's done to put the attacks behind her still amazes me. It shows that muscles don't prove how strong someone is, because she's stronger than Mr. Olympia.

It took two months before we slept together, but I was okay. We took baby steps until she was ready. As long as she was mine, I didn't care. That night when she tried to tell me she loved me first was the best night of my life.

Now we're in Vegas, and it's all I can do not to drag her down to the strip and have Elvis marry us. We're here for a dual bachelor/bachelorette party for my cousin Luca and his fiancée, Lauren. After being apart from Bella all last night, I'm done with this shit. But I'm supposed to go bungee jumping with the guys while she shops with the girls until we all meet up for dinner.

My phone vibrates on the nightstand.

Bella picks it up and hands it to me. "It's Enzo."

I shake my head and put it back on the nightstand, rolling us over so I'm on top of her.

I'm ready for another round of Bella Scott, but she places her hand on my chest. "I have to get pretty. Have you seen these women?"

My lips find her neck. "You're the most beautiful of them all. They're all competing for second place, believe me."

Her legs wrap around my waist. "You're too sweet and just trying to get me to have a quickie when we both know Enzo's calling because they're waiting for you downstairs."

I laugh and roll over because she's right, but I'm not willing to be the idiot who makes everyone late. "When it's my turn for a bachelor party, I don't want all this shit. Let's just elope somewhere. The honeymoon will be my bachelor party."

She shakes her head and disappears into the bathroom. "Oh, how far Carmelo Mancini has fallen, huh?"

After I put on my shorts and T-shirt, I follow her. Wrapping my arms around her waist, I stare at her in the mirror, and she pulls the mascara wand away from her face.

"I don't think I fell," I say. "I rose to new heights."

"Spoken like a guy who wants to get laid." She leans toward the mirror to continue her makeup routine, and my hands mold to her hips. She's in perfect position for me to lift up the skirt of her dress and take her right now.

"I have you, so I can get laid any time I want now."

She raises her eyebrows in the mirror as a challenge.

"I love you," I say to make up for what I just said.

She giggles, turning around. Her hand falls to the bulge in my pants. "Let's see how you feel after sharing a bathroom with me."

I've asked her to move in with me. She wanted to stand on her own for a while after everything that happened—I think to prove that she could—so even though we've been inseparable and wasting money on two places, I waited. She's finally agreed to move in, so as soon as we return to Manhattan, we'll be the Mancini/Scott house. Although Bella says it'll be the Scott/Mancini home. Sometimes arguing isn't worth it, and other times I just like to get her riled up because our sex is extra incredible on nights like those.

"I already love every minute of it. Especially those days when you get ready naked."

She laughs again and pushes my chest. "Go!"

I hold up my hands and back away, but at the last minute, I grab her and kiss her until she's panting and I'm assured she's wet. There. Let her suffer too.

"Love you," I say right before stepping out of the hotel room door.

"Love you," Annie mimics, walking down the hall

toward me.

"Morning," I say to her with a smile.

Once I realized that I was actually jealous of Enzo and Annie's relationship, it was easy to stop busting his balls about it whenever I could. Now Annie and I get along great.

"Enzo is not happy. Grab Dom, because you two are the only ones missing." She tsks while waving her finger.

"Take care of my girl," I holler back as we pass one another.

"She takes care of herself but..." She nods. "Done."

"Thanks, sis."

"Not yet. Except if your brother had his way, I would've been Mrs. Mancini last night." She laughs as though that would never happen.

"Damn, we really do think alike. What about a double wedding?" I circle around and so does she, both of us walking backward away from each other but facing one another.

"You've forgotten one tiny detail. I have this." She holds up her left hand. "Your girl doesn't."

"Minor detail." I shrug. I just got her to move in with me. Baby steps.

"Not that minor," she says and swivels around. "Don't do stupid shit today!"

I laugh, not promising anything, and I press the up button on the elevator instead of down. Once I'm on Dom's floor, I hammer out a text to Enzo that I'm grabbing Dom and will be right down.

I knock on Dom's door, but he doesn't open it. I blow out a breath and call him.

No answer.

I knock again.

Maybe he went down early to play some tables. I turn to

leave, but then hear movement behind the door so I stop.

Dom opens the door, squinting as if the light in the hall hurts his eyes, and oh yeah, he's nude. Dick swinging in the wind. Naked.

"Jesus, bro, I don't wanna see your dick. Although I am happy to know mine's bigger."

Am I telling the truth? Who knows? Dom doesn't need to know.

He steps into the bathroom, and I catch the door and walk in.

He reappears with a towel wrapped around his waist. "Fuck off. What's going on?"

"You're late for bungee jumping. Everyone is waiting. Where'd you disappear to last night anyway? One minute you're sulking at the bar and the next you text us to say you're out."

He looks like shit. His hair's as messy as if he's been... I slide to the side to look farther inside the room. Just as I thought, a foot with red nail polish on the toes is peeking out from under the sheet.

He runs his hands through his hair and down his face, blowing out a breath.

The light from the bathroom glints off the shiny silver band on the ring finger of his left hand.

"What the fuck is that?" I point at it, my eyes wide.

He holds his hand out in front of him and all the color drains from his face.

"Holy shit!" I laugh hysterically.

Dom stares at the ring as if he has no idea how the hell it got there.

Looks like Dom beat Enzo and me to the altar after all.

The End

COCKAMAMIE UNICORN RAMBLINGS

What did you think of the billboard with a half-naked Carm asking if it's your first time? Credit to that goes to Piper's husband. He's a Realtor and many years ago he used that same ad copy for one of his own ads (minus the bare chest). :P

This was a book that took a while to write but we couldn't be happier with the way it turned out. We fell in love with Carm in book one but neither one of us realized how much he'd steal our hearts until he hit the page. After so many books you try to tweak characters to make sure they have their own identity. Carm definitely has his, doesn't he?

We knew Bella and Carm would be opposites, so it was an easy decision to have her move in across the hall. Plus adding Enzo and Annie helped a TON. We loved how much they snuck on the page since there's so many secrets when it comes to Dom (oh just you wait, he'll steal your heart, too). We wanted Carm and Bella to be forced together more than just at the office and since Rayne loves almost all Bravo shows you can probably guess which series was on while she was writing the book. Summer Rental. She's a drama llama addict. What better way to get them together than to get them out of NY for a few weekends?

And as we mentioned, as funny as this book was, Dom's is going to tug at those heartstrings. Since we don't want to give anything away, we're going to leave you hanging, but you don't want to miss Wild Steamy Hook-up!

We can't give you all these books without our awesome team!

Wander Aguiar for an amazing photo
    Thom Panto for modeling being our muse for Carm (newbie).
    Shari Ryan from Mad Hat Covers
    Cassie from Joy Editing
    Ellie from Love N Books
    Shawna from Behind the Writer
    Dani Sanchez and the Wildfire Marketing gang
    All the bloggers who carve out time to read and review our books.
    All our early ARC readers
    And of course, all our unicorns. <3

ABOUT PIPER & RAYNE

Piper Rayne, or Piper and Rayne, whichever you prefer because we're not one author, we're two. Yep, you get two USA Today Bestselling authors for the price of one. Our goal is to bring you romance stories that have "Heartwarming Humor With a Side of Sizzle" (okay...you caught us, that's our tagline). A little about us... We both have kindle's full of one-clickable books. We're both married to husbands who drive us to drink. We're both chauffeurs to our kids. Most of all, we love hot heroes and quirky heroines that make us laugh, and we hope you do, too.

www.piperrayne.com
Amazon
Goodreads
Facebook
Instagram
Pinterest
Bookbub

ALSO BY PIPER RAYNE

You can't kiss the Nanny, Brady Banks

Over my Brother's Dead Body, Chase Andrews

The Baileys

Lessons from a One-Night Stand

Advice from a Jilted Bride

Birth of a Baby Daddy

Operation Bailey Wedding (Novella)

Falling for My Brother's Best Friend

Demise of a Self-Centered Playboy

Confessions of a Naughty Nanny

Operation Bailey Babies (Novella)

Secrets of the World's Worst Matchmaker

Winning My Best Friend's Girl

Rules for Dating your Ex

Operation Bailey Birthday (Novella)

The Greenes

My Beautiful Neighbor

My Almost Ex

My Vegas Groom

The Greene Family Summer Bash

My Sister's Flirty Friend

My Unexpected Surprise

My Famous Frenemy

The Greene Family Vacation

My Scorned Best Friend

My Fake Fiancé

My Brother's Forbidden Friend

The Modern Love World

Charmed by the Bartender

Hooked by the Boxer

Mad about the Banker

The Single Dad's Club

Real Deal

Dirty Talker

Sexy Beast

Hollywood Hearts

Mister Mom

Animal Attraction

Domestic Bliss

Bedroom Games

Cold as Ice

On Thin Ice

Break the Ice

Box Set

Charity Case

Manic Monday

Afternoon Delight

Happy Hour

Blue Collar Brothers

Made in the USA
Coppell, TX
05 April 2023

15283854R00177